SWITCHED

N.R. WALKER

COPYRIGHT

Cover Artist: N.R. Walker
Editor: Labyrinth Bound Edits
Switched © 2016 N.R. Walker
Publisher: BlueHeart Press
Second Edition 2025

ALL RIGHTS RESERVED

This literary work may not be reproduced or transmitted in any form or by any means, including electronic or photographic reproduction, in whole or in part, without express written permission.
This literary work may not be reproduced or transmitted in whole or in part in any form or by any means, including information storage and retrieval systems, or for use in AI training software.
This is a work of fiction, and any resemblance to persons, living or dead, or business establishments, events or locales is coincidental, except in the case of brief quotations embodied in critical articles and reviews.
The Licensed Art Material is being used for illustrative purposes only.

WARNING

Intended for an 18+ audience only. This book is intended for a mature, adult audience. It contains graphic language, explicit content, and adult situations.

The author uses Australian English spelling and grammar.

TRADEMARK ACKNOWLEDGEMENTS:

All trademarks are the property of their respective owners.

GLOSSARY FOR AUSTRALIAN TERMS

Esky: a portable cooler

QC: Queen's Counsel Barrister

DEDICATION

To Family…
No matter what shape or size it comes in.

BLURB

Israel Ingham's life has never been easy. He grew up in a house devoid of love and warmth. Nothing he ever did was good enough. The fact Israel is gay just added to the long list of his father's disappointments.

Then a letter from Eastport Children's Hospital changes everything. A discovery is made, one of gross human error. Twenty-six years ago two baby boys were switched at birth and sent home with the wrong families.

Sam, Israel's best friend, has been his only source of love and support. With Sam beside him every step of the way, Israel decides to meet his birth mother and her son, the man who lived the life Israel should have.

Israel and Sam become closer than ever, amidst the tumultuous emotions of meeting his birth family, and Sam finds himself questioning his feelings toward his best friend. As Israel embraces new possibilities, he needs to dissect his painful relationship with his parents in order to salvage what's left.

Because sometimes it takes proof you're not actually family to become one.

Switched

N.R. WALKER

ONE

I didn't have time for this. I had numbers to crunch, emails to tend to, deadlines to meet, and I knew for every ten minutes of work I missed, I'd have four phone calls to return. As the junior executive manager of iCon Inc., my father's self-made consulting empire, I had pressures from every angle.

At twenty-six, I'd been groomed for my role in my father's business—to follow in his footsteps, whether I wanted to or not. It was expected, assumed. I'd been a constant string of disappointments to my parents in my youth, so as the only child and heir, I swallowed down my pride, accepted my obligation and duty, and did my job.

This meeting, however, was not in my area of expertise. Why on earth I was being requested to attend a fundraising schmooze, I had no idea. Like I said, I didn't have time for it, nor the authority to grant approval for such requests, so I was at a loss as to why I was even there.

My mother had received a letter from Sydney's Eastport Children's Hospital, the very hospital in which I was born, requesting our attendance. She told me nothing more, only that she, my father, and I were asked to attend. I assumed my father would send an apology, citing business dealings elsewhere, so I was surprised to see him alongside my mother in the waiting room. I rushed in, not late for the meeting but later than him, so again, another disappointment to add to the list.

My mother offered me a curt smile. My father's only response was a slight adjustment of one eyebrow, but otherwise he didn't look at me.

A normal day in the life of Israel Ingham. I bit back a sigh and took out my phone, thumbing through messages while pretending not to give a shit that my parents detested me.

"Merrick and Julia Ingham?" a man with grey hair in a grey suit asked from an office doorway. My parents turned to face him, and he looked at me. "Israel Ingham?"

"Yes," I replied, seemingly the only one in my family with manners.

"I'm Phillip Dovich, legal counsel for New South Wales Family and Community Services. Please." He swallowed hard. "Come in."

We walked into his office to find two other people sitting at the side of a large mahogany desk. They were obviously legal people, witnesses or barristers. It was hard to tell. It took me a fraction of a second to figure out this meeting had nothing to do with fundraising.

He chewed on his bottom lip and seemed unsure of where to start. His complexion paled to match the grey of his hair, and I'd sat in on enough exec meetings to know this man was about to deliver news he'd rather not.

"There's no easy way to say this," he started. Then, like he remembered a spiel he'd mentally prepared earlier, he dropped a bombshell that would forever change the three of us.

"It has come to our attention, on the day of Israel's birth, there was a mix up as a direct result of human error." He steeled himself and looked at my parents. "Mr and Mrs Ingham, we believe the child you were given to raise as your own was not your biological child."

We sat in silence as the man across from us explained it had only recently come to light, during an unfortunate circumstance where another woman had required blood testing. Her son had routine blood tests for his place of employment, where the mother noticed an inconsistency. The blood group stated differed from that of his birth records.

As it turned out, this child was born on the same morning of the same day in the same maternity ward as me. And in fact, we were the only two boys born on that day. Further investigation into my medical records from when I'd had my appendix removed as a young boy, in this very hospital, proved my blood type was a match to this other boy's birth records, not mine.

Further DNA testing would be required, of course.

My mother stared at him, unblinking. My father, on the other hand, processed the man's words for about twenty seconds before he erupted in accusations about responsibility and liability. The hospital's legal team would have, without doubt, known who they were meeting before we walked in, which probably explained their nervousness.

As my father ranted and raved and Mr Dovich answered the best he could, my mind swirled. Disjointed, foggy, and disbelieving, my mind struggled to make sense of what I'd just learned. It was so absurd, yet somehow felt so real.

Could it be true? I mean, I looked nothing like my parents. Sure, I had pale skin like my mother and I was tall like my father, but that was where the similarities ended. My eyes were a dark, dark brown, different to my mother's light brown, my father's blue. My hair was darker. I had a different shaped face. I had a different build. Not only that, but I was nothing like my parents. Not in mannerisms, temperament, demeanour, or personality.

My heart was thumping hard in my chest, and my mother silently wiped a tear from the corner of her eye. I'd never seen my mother cry, ever. She normally had a look of profound disinterest on her face. And even now, for the very first time, I wasn't sure whether it was tears of sadness or heartbreak, loss or betrayal, or whatever it was you were supposed to feel under circumstances such as these.

I'm pretty sure she cried because now it all made perfect sense. I wasn't *their* failure, after all.

"Mr Ingham," Phillip Dovich addressed me. I wasn't even aware that my father had stopped talking. When I turned to look for him, I found him at the window with his phone pressed to his ear, no doubt already talking to Nigel, his attorney. "Israel?"

In a daze, I turned back to the man speaking to me. "Yes?"

Mr Dovich gave me a soft, patient smile. "Would you agree to further DNA testing?"

Did I want to know if my entire life had been a lie? Did I want to know that after all the years I'd disappointed my parents that they were finally off the hook? They didn't have a failure of a son, a not-smart-enough, not-disciplined-enough son? That after all these years, they didn't really have a gay son? Did I want to find out if these people, who told me being gay was an "embarrassing smear" on the family name, might not be my parents after all? Did I really want to know? Without understanding what repercussions lay ahead, without any clue where this would leave me, personally, financially, did I really want to know?

I nodded, without doubt. "Yes."

AN HOUR LATER, after we all had buccal swabs and blood drawn, I was back in the waiting room of Mr Dovich, unsure of what to do or where to go. I mean, what did one do after being told they had possibly been switched at birth? After waiting no longer than ten minutes, claiming he was too busy to wait a moment longer, my father left with his phone still pressed to his ear, his mouth an angry slit and his eyes focused and cold. Following him dutifully, my mother offered a quiet goodbye. Unsure of what else to say, I promised I'd call her later, but there was only one person I wanted to speak to.

I pulled out my mobile phone, found Sam's number, and pressed Call.

"Hey," he answered in his always-cheerful voice. "Why are you calling me and not swamped in work? Does your old man know you're making private calls on company time?" He snorted out a laugh.

I smiled as soon as I heard his voice, and tears sprung to my eyes. I sobbed his name. "Sam."

His voice changed to alert and concerned. "What's wrong?"

Just then, Mr Dovich's door opened and he walked out into the waiting room where I sat, followed by a woman and a guy around my age. Mr Dovich stopped cold, clearly not expecting to see me. But it was the woman's reaction behind him that brought me to my feet. As soon as she saw me, she put her hand to her mouth, a quiet cry escaped her and tears welled in her eyes. I had no clue who she was. I'd never seen her before, but she sure as hell knew me.

We stood, facing each other, and she nodded before bursting into tears. The younger guy with her tried to console her, but he couldn't seem to look away from me either, and Phillip Dovich didn't know where to look or what to say. The woman wailed, and silent tears rolled down my cheeks.

"Iz? Israel?" Sam yelled in my ear, his tone thick with concern. "What's going on? Are you okay?"

I shook my head, though he couldn't see. "No. Yes. I think so, I don't know." I never broke eye contact with the crying woman across from me. Disconnected, like I was having some out of body experience, I spoke through my tears into the phone. "Sam, I gotta go."

"Iz, you're starting to scare me. Where are you?"

"Eastport Children's Hospital," I murmured. "Sam, I think I just met my mother."

TWO

I somehow managed to drive myself home. And I'd no sooner walked into my apartment, thrown my keys and phone on the kitchen counter, and run my hands through my hair when I heard the jingle of keys at my front door. There was only one person who it could be—the only other person who had keys to my place—and I smiled, the ache in my chest lessened.

"Iz?"

"Kitchen," I mumbled, my voice sounding detached and weary. So fucking weary.

Sam rounded the corner, like he'd run the whole way, and stopped. He seemed to sag when he saw me—I must've looked like utter crap—and he walked slowly over to me before pulling me into a crushing hug.

Neither of us spoke for a moment. We didn't need to. He'd been my best friend for years, and we were like brothers. *Brother from another mother*, we used to joke, and that now made me laugh, which in turn made me cry.

Sam cupped his hands to my jaw and pulled me back so he could look me in the face. He was clearly shocked by my tears, but his concern won out. "Iz, talk to me."

"I'm a mess," I croaked out.

"What the hell happened?"

"Went to Eastport Hospital today," I started.

"The fundraising thing?"

"It wasn't fundraising. It was family services legal."

"Legal? Family ser... What for?" He was confused and I wasn't making much sense. "You said you met your mother, but she was there with you, wasn't she?"

"My parents aren't my parents," I said, with a fresh wave of tears. "Switched at birth, identity mix-up, human fucking error, whatever you want to call it."

Sam blinked as he processed what I'd said. "Switched at birth? What? *How*?"

I shrugged. "I don't know." A sob of laughter escaped me, despite my tears, and I was pretty sure I sounded crazy. "I was switched at birth. It's kinda funny, isn't it? How it's so unbelievable, but it makes perfect fucking sense." I couldn't stop crying. Once the waterworks started, I was unable to stop it. "I don't even know why I'm crying," I sobbed, and Sam pulled me into his arms once more.

He tightened his hold on me. "Jesus, Iz. You're allowed to cry. You just had your world turned upside down."

He was wearing his blue suit, probably Armani, and I was sobbing snot onto his collar. Yet I couldn't seem to let him go. I mumbled into his neck, "Thank you for coming over."

His reply was calm and soothing. "I wouldn't be anywhere else."

I allowed myself to be held by him. The rise and fall of his chest, his strength and quietness, soothing me until my tears subsided. When he finally pulled away, he fondly tapped my cheek before reaching for a bottle of Chivas from the cabinet where I kept the liquor. He found two tumblers like it was his kitchen and set them in front of me. "Drink with me."

It was half past eleven in the morning. "Don't you have to get back to work?"

He didn't even blink. He simply pulled out his phone, sent a rapid-fire text to someone, and slid his phone onto the countertop. "Nope." He poured two hefty swigs of scotch, kept one, and handed me the other.

I downed it in one go. It burned the whole way down and I gasped, breathing through the heat of it. Without a word, Sam poured me another and handed it to me. Only this time, he nodded toward the lounge room. "Let's go sit down."

He led the way to the sofa. A room he'd been in countless times, watching footy, movies, lounging off a hangover, or simply planting his arse on my three-seater for something to do. He sat in the middle of the sofa and patted the seat next to him. I sat down and he put his hand on my knee and sipped his scotch. He never prodded or pushed for me to speak. Just like always, he'd wait until I was ready.

I'd known him since we were thirteen. We both attended Knox, Sydney's most prestigious boys' school. We weren't best friends straight away, but over the next few years, as we realised our attraction to boys—the only gay guys in our year at school—we became closer, and by the time we were fifteen, we were inseparable.

We understood each other. His family had more money than my father could ever dream of. If you met Samuel Finch or had dinner with his parents, despite their address or exquisite home, you'd have no clue his family business made Forbes Australia's list every year. They were down to earth and the most humble people I'd ever known. When Sam wasn't at work, he wore old jeans and vintage T-shirts. His blond-brown hair was always a stylish, artful mess, and much to his disgust, reminded me of Brad Pitt. His jaw was strong, his eyes were a sharp blue, and everywhere we went, guys threw themselves at his feet. His family was great; his parents loved him, regardless of who he was attracted to. He seemed to have it all. But he was also the nicest, most genuine person I'd ever known. And like just now, the minute I needed him, he would drop everything and come running.

I'd spent most of my older teenage years at his house. Whereas the home I'd grown up in was sterile and cold, his was warm and happy. His parents welcomed me into their lives and home like a second son, while his sisters helped me pick clothes and styled my hair. They knew my family was the polar opposite to theirs: where they were warm, mine were not. Where they were welcoming, mine were curt and closed off. Sam was never welcome in my parents' house, because the only thing worse than having one gay boy under their roof was having two. The Finch family basically adopted me as their own, showing me what a family was supposed to be. Every time my father tore into me about the disappointments of "choosing to be gay" and "ruining his reputation," it was Sam and his family that held me together.

They'd saved me so many times I'd lost count.

But I never felt pitied. I felt loved and welcome.

Sam and I had never been anything more than friends. I dunno whether it was fate, bad timing, or the universe telling us something, but it just never happened between us. We'd dated other guys, left gay bars with random one-nighters, but neither of us had ever been serious about anyone else. I know guys I'd dated a few times were wary of mine and Sam's relationship; whether they were jealous or threatened, I never kept them around long enough to find out. Sam was the number one man in my life. He was the Will to my Grace.

"Thank you for being here," I mumbled, swirling the scotch in my glass.

"It's fine, Iz. It's what family does." He regretted his word choice immediately.

I snorted at that, and it seemed to open the floodgates. "You should've seen them."

I didn't need to explain who *they* were.

"My father's first reaction was to scream about liability

and legal repercussions. Not to see if his wife was okay, or his son. My mother cried silent tears, but for what, is anyone's fucking guess. It certainly wasn't sorrow. The only person who offered me any sympathy or kindness was the lawyer who told us. Actually, I'm pretty fucking sure my mother cried for the son she should have had. And you know what? Maybe she should. Because it's not fair on her. I get that. But Sam, those were not tears of grief for a son she lost or should've had; she cried because she was robbed of having a better son. A son that wasn't me."

Sam put his hand around my neck and gently scratched the back of my head. He never argued because he'd heard the hurtful things my parents had said to me with his own two ears. He knew there was truth in what I was saying.

"I fucking hate your parents," he said. He'd stopped apologising for saying that years ago.

I nodded, and tears fell silently down my cheeks. "She cried because now it all made such perfect sense. I mean, they just had it confirmed that the reason I'm such a fucking disappointment is because I'm not really their son. After all these years, they can now legitimately say it's not their fault."

Sam's hold on my neck tightened and he waited for me to look at him. "That's not true. You're not a disappointment. You never have been. And if they can't see that, then fuck them."

I clung to his words like a life raft. The fear of drowning in a sea of desperation and failure was all too real as the dark waters lapped around me. I gasped for air, and he fought back tears, his fingers clutching my hair at the nape of my neck, as I tried not to succumb to being an all-out fucking mess.

I'm pretty sure it was too late. My ship had been sinking for years.

SAM FED me scotch until I was comfortably numb. He also fed me pizza to soak up some of the alcohol, but the heavy and hazy, chemically dulled feeling in my head and heart was welcome.

"I need to call my mother," I said, fumbling with my phone. "Said I would."

Sam was still across from me. The room was now darkened with evening. He nodded, though his jaw ticked with his barely suppressed distaste at the idea.

I found her number and hit Call, waiting for her to answer while wishing she wouldn't.

The phone clicked and her voice was soft. Not in a kind way, more of a detached sound. "Israel."

"Mother."

I wondered if I would still get to call her that when the DNA tests came back to confirm what we all pretty much knew to be true. Or if she'd even want me to.

She didn't speak, so I had to. "I said I'd call. Today was kinda rough. How're you feeling?"

There was a beat of silence. "You've been drinking."

I snorted. "Yeah. Kinda helps not to feel."

Sam slowly closed his eyes, like my words hurt to hear.

"Maybe we should schedule this phone call for another time."

"You know, most people don't schedule calls with their kids," I said with enough scotch-induced bravado not to care. But I figured she wouldn't care either, so I didn't bother. "I was just calling to see if you were okay. You were upset."

I heard her swallow. "Today was quite unexpected."

I almost laughed. "You could say that."

She was quiet a while. "Are you alone?"

I huffed out a sigh. "Sam's here." I locked eyes with him. Even as my vision swayed and blurred, we never broke eye contact.

"I thought he might be."

Her comment was said in a tone I didn't really care for. "Why wouldn't he be? He's the only one who ever really has been."

Silence.

"Is Dad there?" I pressed. "I mean, are you alone?"

There was the sound of ruffling, like she had to straighten her composure to answer. "He was meeting with Nigel."

Nigel Evans had been my father's lawyer since before I was born. Both had excelled in their chosen fields, and he was the closest thing my father had to a best friend. I shouldn't have been surprised that my father would be discussing legal recourses about all we'd learned today instead of being at home with his wife.

"Of course he is."

"Yes, well, I'd imagine they have a lot to discuss."

I tried to keep my tone civil, but it was strained at best. "Not everything's a matter of liability. Sometimes the collateral damage is more important."

Silence, and I knew this time the conversation was over. I swallowed down my anger and inhaled slowly. "Well, clearly you're okay, so my phone call was unwarranted. If there are any briefs or disclosures I need to sign, I'm sure he'll have his secretary forward them to me."

"Israel…"

My breath was shaky as I fought more tears. "Goodnight, Mother."

I disconnected the call and threw my phone onto the sofa beside me. I put my head in my hands and growled in frustration. I wanted to punch something. I wanted to make something pay for the way I felt, but I knew it was futile. I leaned back on the sofa, letting my head loll back, pulled at my hair, and let out a roar of pent up emotion. "I'm so fucking angry!"

When I felt a tap on my knee, I looked up. My vision swam a little, but I found Sam now sitting on the coffee table between my legs, and his hand was on my knee. "You're allowed to be angry. You should be angry."

"I am." I wiped the tears from my cheeks and shook my head. "And fuck these stupid tears."

He rubbed my knee and looked at me for a long moment. "You're not collateral damage."

"I am to them."

Sam shook his head slowly. "You're worth more than that."

"They don't even give a shit. My father'll have a lawsuit on the table by 8:00 a.m. I'm pretty sure he isn't even human. He has zero emotional capabilities."

"You're not like him."

I barked out a laugh. "Clearly. Because I'm a fucking mess, while he's all about strategy for the best financial gain. At least I'll have been useful to him once in my life."

Sam flinched. "Iz."

"I'm tired. I'm tired of never being good enough. I'm tired of being an afterthought. I'm tired of being wrong all the time. I'm so fucking tired of it all."

I couldn't explain the exhaustion I felt in my bones, the weariness that held me down. I was sick of trying to prove my worth to parents who were too cold to care. "I don't want to fight any of it anymore."

I didn't mean to say that out loud.

"Iz," Sam said gently. He held out his hand and I took it. He squeezed my fingers, and it was that touch, that human connection that saved me. His touch that saved me every damn time. "Come on. Let's get you to bed."

He stood and pulled me to my feet. I felt heavy and really drunk, but he managed to get me to my room. We stood facing each other at the side of my bed, and I swayed into him. He held me upright, our chests flush together, and I rested my forehead on his shoulder. It was a quiet moment between us. His hands fell to my waist, and I could feel the rise and fall of his chest against mine. He was my absolute rock, my calm in a world of chaos. "Not sure what I did to deserve you."

I felt the press of his lips at my temple before he was helping me onto my bed. I fell back heavily, drunk and weary, and he lifted my feet, one at a time, to remove my shoes.

"Thank you." My words sounded tired and slurred, even to me.

He gently lowered my socked foot onto the bed. "You're more than welcome."

"For everything."

Sam nodded but didn't say anything. He looked sad, and I hated that.

"Sorry."

"What for?"

"Being a mess."

"Iz…"

"Thank you for being here."

He smiled that sad fucking smile again. The one he gave when I thanked him for being around. Like it hurt him that I was so grateful. And I was, so fucking grateful. He had no idea just how much. I closed my eyes. I tried to fight sleep but I was too drunk and too tired. "Love you," I mumbled.

He didn't reply for so long, I'd wondered if I'd said it, or just thought it, or if he'd gone already.

I managed to open my eyes, and he was standing there with a look on his face I wasn't sure I'd seen before. Maybe I was too drunk to focus…

"Love you too, Iz."

THREE

I woke to the smell of coffee and a rather loud, "Iz, get your arse outta bed or you'll be late."

It took me a little while to realise it was Sam hollering at me from the doorway. He was holding a coffee.

"Mmm, coffee."

"Good morning to you too, arsehole."

I sat up, ignoring the thump in my head and the wave of nausea in the back of my throat. "You stayed?"

His eyes were soft, but he rolled them anyway. "Of course I did."

"Is that coffee for me?"

"Yes, but you need to get out of bed to have it."

"You're an arsehole."

His grin got wider. "You're welcome."

"Is that my shirt?" I only just realised he was wearing my new Banana Republic tailored shirt. It looked good on him; better than it did on me anyway. The sales guy told me it was the new season lilac or some shit. Sam wore his grey suit pants from yesterday, and I made a mental note to wear that shirt with my grey pants too. If I ever got it back. "I had to borrow one."

"So you picked the most expensive one I own."

"Most expensive? Oh please. I was gonna wear the Armani. Now do you want this coffee before a shower or after?"

"Before."

He walked into my room and handed me the cup. I inhaled the aroma before taking a sip.

"You don't want to be late today," Sam said gently. "Given the mood your old man's likely to be in."

Jesus. I'd forgotten...

Sam must have seen the moment the events of yesterday dawned on me. "Get showered and dressed. I'll make you some toast. I'll drop you off at work. How's your head?"

"Sore."

"Thought it might be."

I sipped the coffee. "Thank you."

He waved me off as he walked out of my room. "Shower, Iz."

It was only a short drive from my apartment in Woolloomooloo into the office. Sam lived in Potts Point, not far from his family home in Elizabeth Bay. The Finches were old money, and their address reinforced that. Something that, no matter how hard he tried, my father would never have.

Sam stopped in the no-stopping zone. "Call me if you need anything. Let me know what game he's playing at."

"I will." I opened the car door. "And Sam?"

"Yeah, I know what you're about to say. And you're welcome."

I smiled and got out of his car just as a cab honked behind him. He saluted me. "Capt'n," he said with a smile.

It made me smile. Captain, or Cap, as it was shortened to: the nickname I'd been given in high school had stuck. Once a thorn in my side, it had grown on me. From my initials being I I, it didn't take long for that to become aye aye, and the obligatory "Captain" followed, and stayed.

Sam grinned right back at me, seemingly happy that I'd managed a smile, and drove off in the direction of his office, which admittedly, wasn't too far. Seven blocks, if you had to walk. And I had, many times.

But with a deep breath and my professional mask in place, I turned and walked through the front doors of my work. My father's empire. His first love, his brainchild, the one he could shape and mould, the one he wanted to thrive, the one he encouraged, and the one that hadn't let him down yet.

"Mr Ingham," Valarie, the lady behind the reception desk, greeted me. She'd been there forever, her face professionally stoic.

"Morning." I nodded as I walked to the elevator. Though here, I was only ever addressed as Mr Ingham. Never Israel, and certainly never Captain.

My father would breathe fire every time he heard one of my mates call me that. I wasn't too sure what he expected to happen when they'd given me the initials I I. Though every time someone called me Mr Ingham, I straightened and looked behind me for my father. It was an ingrained fear, trepidation, dread. One I had worked hard at masking but never could quite get right.

iCon Inc. was on the thirty-fifth, thirty-sixth, and thirty-seventh floors. My office was on the thirty-seventh with the other executive and upper-management offices. My father had taken a risk by launching an e-based tech-consulting business at precisely the right time. Whether it was luck or extrinsic planning on his behalf, I wasn't sure. But he'd grabbed the e-commerce world by the coattails and had somehow managed to hold on. Over the last twenty-odd years, he had grown iCon Inc. into the world-class initiative, front-running business it was today.

Starting out in e-consulting small business and the human element of technology, he'd known exactly in which direction the world was heading, and with one foot in the door, he'd branched out into silicone-based arenas. He'd set his sights on what others told him were unobtainable IT goals, and he'd stopped at nothing until he'd conquered them.

It was all about management. Management of businesses, information, advice, technology, systems, money. People. There wasn't anything in the IT consulting world he couldn't estimate, manage, implement, deploy, administer, or outsource.

I had to give it to him. He was an incredibly astute businessman. He just sucked at being a father. He'd groomed me for my job here, which I was sure he insisted on just so I wouldn't land some dead-end job and be an embarrassment to his reputation. The real kicker was, I actually liked my job. I was good at it, and it was the closest to a level-playing field with my father I would ever get.

The elevator dinged, like I'd won a prize for turning up before everyone else. The floor was almost empty, save for my personal assistant. Prue was the same age as me. Twenty-six years old, cautious, and very intelligent. Her long brown hair was always pulled into some kind of scroll at the back of her head, her make-up subtle, and her attire and pose were always impeccable.

Apart from that, I didn't know the first thing about her.

"Morning," I said in greeting.

"Good morning." She looked up from her computer. "Your father wishes to speak with you."

The lump in my gut expanded. "Of course."

"Coffee first?"

I smiled at her, which she seemed to like. "Yes please."

I went to walk into my office, but stopped. I turned back to Prue's desk and she looked up at me, politely surprised.

"Sorry for cancelling my day yesterday. Must have made your day more painful."

"My days aren't painful—" she started to say.

I put my hand up and smiled at her. "You know what I mean. I'm sure I have twice as much to do today, which means you do too. And for that, I'm sorry."

"It's more than fine," she said, a pleasant smile crossing her face. I think this was the most I'd ever spoken to her at length that wasn't case related.

"If you need some time off in lieu, that's fine."

"Oh no," she replied quickly, rising to her feet.

"Not even an hour early on a Friday?"

She finally smiled and conceded a nod. "I'll keep it in mind."

I found myself smiling back at her, despite knowing I had to face my father. "Good." I went into my office and opened my laptop, watching as my inbox filled with yesterday's mail. My hangover made itself known with a wash of nausea and dull stabbing behind my eyes.

Prue entered gracefully and silently placed a coffee on my desk. She paused a moment. "Your father knows you're here."

I sighed without really meaning to, and it caused Prue to stop. "Mr Ingham, is everything okay?"

I must have looked like shit, and my façade had slipped. It wasn't my best day. I gave her a tight smile. "Everything's fine."

She didn't press. Thankfully. "I'll hold all calls until you tell me otherwise."

I sipped my coffee. "Thank you."

She left without another word, and leaving my coffee on my desk, I followed her out. I doubted I'd be long enough for it to cool and even then, after seeing my father, if I'd have the stomach for it.

I passed his personal reception desk, garnering no more

than a nod from Maxine, one of my father's many personal assistants. I knocked, waited for his gruff welcome, and opened the door. His office was the master suite, as it should be. Sparse, minimalist décor; his large dark wood desk sat isolated before the floor-to-ceiling windows, not one thing out of place. My father sat, straight-backed and poised for coffee and a chat, or all-out war: it was hard to tell.

He offered me a tight smile. "Israel. Please, take a seat."

I did as bid and was morbidly curious to see how he'd address the bombshell from yesterday. Though in hindsight, I should have known better.

"As you know, the Yokonami project deadline is this Friday. The system requirements…"

And for the next five minutes, I listened to him give me a rundown of my biggest portfolio, the very job I had lived and breathed for the last month. It was almost time to close it, and I had done this a hundred times. Not once did he mention anything about our family. He didn't ask if I was okay. He offered no insight into his meeting with Nigel. I realised then, that he wasn't reminding me of network design and monitoring platforms. He was reminding me that what happened in our personal life yesterday had no place here.

And who knows. Maybe it didn't.

But I wasn't like him. I couldn't detach myself. I wasn't devoid of emotion. I wasn't a fucking robot.

I was pretty sure I didn't need the DNA test to confirm I was not this man's son.

He was done talking to me, I realised, because he was looking at his computer screen. He glanced at me like I was already wasting his time. "Any questions?"

I smiled. "None."

FOUR

By Friday afternoon, I'd had enough. Of every fucking thing. I'd heard no more from Mr Dovich, no more from my mother, and certainly nothing from my father. Well, not counting the professional obligations he seemed more intent on reminding me of. Even Prue was more wary of his presence. Maybe it was because I was on edge around him, or maybe it was because I was so high-strung.

The not knowing was like an itch under my skin. Being in limbo, not knowing where I truly came from or where I belonged, was unsettling to say the very least. The fact my parents acted like they couldn't have cared either way was a stark reminder of the void between us.

Sam called and messaged me every chance he got. And I even had a few messages from the other guys in our group of friends, so I was fairly certain Sam had told them something had gone down. I doubted he'd have told them *exactly* what had happened, but it was true to form for Sam to say something along the lines of "Cap's had a shit run of late. Let him know you're around" kind of thing.

It wouldn't be the first time he'd done that. And I was grateful. Just knowing there was someone who had my back meant more than I could explain. Our other mates, Jamie, Millsy, and Connor, were old uni friends, and we hung out as often as our careers allowed. They were good guys, and although they knew of my parental issues, they'd never really seen them firsthand. Not like Sam had. In school, he'd been at my house countless times. No, he wasn't always made welcome, but that didn't stop him. And it blew his mind that it was my carers, my nanny or driver, who knew me better than my parents, the fact he'd stay for dinners and it would be me and him with the nanny and chauffeur sitting at the table, asking me about my day.

Not that I minded. I liked dinners with them better than trying to stomach food under the suffocating silence when my parents were there.

My stomach knotted at the memory. I pushed against my abdomen, sure I'd be the only twenty-six-year-old I knew to get an ulcer. My phone buzzed in my desk drawer. Instinctively, I checked the time. It was almost five. I checked the message to see it was from Sam.

Can you talk?

I replied. *Sure.*

My phone rang immediately. "Hey."

"What's up?"

"Just letting you know you need to be packed and ready when I get to yours at six."

"What?"

"Two days. Pack outdoors stuff. Boardies, beach towel, that kind of thing. Maybe a hoodie if we can light a fire on the beach."

"Sam," I started to say.

"Shut the fuck up, Cap. Just be ready."

I smiled and could feel the tension in my shoulders loosen a little already. "Okay."

"You can set your Out of Office Reply too," he added. "Leave your phone at home."

Well shit. I couldn't remember a time since I'd started my internship under my father that I hadn't had my phone within reach. The notion of ignoring my father's calls or texts about work gave me a cold sweat. "Oh. Well—"

"No phone. No work. No stress."

"Sam, I can't just—"

"Did you close the Yokonami file today?"

"Yes."

"Then you can have a fucking weekend off, Iz. Six o'clock. Be ready. It's already five. Don't be late."

The call clicked off in my ear, and I found myself smiling at the screen. Before I could change my mind, I set the Out of Office Reply on my emails, closed my laptop, and walked out of my office.

Prue was still entering data like a dedicated madwoman, and after telling her to finish up and enjoy her weekend, I made a mental note to show my appreciation more often for her efforts.

But by six o'clock, I'd changed from my suit to shorts and a T-shirt, with my duffle bag sitting at the front door. I had a fair idea where Sam was going, and like always, he was right. If he'd asked me if I wanted to spend the weekend at his parents' beach house at Palm Beach, I'd have said no. I would have given a dozen excuses as to why it was a bad idea. But he didn't ask me. He *told me* I was going, and the fact he knew me that well made me smile.

Right on time, I heard the familiar sound of keys in my front door. Then Sam's voice sounded from the door. "You better be ready, Cap."

"Bag's at the door," I yelled from the kitchen. I walked out holding a six-pack of beer in each hand. "Corona's okay?"

His grin was instant. "Perfect." Then his eyes gave me the once over, and he seemed to like what he saw.

"What?" I asked. I looked down at my long cargos. They

were a faded blue and I thought they matched my T-shirt okay. "I've had these for ages."

His eyes shot to mine and he smiled, one-sided. "Just been a while since I've seen your legs. Jesus. You need some sun."

I rolled my eyes. "Fuck you." He laughed and held his hand out for one of the six-packs. I scoffed at him. "I can carry two. I'm a big boy."

He snatched one anyway. "No, idiot. Now hand over your phone."

I froze, but knowing it was quicker to not argue with him, I fished it out of my back pocket. He snatched it from me and handed me the six-pack back. Then he collected my duffel bag and tossed my phone onto the sofa and pushed me out the door.

"Right then. You weren't kidding about the no phone."

He just smiled at me. "Nope." He started to walk toward the elevator. "You need this, Iz."

I couldn't argue with that.

THE DRIVE to the Northern Beaches was slow in Friday-night peak-hour traffic, but with every minute, I was feeling better.

Sam told me about the funny afternoon he'd had, and it felt good to laugh.

"What do twenty-six-year-old women like?" I asked.

His eyes went from the traffic in front of us to mine, his expression concerned and curious. "Why?"

"My assistant. I think I should buy her something. Like a small gift."

He frowned. "What kind of message are you trying to send?"

"Um, a thank you?"

"Yeah, but why now? I mean, how long has she been your PA for?"

"A year or so."

"And this is the first time I've ever heard you talk of her."

I shrugged. "Dunno. It just occurred to me that she's worked her arse off for me for twelve months, and I don't know anything about her."

Sam considered that for a moment. "Her name is Prue. Last I spoke to her, which was about two months ago, she was single and spending a weekend in the Hunter Valley at some Jazz in the Vines thing with the girls."

"You spoke to her?" I blinked in surprise.

"Well yeah, I had to leave you a message about my mum's dinner party, remember? Because you wouldn't answer your phone."

"I was in a meeting with some multimillion dollar optic cable company, if you'll recall. They kind of like undivided attention. And anyway, I'd already agreed to get the wine on the way to your parents' house."

"Yeah, but I was just reminding you."

I chuckled. "And you got chatty with my PA?"

"Well, yeah. It's called conversation."

"I know. I think she's scared of me. She's faultless, utterly professional. And we've never exchanged more than pleasantries or details about contracts or appointments."

Sam frowned again, then seemed to choose his words carefully. "Well, you're very different at work to who you are outside of work."

"I know." I nodded slowly. "Despite all the shit and having my old man breathing down my neck and watching every single thing I do, I actually like my job. I'm good at it. I understand the dedication it takes to make it in the big league. I'm not afraid of that."

Sam glanced at me as he drove, waiting for me to finish.

"I just didn't realise how impersonal I was, especially with Prue. I think I scare her, you know, being the boss' son and all. But after everything that's happened this week, well something was different. I was different. I think she saw how he affects me. It's getting harder and harder to hide."

I sighed, and he listened.

"I don't want to be like him," I said. Sam's gaze shot to mine, and I explained. "When I realised I didn't have the first clue what Prue might do in her time off, I thought *Jesus, she must think I'm just like him.* You know what he's like, just treats everyone like a number, like they bleed binary codes instead of blood. And I don't want to be like that. I'm not like that. Only, I guess I was, or am. I don't know."

Sam's smile was brief at the binary comment. Then he was dead serious. "Iz, you're nothing like him."

"I know." I stretched out my legs. "Which is why I wanted to send Prue something. You said she was single?"

A flicker of something crossed his features. "That was a little while back. It might have changed." He shifted in his seat. "Um, why? Are you interested in her?"

I think my mouth fell open. "What?"

"Well, I mean, I get it. Attraction is to the person, not the gender. I get that. There are no rules to define that shit. So if you want to send her something that says you're interested, you—"

"Have you lost your fucking mind?"

He stopped talking.

"No, seriously, Sam. Have I ever told you I was bi?"

"Well, no."

"And you know what *gay* is, right?"

"Uh yeah, pretty sure."

"Because as a gay man yourself, you seem to be confused about what we like." I waited for him to smile. "We like dick, Sam. And arse and balls. And a whole range of masculine things. But mostly dick."

Now he laughed. "I'm pretty sure the definition of gay doesn't actually include the words dick, arse, or balls, Iz."

"Maybe not. But maybe it should. For gay men who like

dick, arse and balls, at least. As a sub-clause, not inclusive, non-binding constitutional amendment. In the fine print, ya know? You're a lawyer. I thought you'd like that."

"You're a dickhead."

"Yes, dick and head are two of my favourite things."

He grinned at me, and I knew the seriousness of our conversation was over. For now, at least.

IT ONLY TOOK us fifty minutes to get to the Finch family weekender up off Barrenjoey Road at Palm Beach, even in heavy traffic. I had spent many summers here as a teenager. The Finches were, after all, my surrogate family. The house was a gorgeous waterfront split-level design that felt like a second home, even if it had been a year or so since my last visit. Sam and I threw our bags into a bedroom each and soon found ourselves in the kitchen sorting out dinner over a few beers.

But the week soon caught up with me, because after four beers and a belly full of pasta, I could barely keep my eyes open.

"Go to bed, Iz," Sam offered gently.

"You sure? I don't wanna leave you up by yourself. It's only kinda early…"

"Jesus, Cap. Imma big boy. I can watch the footy by myself."

I looked at the TV screen and, more importantly, the men in tight shorts all sweaty and breathing hard. "If you want to jerk off in private…"

He threw a cushion at me. "Fuck off. And you're getting up early. We can walk the beach in the morning before breakfast. I thought we might go kayaking if it's not too windy, then we can light a fire on the beach tomorrow night. Cook a barbie or something."

"Did you plan everything?" I fought a smile. "What if I have to take a piss and it's not on your schedule?"

Sam sighed. "Just go to bed."

I clapped his shoulder as I walked past the back of his sofa, and as I got to the hall, I stopped and faced him. He looked at me expectantly. "Thanks," I said, my voice quiet and serious. "For doing this."

He smiled at me for a long moment. "Anytime."

I woke to Sam singing from my doorway, really loudly and really fucking badly. "Aye, aye, Captain." He took a deep breath and bellowed, "Whoooooooooo," before he launched into the theme song to SpongeBob SquarePants.

I pulled the pillow over my head. "Fuck you."

He barked out a laugh. "Come on, Cap. Time to get up."

Jesus. "Is the sun even up yet?"

"Almost. That's why you need to hurry."

"If I was at home, I'd be sleeping in till nine."

"If you were at home, you'd be at the office by eight."

I groaned and rolled over, kicking the blankets off me. I kinda forgot I slept in my undies until Sam's eyes went straight to my groin. I was expecting some smartarse comment, but he looked away and swallowed hard before licking his lips.

I sat up with my feet on the floor, hiding my morning wood the best I could with the blankets around my hips. But his reaction surprised me. "Jesus. How long since you've been laid?" I asked.

He totally fucking blushed. "Not as long as you."

"Keeping tabs?"

"Just fucking get dressed," he said, walking down the hall. Then he yelled, "And just for that, you're cooking breakfast when we get back."

THERE WAS something to be said about walking along the water's edge as the sun came up. The fresh sea air was invigorating; the sand between my toes was cathartic. The ebb and flow of the water pulsed a gentle beat, and Sam and I walked the length of the shoreline and back again and never said a word.

We didn't need to speak. We had that easy, amicable way about us where we could just hang out. We'd always been that way. He threw some rocks into the water, skimming them over the waves, while I was happy to just walk and enjoy the feel of early morning sunlight on my skin.

I cooked us breakfast, and Sam made me go with him to the market to buy meat for the barbeque dinner he had planned, then we kayaked around Sand Point up to Observation. It was the sheltered side of the headland, and the water, the sunshine, using muscles I hadn't used in far too long, felt amazing.

We spent the afternoon laughing and lazing about, watching the American NFL on TV. And just when I began to doze off, Sam kicked my foot. "Hey, sleeping beauty."

"Mmm."

"Help me with this."

I groaned and rolled off the couch, wearily getting to my feet. "Why are you always waking me up?"

"Because you're always falling asleep." He had packed a small Esky, and as he grabbed the open fire grill plate with the meat we'd bought earlier, he nodded toward the cooler. "Can you grab that?"

I lifted the Esky and followed him down to the beach. He had somehow started a fire. "Jeez, did I actually fall asleep? I thought I was resting my eyes."

He snorted out a laugh. "It's all good."

I fought a yawn. "I'm still exhausted."

"It's been a rough week," he said. "I'm not surprised you're so freakin' tired."

"And you've been running me around all day."

Sam put the grill plate on the fire and stoked the embers. "It's been good though, yeah?"

"It's been great," I admitted. His grin was instant, and I knew then his entire motive was to bring me up here, get me out in the sun and sand, and to expend some pent-up energy. "Which was your plan all along, wasn't it?"

"You needed this, Iz."

The quiet emotion in his voice surprised me, and it took a while for him to look at me. When he did, he gave me an uncertain smile before he replaced it with his usual smartarse smirk. "Beer me, Captain."

I fished two beers from the Esky, topped them both, and handed him one. He waited for the grill to get hot, threw the steaks on, and we settled back in the sand, watching the sun set. Right here, right now, I would have thought my life was close to perfect. But it was far from it, and that reminder sent my thoughts back to square one.

Sam was obviously on the same page as me. He sat back, resting on one elbow, quietly scratching at the beer bottle. He chewed his lip and his brow furrowed, and before I could ask him what he was thinking, he said, "The woman you saw, the one who you thought was your birth mother?"

"She looked at me like she'd seen a ghost. She nodded like she knew it was me."

"Did you get her name?"

"No. She was ushered out before I could speak to her. And Dovich said he couldn't release names until results were back and both parties agreed to meet."

"Do you want to meet her? Like for real? If the results come back and she is your mother, do you want to meet her?" He swallowed hard. "I mean, that's huge, and you can't undo that."

I'd be lying if I said I hadn't thought about that. "Yeah. I want to meet her. For sure."

"Iz," he said softly. "What if she doesn't want to meet you? What if she's not interested in any of it?"

I hadn't thought of that.

"Or what if she wants money?"

I frowned at that.

"Iz, I don't mean to imply she's a horrible person. That's not what I'm saying. I'm just worried for you, that's all. I can't stand the thought of you going through all this only to find out she's not everything you want her to be."

"Well, she certainly can't be any worse than the parents I already have."

Sam snorted out a laugh. "True."

We were quiet again for a while. Then he said, "Do you want me to come with you?"

God, was he even kidding? There was no way I could go through with that without him. He had always been my life-line, the one to save me. I wasn't sure why he expected that to change now. I nodded. "Yeah. Of course."

He gave me a warm smile. "Just let me know when and where, and I'll be there."

FIVE

On Wednesday morning, I received a phone call to advise me the DNA testing results had been determined, and by lunch time that day, I found myself sitting in Mr Dovich's office once more.

My parents were there, of course. The three of us sitting stoically, and if Mr Dovich had even the slightest inkling of body language, he'd know the distance between our three chairs was symbolic of the distance between us in person.

He wasted no time in delivering the news. Like he was reading a legal finding, he listed our names and case number. The report he read from showed a table of rows and columns, filled with letters and numbers, that I couldn't read or understand from where I sat. One page I saw had another table of numbers under the words Paternal Index, and on the third page I saw the same under the heading Maternal Index, though Dovich didn't stop to explain. He simply turned to the last page and finished with, "It is conclusive from the DNA analysis that the alleged father and mother, pertained to within this finding, are deemed excluded as the biological parents of the child."

We three sat unmoving, unblinking. I felt cold all over. "Excluded?" I asked.

He looked right at me. "You are not the biological child of your parents."

And even though I'd suspected as much, and even though part of me *knew* it, having it confirmed was still hard.

"However," Dovich went on to say, "Israel, you were a conclusive match to the separate DNA results of the woman who gave birth to a son on the same day. And after cross-referencing both buccal and blood samples, the child she was given to take home and raise as her own, was indeed a match to the DNA found in this test. Mr and Mrs Ingham, I'm very sorry to tell you, the results are indisputable. You are not the biological parents of your son."

There wasn't a sound to be heard. Even the noises from outside the room faded away, and all I could hear was the pounding of the blood in my ears.

I really was switched at birth.

These parents were not my own.

Every single thing I had known in my life was wrong.

And I don't know why, and I truly do think for a moment something shut off in my brain, because I laughed.

I fucking laughed.

Everyone in the room turned to look at me. Clearly it was not the expected reaction. "Sorry," I managed to say. "It's just..." I clamped my mouth shut to stop myself from laughing any more.

"A lot to take in," Dovich finished for me. "Understandably."

I don't know why, but I was surprised my father hadn't already threatened to sue someone and stormed out by now. I'd expected him to rant and rave and throw around his financial and legal prowess, but he didn't. He sat, stunned, alongside my equally shocked and silent mother.

Dovich spoke for a while, about what, I really couldn't say. My mind was spinning in circles, a thousand miles an hour. "Israel." My name snapped me from my thoughts, and I found Dovich looking at me. His composure was professional, but there was concern in his eyes. He gave me a moment to focus. "Your biological mother has expressed interest in arranging to meet you. She doesn't expect an answer right away, only for you to consider it at a time you're comfortable with. Whether it be done through solicitors or mediation, I—"

"Yes." I ignored the looks from my parents and cleared my throat. "Yes. I'd like to meet her as well."

"It might take some time to arrange," he went on to say.

I smiled anyway. "That's fine." Then I thought of something. "And of my biological father?"

Dovich's face softened. "He was killed in a motor vehicle accident in 1998. Sorry."

It was strange to feel a pang of loss for a person I never knew. "That's a shame."

"The boy," my mother said softly. Her voice surprised me. "What did she name him?"

Dovich looked torn. Like he wanted to tell her but wasn't sure if he should. In the end, whether it was my mother's raw expression that won him over, I wasn't sure. "His first name is Nicholas. However, he has asked not to be contacted at this time. He's not opposed to the idea of meeting with you, but he has asked to be given some time to come to terms with everything."

"Of course," my mother said. She nodded and smiled sadly. "Nicholas is a nice name." And then came her tears. She wept openly, and my father never moved to console her, so I put my arm around her shoulders. It felt clumsy and awkward, and I couldn't rightly remember the last time I'd hugged my mother, or her me, for that matter.

We stayed for a little while longer. Mr Dovich offered an

array of counselling services and support groups, though we left in a daze.

My father still hadn't spoken. I'd never seen him so uncertain of anything. My mother had stopped crying, and after I'd told her I'd be in touch, she climbed into the waiting car. My father leaned on the open car door and looked at me. He swallowed hard and frowned. "If you need time off…"

I shook my head. "No." I checked my watch. It was after two. "I have a meeting at four."

He stared at me, like he was trying to figure out what was worse: whether I didn't care he wasn't my actual father or that I was so like him, I kept my emotions in check.

My father's frown remained in place, and he gave a hard nod before getting into the car.

The truth was, I felt so detached, I couldn't describe anything I was feeling. It was almost a relief to have it confirmed that I wasn't their son, even if that left me without an identity. Without any clue of where I came from or what direction my future was headed; it was the most bizarre feeling in the world.

I was lost but somehow found.

I drove back to work on mental autopilot but had the compass of mind to call Sam. "Hey, Cap," his voice came through the speakers. "I was just about to text you. What's up?"

"Can we meet after work?

"That's what I was texting you for. The guys are heading to McGee's to watch the Twenty20. You wanna come with?"

"That actually sounds pretty perfect."

"Iz, you okay?"

"I think so."

There was a shuffling sound, like he was changing which ear he was listening with or walking to a quieter spot. "Iz?"

I pulled up at the parking garage and drove into my

reserved space. "I'm okay. I just pulled up at work, so I better get in there. See you at McGee's at six?"

"Sure thing."

"Thanks, Sam."

"Iz, you sure you're okay?"

"Yeah. I'll see you at six."

"I'll have your first Stella Artois ready and waiting."

"You are one of a kind."

"That's not a compliment. I could be one of a kind of arsehole. Or one of a kind of wanker."

"Or one of a kind of irreplaceable."

"That is the correct answer, my friend."

I laughed, despite the kaleidoscope of emotions swirling through me. I disconnected the call, and by the time I walked into my office, I had my game face on. I met with new clients, Midco, and orchestrated a kick-arse portfolio for them. I spent ten minutes talking with Prue about kayaking with Sam on the weekend, and I walked into Patty McGee's Irish Pub at two minutes to six.

True to his word, Sam had a beer waiting, and after a round of hellos to the guys, I threw myself into a chair at the table they'd claimed for the night and I smiled as I took a swig of my drink.

"Oh Captain, my Captain," Connor said. It was his usual greeting for me.

"Look at you," Jamie said with a knowing smile. "Did you get laid last night?"

I snorted out a laugh. "No."

"At lunch time with some hot courier dude in the boardroom?" Millsy added with a shit-eating grin.

"No."

Sam eyed me cautiously. "Iz?"

I took a deep breath and let it out real slow. Sam knew everything that had been going on with me but the others didn't, so I thought I'd fill them in. "So, I had some DNA testing done because apparently my parents aren't my parents at all. Results came back today." I took another mouthful of beer, and the four of them stared at me, unblinking. I swallowed my mouthful. "Makes sense though, doesn't it? I mean, how many years have we all thought I was adopted? Or wished I was, in my case. Except you see, I wasn't adopted. I was switched at birth. Apparently. And I've agreed to meet my birth mother."

Jaime, Connor, and Millsy still hadn't blinked, but the look on Sam's face was one of hurt and sadness. "Iz…"

"No, it's good," I reassured him. "I feel… well, I don't know what the fuck I feel if I'm being completely honest. But I'm not freaking out. Okay, well, maybe just a little. And even though I can't make sense of it, or given that I now have no clue who I really am or where I belong, I really do think I'm okay with it. I mean, it's scary as fuck, but it's exciting too. Because it might be kinda cool to have a family that doesn't make me feel alone."

Sam looked like he was ready to cry or scream or punch something. "You're not alone," he said.

"Not with you guys," I conceded.

Jamie scrubbed his hand over his face, still trying to process what I'd just told him. "Jesus, Cap. What the fuck?"

"I know, right?"

"When did this happen?" Millsy asked. Then he looked at Sam. "You knew? This is what the whole 'Cap needs his mates right now' speech the other day was all about. You knew?" Then he seemed to answer his own question. "Of course you knew. Sorry. But Jesus, Cap. This is huge!"

Sam ignored Millsy's outburst and subsequent apology. He hadn't taken his eyes off me. "Were your parents there?"

I nodded and took another sip of my beer. "The other guy, their real son, isn't sure if he wants to meet them. My mother cried and my father… well, he was just quiet. Like, not a word. Which is very odd for him. And he didn't come back to work."

"And you did?" Sam clearly couldn't believe it. "After finding out all that… everything… you went back to work?"

"Well yeah. I actually had a really productive afternoon." They were all looking at me like I'd lost my mind. "Seriously. I actually feel okay. Like, better than okay, I think. I don't know. I'm expecting it'll hit me at some point. But the truth is, I've always felt like I was a stranger in my family, and now I know why. I'm actually kind of relieved."

No one spoke for a while, but everyone looked at me like I was a puzzle to solve. Then Connor held his hand up to get the bartender's attention. "Five shots of tequila, straight up."

I laughed at that and drained my beer. "My shout?" I asked around the table.

No one answered. Sam's brow furrowed. "So she wants to meet you?"

"Yeah, apparently. I mean, we've seen each other, but I guess it needs to be official at some point."

Sam's eyes narrowed; his voice was soft and serious. "When?"

"I don't know. Soon probably." Then I added, "I know you have concerns about that. But I've seen her. She looked… kind. If someone can even look kind, I dunno. I want to meet her."

"Promise me you'll let me come with you."

His eyes were so imploring, all I could do was nod.

"Jesus," Millsy said. "Would you two just get married already?"

I'd kind of forgotten they were there, but I laughed and Sam smiled, almost shy-like. I could have sworn he blushed, but it might have been the lights. Before I could think any more of it, Connor came back to the table and expertly put the five shot glasses of tequila on our table. We each picked one up and I raised mine into the air. "To family. And in case you're fucking stupid, I'm talking about you bitches."

They all laughed and clinked their glass to mine. "To family."

THE NEXT MORNING, my father wasn't in the office again. Not even his personal staff knew where he was or why, and that was so out of character, I started to worry.

It wasn't worry for his well-being. I was more worried about what he was up to. I felt a stab of guilt for that; he had just been dealt life-changing news. I was hesitant to say he'd just lost a son, because he hadn't lost me, as such. He never really had me. We certainly weren't close. I couldn't remember a birthday party of mine he attended, ever. I couldn't remember him offering any gentle words to heal my teen-worried heart. I couldn't recall a time when he personally drove me to sport or training, and he certainly never tended to me if I was sick.

I actually couldn't recall one fond memory of him.

I did, however, have the perfectly clear memory of him telling me I was a disgrace to the Ingham name when my high school principal alerted my parents that I'd been caught in a compromising position with another boy. I was a senior and had already been accepted into university—albeit of my father's choosing—but I could almost taste freedom from his suffocating scrutiny. And in a rare outburst from me, I'd told him I was gay. I liked guys, and that wouldn't ever change.

He looked at me like I was dog shit on his expensive Italian shoes.

Though his distaste for me was there, long before my coming out. I remembered with perfect clarity when I was eight, the look of unpleasant puzzlement he didn't even try to hide when I'd cried watching *Toy Story*. Nothing I ever did pleased him. My grades were never good enough. Even straight A's weren't a thing to be congratulated. They were something to be maintained.

It seemed every bar of expectation he set for me was simply too high. I didn't know if he actually resented me being born, but he certainly never warmed to me. He never called me names, but in many ways I wished he had.

The coldness, the silence, the looks of disdain were, in many ways, so much worse.

I was sure he thought of me as no more than an investment in his company. The cost of my education, the nannies and personal drivers, food and clothing, were simply a long-term investment for the betterment of iCon Inc.

And that got me thinking…

Ignoring my inbox and the job file in front of me, I pulled out my phone and sent a quick text to my mother.

Just thinking of you. Hope you're okay.

It felt a little trite, but I did hope she was okay. I also hoped she'd reply and maybe explain where my father was without me having to ask.

Next, I called Sam.

He answered with, "Please tell me you're hung-over and feel like shit?"

I snorted. "I feel fine. I actually stopped drinking at nine, remember?"

He groaned, a painful sound. "Why didn't you stop me?"

"I tried, but you were on a mission."

And that was true. He was on a mission last night. When he wasn't watching me like I was a ticking time bomb, he was downing beers. Or shots of tequila. Then watching me again, like he was expecting me to lose my shit any second.

"Any reason I should know about for the Operation Get Shitfaced last night?" I asked.

He sighed into the phone. "Nah. I was just in the mood for

it. Which is something I'm deeply regretting today, let me tell you."

I realised then that I very rarely ever asked him how he was. Normally subjects just evolved in conversations, but I didn't ask him outright often enough. I needed to change that. "So, how is everything in the world of Samuel Finch, corporate lawyer extraordinaire? Hangover, notwithstanding."

He took a little while to answer. "I'm okay, Iz."

I frowned. "Just okay?"

He brightened considerably. "Yeah, yeah, I'm fine. Work's work, and my head is killing me. How you're doing is the more important question." His voice went quiet. "I can't believe you didn't tell me you got the test results back before you got to the bar. You always tell me things first."

Oh. Was that his reason for drinking so much last night? "I called you when I left the meeting. I'd literally just found out myself, and I didn't know what to feel. But then I talked to you and I felt better." I laughed at myself. "That sounds so fucking corny. Sorry. But just talking to you helped."

He was silent so long, I checked my phone to see if the call had been disconnected. "Sam?"

"Don't ever apologise." His voice sounded different. Gruff and warm. "I'm glad I could help."

"Sorry for the emo-dump," I said, trying to laugh it off. My dependence on him was embarrassing. "I'll stand on my own two feet one day. Just you watch."

"It's fine, Iz. Really, it's more than fine with me." Then he changed subjects. "So, were you just calling to see how hung-over I was?"

"No, actually, that's just a bonus."

"Gee, thanks."

I smiled and scrubbed my free hand over my face. "My old man didn't show again today. Not even his PA knows where he is."

"Fuck. Do you think he's okay?"

"I don't doubt he is."

It didn't take him long to catch on. "Who do you reckon he's meeting with?"

"I'd have a fair guess it involves Nigel." Sam knew of my father's lawyer slash friend. "And probably a QC or two."

"Fuck," he mumbled again. "Iz, we should meet for lunch. The Emporium at twelve. You're buying me the biggest, greasiest burger and fries on the menu."

"See you then."

***

It never really occurred to me, but I truly wasn't surprised it was the first thing Sam thought of.

"You need to protect yourself," he said. I knew his business face, and the seriousness with which he spoke alarmed me. "Not only financially, but your professional reputation as well."

Sam had told me, no holds barred, what he thought my father was capable of. Now I was officially not my father's son, he could have me struck from his will and, more importantly, evicted from iCon, or make my job so unpleasant I'd leave. He was under no obligation to keep me around, not to mention the fact he could barely stand to look at me, so it kind of made sense he'd get rid of me from his life.

I felt a bit stupid for not thinking of that first. I mean, it wouldn't surprise me. I didn't even question if it was something he was capable of. That went without saying. But for one thing…

"He can't hurt me professionally without hurting himself or his company. Surely he knows that. Even if his pride is dictating right now, Nigel will see reason. He won't let him do anything brash."

"But he can hurt you."

"No more than he already has."

Sam pushed his half-eaten burger away and leaned back in his seat. "Your apartment is in your name, yes?"

He was there when I bought it, so he already knew this. "Yes."

"Your car's company owned though, right?"

He knew that too. "Yes."

"Your position at the company?"

"Junior Executive Manager. Shares, dividends, ten per cent shareholder."

"Let me make some calls on that," he said, his brow furrowed. "There are director insurances and protection laws. I'd imagine Nigel is all over that, but I'll let you know something by this afternoon."

"Sam," I said quietly. "If he wanted me gone that bad, believe me, I'd go."

"Not without a fight."

"I won't beg him for acceptance or approval." I shook my head. "I certainly won't give him the benefit of mopping a courtroom floor with my arse. Don't think for one second that's a fight I'd win. He's never lost a damn thing in his life."

Sam's jaw bulged. "Fuck him. If he tries, then we'll take it to the Supreme Court and let all the QC's in the country fight it out. We'll have his company assets frozen for the duration, until he folds to save his own arse."

I couldn't help but smile at him. "You know you're hot when you get mad. Have you ever had courtroom sex? Because I'm pretty sure if you get riled up like that at work, wearing suits like the one you're wearing, I'm sure someone's bent over a desk for you more than once."

He stared at me for a second, then he scoffed, but a faint blush coloured his cheeks. "Uh, no." He shifted in his seat, then refocused. "Iz, I'm just worried about you, that's all. You know, to be forewarned is to be forearmed. I certainly hope he wouldn't do anything like this, with all of my heart, Iz. But we both know what he's capable of."

I nodded slowly. "I know."

"And if he's having secret meetings out of office that even his staff don't know about, then that's a red flag for me. He's up to something, and I don't trust him. Especially when you're involved."

I smiled at him. "Thank you."

Sam tapped the table with his finger. "And what about his will?"

"I don't know. I wouldn't know the first thing about it."

"He could do one of three things with his beneficiaries. He could either do absolutely nothing. Just leave everything as is. Or he could include his birth son into his will, which will effectively cut all entitlements to you by whatever percentage he deems appropriate. Possibly fifty per cent, Iz. That means you only get half."

I snorted out a laugh. "I know what fifty per cent is."

"Iz, I'm being serious."

"So am I. I really do know what fifty per cent is."

Sam rolled his eyes. "I'm trying to offer professional counsel here. His third likely option would be to cut you out completely, citing he'd paid enough money for a child that wasn't his, and you get nothing."

I sighed, long and loud. "Sam, I don't care."

He blinked. "What?"

"I don't care. I think it'd probably be smart for me to assume he'll leave me nothing anyway. And I'm okay with that. It's not my money anyway. I have no claim to it, so if he wants to give every cent to charity, then who am I to argue?"

"You know that'd never happen. He's never given anything away for free in his life."

I smirked. "True. And if he wants to give his real son fifty per cent, then he should. Hell, give him the lot. I don't want his money." I thought about it and shuddered. "I'd feel kinda dirty."

"And if he gave him one hundred per cent control of iCon?"

I considered that and nodded slowly. "That, I'd have an issue with."

Sam finally smiled. "And there I was thinking you'd completely lost your mind."

I picked some fries off his plate and stuffed them in my mouth. "I've worked hard for that company. I spent hours learning the ropes from the mailroom up, as an unpaid intern to where I am now. I'll admit, I wouldn't have my title if it weren't for my father, but no one can argue that I haven't worked hard. I've earned my job."

"And if he decides to bring in his new son and offers him the same job and title?"

I shrugged. "If the guy can do the job, then I have no problem with that."

Sam shook his head with a smile. "You're a good man, Israel Ingham. Plenty of other people wouldn't be so gracious under fire."

"What else can I do, Sam? The only two things I wanted from my father were love and acceptance. And considering he's never given me either, he can hardly take them from me. If he wants to take away my job and inheritance, then that says more about him than it does about me. And if his real son wants into the Ingham family mental institution, then he can have at it."

Sam almost smiled. "You saw him, didn't you? The son. Well, if that was the guy our age with the woman you saw, who you believe to be your birth mother. You'd think it would be her son."

I nodded. "Yeah. I'm pretty sure it was him. I was focused on her more than him, but in my mind's eye, I can see him. I think he has my mother's nose, but it's hard to tell if that's real or my memory playing tricks on me." I smiled sadly. "It's a bit of a mindfuck."

Sam shook his head in wonder. "Just a bit? It's a colossal mindfuck, Iz. I don't know how you're not in a padded cell by now."

"Some days I think I should be." I chuckled wryly and let out a long sigh. "You know what the hardest part is? It's not knowing who you really are. It's hard to explain, but you think you know your fundamental self, right? Your name, your parents, your heredity. It's just ingrained. You know it. You accept it. It just is. You know what you like, what you don't like, you know the fundamental truths of who you are. God, you even know your reflection. You know these things, right?"

Sam nodded.

"Well, I don't know that anymore. And as shitty as my family's been, they were still mine, ya know? But now I don't even have that." I looked around the busy café and let out a sigh. "I don't know who I am anymore."

Sam frowned. "You've never felt like you belonged with your parents."

I nodded. "I always felt more at home with your family."

He gave me a slow spreading smile. "And at the end of all this, Iz, if things with your birth mother don't work out like you hope, and if things fall to shit with your parents, you'll always have my family."

"Will you adopt me?"

He barked out a laugh. "Then your initials would be IF. That'd be very iffy."

I rolled my eyes. "Can't be worse than I I."

We stood up from the table and he fixed his jacket button. "Aye aye, Captain." Then he started singing the SpongeBob theme song, very, very loudly.

I pushed him toward the door. "I fucking hate you."

SIX

I HADN'T HEARD BACK FROM MY MOTHER BY THE TIME I WENT home, so instead of texting again, I called. She answered on the sixth ring. "Israel."

"Mother. I'm just checking up on you. I texted you earlier."

"Oh yes. I did receive your text. I meant to reply."

"Everything okay?"

She paused. "Oh yes. As well as can be expected, I guess. It's all been a bit of a shock, hasn't it?"

That was the most honest, up-front response, and one I was not expecting. "Yes, it has been."

"Are you… how are you?" she asked.

I had to stop myself from looking around my lounge room, as if a *Punk'd* camera was hidden somewhere. "I'm okay. Like you said, it's been a shock." I licked my lips. "I was hoping to speak to Dad today at work, but I must have missed him…"

It wasn't exactly a lie.

"Oh yes. Well, he took a day of leave. He'll be back tomorrow, I believe." She sounded distracted. "He's not in right now. I can ask him to call you."

"No, it's okay. I can catch up with him in the morning." Then I asked something I wasn't sure I wanted to know the answer to. "Is he okay?"

She didn't answer for a while, though I could hear her breathe, so I knew she was there. Eventually she said, "He has a lot on his mind right now."

Well, that was a diplomatic way to say no.

She daintily cleared her throat. "So, you agreed to meet… your mother?"

I would've preferred to have this conversation face to face, but if she wanted to talk about it now, I wouldn't pass on the opportunity. "Yes. I'm sorry if that upsets you. That was never my intention. I just want to see where I come from, that's all."

"It wasn't any of our intentions, Israel. None of us asked for this, so don't apologise. No one can blame you for wanting to know."

"Well, I'm sorry. And I'm sure Nicholas will want to do the same, once he's had some time to adjust."

"Possibly," she replied softly. "One couldn't blame him if he didn't. He would have his reasons, whichever he chooses."

"If he wanted to meet you, would you agree to it?"

I heard her swallow. "I… Well, I'm not sure. I'm curious, of course. I don't want to further upset him or to give him false hope."

"False hope of what?"

"I don't know what he would want from me."

I shook my head and pulled at my hair in frustration, thankful she couldn't see me. "Not everyone wants material things."

"I know that," she replied, her tone frosty.

Before our conversation could completely implode, I heard the jingle of keys at my front door. "Mum, I have to go. Sam's here."

We said tight goodbyes with no promise to talk again

soon, and I slid my phone across the coffee table just as Sam walked in. He was grinning, held a bag of Chinese takeaway in one hand, and a manila folder was tucked under his arm. "Surprise!"

"Perfect timing."

"Oh really?" he asked, walking in and heading to the kitchen.

I followed him. He'd taken his tie and jacket off that he had on at lunchtime, wearing only his navy suit pants, that sculpted his arse beautifully, and a white, fitted business shirt that looked like it was made just for him. It wasn't weird to check him out, I reasoned, because best friend or not, he was fucking gorgeous and I wasn't dead. I looked away before he caught me staring. "I was on the phone to my mother. It was possibly the longest conversation we've ever had, but…"

"But what?"

I groaned. "Ugh, she does my head in."

He put the Chinese food on the kitchen bench and handed the folder to me. "I have things to discuss and for you to look over. No pressure. I'm just giving you the information for you to do with what you wish."

My curiosity was piqued.

"It's just a brief on what we discussed today. What your rights are, and what options you have depending on your father's first move."

I opened the folder, and it was easy to see the professionalism and time he'd put into it from the first page alone. "Thanks, man. I really appreciate this."

"You don't have to read it right now," he added. "Though you should be prepared. He might do nothing, but he also might be a total prick about it."

"I know." I sighed. "But if he does try to cut me out of everything, I'm not sure I'd want to fight it."

Sam looked like he wanted to say an awful lot about that, but he let me finish.

"If he disowns me, severs all ties, whatever, *then* fires me from iCon, why would I want to keep working for him?"

"Because he can't fire you without reason."

"I wouldn't want to work for someone who despises everything about me, Sam. If he doesn't already. Somehow, like a freakin' miracle or something, I survived my childhood with enough self-respect to want better than that."

He surprised me by sliding his hand over mine, giving it a squeeze. "You do deserve better than that." He pulled his hand away, and with a nervous smile, he took two forks from the top drawer and handed one to me. "Which is why, if he does decide to be a prick, you should stand up to him."

I took the fork. "Maybe. I'll think about it. And who knows, maybe his being away from the office has absolutely nothing to do with him secretly conspiring to protect his business, assets, and reputation."

Sam snorted at my sarcasm and slid a takeaway container to me. "Your favourite."

I took my Singapore Chicken. "Thank you, Sam."

"You know," he said quietly. "One day, you won't thank me like I just saved your life."

If only he knew.

With my dinner in one hand, I grabbed two bottles of water from the fridge and nodded toward the lounge room. "I think there's NBA highlights on ESPN tonight. Wanna watch?"

He grinned. "Hell yes."

THE NEXT MORNING, I could tell by Prue's nervous smile when I walked in that my father was back in the office. "Good morning," I said, still aiming to be more personable.

"Morning," she said. "The Hallicott file is on your desk for your ten o'clock, though your father wants to speak to you first thing."

"I'm sure he does."

"I'll wait until you're back in your office before I bring in coffee, shall I?"

I gave her a smile that hopefully hid the way my stomach was in knots. "Yes. Thank you."

Not even pausing to drop my satchel in my office, I walked straight to my father's double doors and knocked.

"Yes," came his blunt acknowledgement.

I opened the door and walked inside. "You wanted to see me first thing?"

He noted the bag still slung over my shoulder before making eye contact. "Israel, take a seat."

He looked tired. Though his demeanour was always stoic, his eyes gave away his weariness. I wasn't sure what to make of that. Was it lack of sleep due to the heart-wrenching discovery of finding out his only child wasn't his at all? Or was it because he'd been up late determining the best and most efficient way to spear me.

"What's up?" I asked him.

He eyed me cautiously. "You secured the Midco contract."

"I did."

His eyes flinched. "On the afternoon we found out the test results." It wasn't a question.

I answered anyway. "Yes." Was he happy with this development, or hurt? I wasn't sure. "The paperwork should be finalised next week."

He nodded slowly. "And you worked yesterday?"

"Yes." I wasn't sure where he was headed with this. "Is that a problem?"

He took a moment to answer but looked away before he spoke. "No."

"I spoke to Mother last night. She seemed to be handling things okay."

He looked out the window at the sunny Sydney morning, then took a deep breath. "As well as to be expected."

Did he even know how his wife was holding up? I seriously doubted it, and I'm pretty sure he knew it. God, this was awkward.

"You should know that I've sought counsel against Eastport and the NSW Health Department."

Aaaaaand there it was. "I expected as much."

"We're not expecting it to be contested."

By me or the hospital? I thought sardonically.

"And we assume the matter to be settled before it goes to court."

I forced a tight smile. "Well, that would be..." Tidy. Convenient. "...best, really."

He studied me for a moment. "You don't approve?"

Somewhere inside me a levy bank broke and a lifetime of hurt, a torrent, flooded over. "Honestly," I said. "I don't give a shit. Sure, what the hospital did was wrong, grossly so, but suing them isn't going to fix anything."

He stared at me, then he smiled like I was a foolish, stupid child. And that just made me angry. So before he could reply, I said, "And quite frankly, my first reaction isn't to blame and seek remuneration. But yours is, and that's fine. So sue them. Do what you have to do. Whatever. If that's all you have to speak to me about," I said, getting to my feet, indicating I was done. "But in case you were wondering how I was holding up, if it has *even* crossed your mind at all, I'm not really doing okay. Thanks for not asking. And despite my personal life being a complete shambles, I can come into work and operate on autopilot because, after all, that's how you raised me to be." I ignored the steel of his eyes. "So rest assured, despite being a great disappointment to you, I won't let this company down. But by all means, if you need to sue them because getting me as a son was damaging to you, then go right ahead."

Ignoring the hurt and anger in his eyes, I turned and walked to the door. And even though my hand shook when I grasped the doorhandle, and even though my heart was hammering so hard and my adrenaline was pumping, I smiled as I left his office.

Prue followed me to my desk, quietly placed a coffee in front of me, and gave me a wary smile. Whether she could pick up on my mood or if she could feel the waves of adrenaline rolling off me, I wasn't sure. Although I aimed for complete composure, I highly doubted I pulled it off. I was positively buzzing.

"Do you need me to hold any calls?" she asked.

"No, no, I'm fine." And I was fine. I got through some prelim data findings and led my ten o'clock meeting with confidence and competence. I ate a few bites of lunch at my desk, not wanting to risk running into my father in the hall even though Prue told me she hadn't seen him leave his office either.

But by four o'clock, the adrenaline had well and truly worn off and the "What the fuck have I done?" had set in. I wanted to speak to Sam but couldn't bring myself to make the call. As I turned my phone over in my hands, I wondered if I was too dependent on him. I mean, I *knew* I was, but more to the point, I wondered if he was sick of babysitting me. I considered texting him instead when my phone rang in my hand.

It was Mr Dovich's office.

"Your birth mother wants to meet you," a mediator told me. "Would this weekend be okay? Or is it too soon? She didn't want to waste another minute, but she would understand," the mediator relayed.

I was so not mentally prepared to make that decision, but I knew I didn't want to put it off. I needed to move forward. Regardless of how it ended, I knew I couldn't stay where I was any more.

I said, "Yes. This weekend's fine. Just tell me where and when."

When I disconnected the call, I had no choice. The ache in my chest wouldn't let me do anything else. My fingers dialled his number without conscious thought. "Sam?"

"Hey."

"Hey. I lost my shit at my father this morning. He's suing the hospital, which we assumed he would, but I told him I didn't agree with it. I said if he needed financial compensation because he was unlucky when he got me as a son, then he should fucking have at it. I told him it was duly noted that his first concern was remuneration and not how his son or wife were holding up."

Sam let out a gasp. "Oh my God."

"Yeah. And I might have said he raised me to run on autopilot, and even though I was a huge disappointment to him, I wouldn't let the company down."

"Jesus, Iz. What did he say?"

"Nothing. Not a word."

"I can't believe you told him that."

"Neither can I."

"Did he imply anything on your standing?"

"He literally said nothing." I ran my hand through my hair for what must've been the hundredth time that day. "I felt good earlier, but now I kinda feel nauseous. I wanted to speak to you earlier, but I thought I'd try and handle this one on my own, ya know?"

"Iz. You don't have to do that. If you need me, you call. Simple as that."

"Well then, just now, a mediator from family services called. I'm meeting my birth mother this weekend."

He was silent a moment. "That's fast."

"I know. I thought that too, but then I thought I don't want to wait either. I can't stay in this limbo any longer. I need to move forward. Whether it turns out to be a good or bad thing, I need things to move forward. Being stuck in this in-between-knowing stage is suffocating." My voice was shaking and I let out an unsteady breath.

"Come to my place tonight for dinner. Sleep in the spare room."

"Sam, you babysat me last night. Don't you have a date or something?"

He huffed, like I'd made a bad joke. "Yeah. Tonight you're my date. You can help me cook."

"Sam—"

"Don't argue with me, Iz." Then his voice was quiet, anguished. "I don't want you to be alone right now."

His words hit me like a punch to the gut. I took a shaky breath and somehow pulled myself together. Even hearing his voice and knowing I'd see him soon calmed me, fixed me. I was kidding myself to think I could do this without him. "Okay."

"Good. Come around after six."

"Okay. Sam?"

"Yeah?"

"Do you really make your dates help you cook? Because that could explain why you're single…"

"Shut up, Captain. My place, six o'clock. Don't be late."

SAM'S ADDRESS in Potts Point was only a short drive from my place, but in terms of exclusivity and income, it was miles apart. Sure, my place was nice. I had more disposable income than the national average, and I was what most people would probably call rich.

But Sam's level of wealth far exceeded mine. Not just from his family's old-money, generations amassing more growth with each decade, but his own career and insightful financial decisions had made him more money than I could probably fathom.

He had more personal wealth than a small country, yet there he stood in his kitchen barefoot, wearing old sweatpants and an old rugby shirt that was almost threadbare, riddled with small holes along the seams. He was totally comfortable and never looked hotter.

Sure, I'd seen him wearing the most expensive tailored suits money could buy. And by God, he wore them well. But nothing beat seeing him relaxed and laughing in his oldest, daggiest clothes, standing in his kitchen, slicing vegetables and sipping a beer.

"Are you gonna halve those squash or are we eating them whole?"

His question snapped me out of my delusional daydreaming. Sam was my closest friend, my everything. I wasn't sure when I started to think of him as hot, or sexy, or fucking gorgeous, but it had to stop.

I couldn't risk ruining what I had with him. So, instead, I put up my first and best defence mechanism: humour.

"So, you not only make your dates cook, but you get pissy about it too?" I joked. "I'm pretty sure that's why you're single."

He paused, mid-slice of a zucchini, and pointed the knife at me. "I'll have you know, I'm single because every time we go out, guys assume we're a couple."

That had happened so many times, our mates now told people we were married. "True. Though we don't even dirty dance together. I mean, if I was grinding on your dick or on my knees sucking it, I could probably see where they might get that idea. But all we do is talk."

Sam stared at me, his vegetable slicing forgotten. The tips of his ears grew red, and he licked his lips before he cleared his throat. "Thanks for a mental image no amount of brain bleach or vodka will erase."

I snorted out a laugh. "Are you slicing that zucchini or are we eating them whole?"

"You're an arsehole."

I grinned. "Thanks! I love arseholes."

He laughed at that and continued to slice the vegetables. "Can you grab the steamer?"

I went directly to the cupboard it was kept in, the second drawer under the wall oven. I knew where everything was in his place, as he did in mine. I filled the bottom of the steamer with water, then switched the grill skillet on to get it as hot as possible before he cooked the steak.

We worked well together in the kitchen, like a left and right hand. Perfectly in tune. By the time we sat down to eat, we'd had two beers, and I hadn't laughed that much in what felt like forever.

He never asked about my father, and he never once mentioned how my life had turned to shit. He seemed to know when to push, and he seemed to know when to hold back and give me just what I needed. And right then, I needed to feel normal. Like the old me, the me I was just a few weeks ago.

Long after dinner was done and the kitchen cleaned up, we sat on his sofa with our feet stretched out on the coffee table, watching some crap show on TV that neither of us were really paying much attention to.

"So, how did I stack up as a date?" I asked.

"Cooking skills are okay, conversation skills aren't too bad. Company is pleasant. But as it's a first date and I have a strict moral code of no fucking on the first date, I'm afraid I can't give you a ten out of ten."

I snorted out a laugh. "You? Moral code?"

He looked offended. Almost. "I'll have you know, I'm a complete and utter gentleman."

"But your moral code requires sex before giving a full score. That's hardly moral."

He laughed and let his head fall onto the back of the sofa, completely relaxed. "On a second or third date sex would up the rating, yes. But if you're being pedantic, I'll concede to strictly dancing and kissing on a first date."

"Then you failed as a first date for me. No dancing, no kissing, definitely no fucking. But the steak was *really* good."

He looked at me for a long moment, like he was trying to decide something. Then changed the TV to some random music channel, got to his feet, and pushed the coffee table to one side. When he was done, he held his hand out to me.

"What are you doing?" I asked.

"You're going to dance with me."

I almost laughed. "What?"

"Just give me your hand, dumbarse."

"We really need to work on your pick up lines," I joked but put my hand in his. He pulled me up so I stood in front of him. "Are we seriously going to dance?"

"Yep."

"This music is kinda crap," I said. Because it was.

He picked up the remote, but instead of changing the channel, he just turned it up. Really fucking loudly. Then he grabbed my hands and spun me around, and when I had righted myself, he was moving to the rhythm. The beat wasn't too bad, kinda groovy, and seriously, you could dance to anything if it was loud enough.

So we danced.

It was strange but oddly freeing at the same time. We'd do stupid moves to make each other laugh, and when Kylie's "Can't Get You Out Of My Head" came on, he did a perfect impersonation of her dance moves that made me roar with laughter. The next song was Bruno Mars' "Uptown Funk," and it was my turn to put on a show. Sam laughed so much, he held his side like it hurt, but he never stopped dancing.

But then Tracy Chapman's "Give Me One Reason" came on, and of course the tempo changed completely. It wasn't really a slow song. It was more of a groove song. It was a hip grinding song. And Sam gave me a wicked grin and held his hand out for me. I half expected him to spin me around again, only slower this time, but he didn't. He pulled me flush against him, so our bodies met from thigh to chest. He slid one arm around my waist and pushed a palm against my lower back, keeping me right where I was. His other hand ran over the swell of my arse, and I could have sworn I heard him groan.

I ran my hands under his shirt and over his back, feeling his muscles and warmth, hard planes and soft skin. He felt incredible.

We rocked and swayed, grinding to the music. Sure, we'd danced plenty of times in nightclubs, but not like this. Never like this.

He wore a lopsided smirk and ran his nose up my neck, and my brain almost short-circuited. My whole body buzzed at the contact. But knowing this was Sam, my Sam, getting his filthy on with me, really turned me on. It was a heady feeling, a dizzying, heightened feeling. He was everything familiar and new and exciting at the same time.

He let his breath wash over the shell of my ear and my cock responded. I had no doubt he felt it. I could feel him, *all* of him, and he pulled our hips harder together. Fuck. He was definitely enjoying this. Whatever the fuck this was.

The song was hypnotic, or maybe he was. I wasn't sure. But he pressed harder against me, swaying our hips to the rhythm, and as the song drew to an end, he rested his forehead against mine. His breathing was rough, but his smile was... his lips were... so close, and so perfectly pink and plump.

I don't know why I did it. It wasn't a conscious decision. I acted purely on instinct. But with the softest of nudges, the lightest of touches, I ghosted my lips over his.

He gasped and his fingers dug into my skin. His heated

gaze flickered to mine, and *oh fuck*, his eyes were sex and smoulder.

And that one moment could have gone either way. We could have kissed again, properly and deeply, and crashed to the sofa in a frenzy of mouths and hands, bringing each other to climax. Or we could each take a step back and a deep breath.

At least he had the presence of mind to act first. He let out a gentle laugh and pulled away. I missed his warmth and touch instantly, but I knew he'd done the right thing.

"Fuck," he said with a chuckle. "That was…"

"Unexpected," I provided. "Hot. And fucking crazy. What *was* that?" I asked.

He scrubbed one hand over his face and shook his head. Then he palmed his dick, which, in sweatpants wasn't exactly easy to hide. He was hard, as was I, but at least I was wearing jeans. The thicker denim saved my dignity.

"It's been a long time between drinks," he said, laughing off his embarrassment at being turned on. "That's what that was."

There was no point in denying I was in a similar state. He'd felt how hard I was, and I didn't want him to be embarrassed. "Like I said, it was hot."

His eyes were filled with uncertainty. "And crazy, right?" He didn't wait for me to answer. "I think we should call it a night, yeah?"

I nodded. It was kinda late. But I didn't want him to feel bad for anything. I mean, after all, it was me who kissed him. I walked to the lounge room light switch and turned it off. "Well, as a first date, I'd give you a ten out of ten. Dinner, dancing, and a kiss. Though you did call me dumbarse. Maybe I should deduct a point for that."

Thankfully, he laughed. It was my intention, and it worked. The tension between us lightened considerably. He flipped off the kitchen light and we walked up the hall. "But I did the moves to Kylie. I get plus two points for that. So technically, that's eleven out of ten."

I stopped at the spare room, my bedroom door. "Doesn't count unless you're wearing tiny gold hotpants. Which you weren't. Because if you were, I'd have totally given you tongue when I kissed you."

He shoved my shoulder, hard, pushing me into my room. "Fuck off."

I burst out laughing. "Night, Sam."

He mumbled something unintelligible, but I chuckled nonetheless. With the door shut and the lights off, I stripped to my underwear and climbed into bed. I was still hard, and my cock was aching for friction. As soon as I wrapped my hand around myself, I thought of blue eyes and a lopsided smirk. I thought of how his back felt under my hands, his warmth, his smell, and how his cock felt pressed against mine through our clothes. I remembered how his hands clawed at my back and squeezed my arse, and I remembered the sweetness of the kiss, his lips against mine. I came in thick bursts of bliss and heaven.

And even as my cognitive realms came back to me, I cleaned myself up and drifted off into a boneless slumber. I refused to let myself worry that I'd just jerked off to fantasies of my best friend.

BREAKFAST COULD HAVE BEEN AWKWARD. In the cold light of day, the realisation that we'd basically dirty-danced and kissed last night could have been devastating to our friendship. And I couldn't let that happen. Because I couldn't bear the thought of losing him, I would carry on like nothing had happened. Given I'd barely slept, I was up long before Sam, and by the time he shuffled into the kitchen, I was sitting at his island bench, showered, dressed, and ready for work. I had a coffee in one hand and an iPad with the *Daily Telegraph* on screen in the other.

"What kind of government makes these decisions?" I asked, reading through the day's morning news headlines. "And how has there not been a federal inquest into the Reserve Bank? I'm telling you, someone is getting their dick sucked under the table."

Sam, looking half-asleep, shirtless, given he was wearing only sleep pants, squinted at me through one eye. His hair was sticking up at all angles, and he even still had a crease line down his cheek from his pillow.

"Morning," I said.

"Who's sucking whose dick?"

"That's what I want to know."

He looked at me then, still squinting. Then he looked at his wrist for a watch he wasn't wearing, then looked at the clock on the microwave. "Shit, Iz. It's six-thirty."

I was smiling at him. Was he always so damn cute in the mornings? "Go shower. I'll make fresh coffee and have breakfast ready by the time you get out."

"Hmm." He made a face. Then he walked over to where I was sitting, and without a word, he simply took my half-full coffee cup, turned, and walked back to his room.

Still grinning, I refilled his coffee machine and put in one of his favourite pods. I cut up some fruit and popped some bread into the toaster. By the time he came back into the kitchen, I had everything spread out on the island bench and was rewarded with a full-blown grin. He pulled up a stool next to me, and a wave of his subtle aftershave washed over me.

Something I'm sure I'd never noticed before.

His suit pants were charcoal grey; his shirt, a crisp white; his tie, royal blue. He was cleanly shaven, his hair now wet and combed into place, and I wasn't sure which version was more beautiful: the sleek-and-suave Sam or the sleep-rumpled Sam.

He stabbed a strawberry, shoved it in his mouth, and washed it down with coffee. "What time are we leaving tomorrow?"

Oh. I'd kinda forgotten about that. "Um. The meeting is at 10:00 a.m. In Penrith."

"Penrith?"

I shrugged. "They must live out west. I don't know."

"Do you know her name?"

I let out a slow breath. "I do."

"And you never told me?"

"If I disclosed that information, what would you have done?"

His toast stopped halfway to his mouth. He pouted thoughtfully.

"Exactly," I said, holding my coffee in a cheers motion.

"Well, of course I'd try and find out everything I could, Iz. And you wouldn't?"

"Nope."

"What if she's a psycho?"

"Sam."

"Sorry, Iz. But we have no idea who we're meeting tomorrow. And my first concern is you." He frowned and put his toast down. "I want it to work out, Iz. More than I can say. But I worry you'll be disappointed and heartbroken. And that scares me."

"Scares you?"

"Yes." His eyes were an imploring blue. "I don't know how much more you can take. Because if it were me in your shoes, I'd have lost my shit years ago."

"No, you wouldn't have."

He barked out a humourless laugh. "Ah, yeah. I would have."

We were quiet for a little while. He sipped his coffee and finished his toast and some melon. I slowly turned my coffee in my hand. "Her name is Donna. Donna Westbrook. The son, the guy I was switched with, his name is Nick. Nicholas Westbrook."

I had Sam's undivided attention.

"I guess that's my real name. That's who I was born as. Who I should have been. Nicholas Westbrook."

"Do you honestly feel like you should have been someone else? I mean, I know it's true, but I can't imagine you being anyone else." Sam shook his head slowly. "You're Israel Ingham to me."

I gave him a smile. "I don't know how I feel. Well, that's not true. I feel betrayed, pissed off, just for starters. To be honest, I don't think I'll know how I really feel until I meet them. It's like it's not real yet. Or something." I shrugged. "But it's weird, huh? To think I could have had a very different life. Different name, different parents, different friends."

"It is weird," he allowed. He pushed his plate away and frowned at his coffee. "I can't imagine that. You know, singing the SpongeBob SquarePants song to anyone else would just feel wrong."

I chuckled. "God forbid."

His smile turned serious. "Whatever happens tomorrow, Iz, we'll be okay, okay?"

"When are we never okay?"

"Well, there was that time we went skiing. You know, what is now regarded as the Thredbo Incident of 2011."

I rolled my eyes. "You locked me out of the lodge at two in the morning, in the snow. In my underwear."

"Technically, it was my underwear. I paid for it."

"It was SpongeBob underwear, and I did wear it. And let's be honest. I think we both agree that it was me who paid in the end. My feet were frozen solid, and it took two hours at room temperature for my dick to reappear. Jesus, it was cold out there."

He burst out laughing. "You lost at poker. It was the bet going in. You knew that."

"You stacked the cards when I went to the bathroom. I know you did. Connor told me. And even though you totally cheated me out, I still put on those damn underpants."

He grinned without shame. "You have to admit. It was funny. You were laughing doing that Squidward thing."

"But then you pushed me outside. Luckily for me, that guy from the chalet next door let me into his place. He kept me warm till morning."

Sam glared at me. "Thought you said your dick disappeared for two hours."

"Mine did. Not his," I clarified.

His smile was tight. "Only you could get laid wearing nothing but SpongeBob undies."

I stood up and put the plates in the sink and changed the subject. "Promise me you won't look into Donna's history. I want to meet her without judgement. I want an honest first impression."

He was suddenly beside me, putting his cup in the sink. "Sure thing, Iz." Then, hesitantly he said, "Can I ask you something?"

"Sure."

"Have you researched what to expect? Or what not to expect? I mean, there has to be other documented cases of people being switched. Have you read their experiences?"

"No. Why would I have?"

"Because what you're going through is isolated to a very specific few. There's no right or wrong way to feel. And maybe reading about what others went through will help you understand or better appreciate the gravity of what you're about to do tomorrow."

I let his words turn over in my head a few times, but

before I could respond, he clapped my shoulder. "Come on. We better get going."

Sam dropped me off at work and tried to convince me that he should come over to my place for dinner. He didn't say it again, but I knew he was worried about me being alone. The thing was, I really needed some time to clear my head. I apologised about five times, and I promised to call him tonight. He said he understood, and I tried to ignore the flash of hurt in his eyes.

Then I went into my office and spent the day reading websites of people who met their biological parents. Ironically, I didn't see my own father all day, even though he was in his office right next door to mine.

But Sam was right. Reading similar cases gave me a better understanding of what to expect and a greater empathy of people who, like me, had had their worlds turned upside down. Some cases had happy endings; most did not.

I read of cases in America, England, Russia, South Africa. Each case was different, yet the collateral damage was always the same; each and every person was forever changed.

But it also gave me expectations, as a whole. Which is something I truly hadn't allowed myself to feel.

Up until then, I had no expectations of my biological mother. I hadn't wondered what I'd do if she was a heroin addict or an alcoholic gambler, like some of the case studies I read. Or if she was some religious fanatic who hated LGBT people. I hadn't even considered what I'd do if she outright rejected me.

I was pretty sure I wouldn't cope with that very well at all.

I didn't know if I was better or worse off for reading those case studies. Part of me knew that it was best to be mentally prepared, yet part of me wished I didn't know at all. I printed off the psychologists' reports on some case studies, giving their findings on the impact of being switched at birth, and Prue stuck her head through the door after five and reminded me it was home time. I packed up my things and took the printouts with me.

Needless to say, I didn't get much sleep.

And when Sam arrived at a little after eight the next morning, he gave me a sympathetic smile to my obvious lack of sleep. "How you holding up?"

"Okay," I offered lamely. I pushed the neat pile of case studies on the kitchen counter to face him. He read the top page, *"Switched At Birth: Psychological Findings and Evaluations."* He glanced at me, alarm and caution in his eyes. "Though I don't think I should have read those."

"Oh, Iz," he murmured.

"I'm kinda glad I know what to expect. But I also kinda wanted to go into this meeting with an open mind, and now it's too late. Now I'll be reading into every little thing, wondering which one's gonna fuck me up the most."

He walked over to me and put his hand on my arm. "If you don't want to do this, you don't have to. I'll call them right now and tell them you need more time or whatever you want me to tell them."

I shook my head. "No. Today. I need to do this today. I need to move forward. I can't stay stuck here any longer."

His eyes sparked with concern and understanding. "Okay. You ready to go?"

I took a deep breath and exhaled slowly. "As I'll ever be."

I SPENT the hour-long drive to Penrith staring out the window while Sam drove, mostly in silence, peppered with concerned looks in my direction.

The place we were to meet was a large park with an open café. Busy with Saturday morning joggers, families, and dog-walkers, it made sense to meet in such a public space that afforded privacy if required.

Sam pulled up nearby, and even though I could see the café and the outdoor tables and chairs, I couldn't bring myself to get out of the car. I took a deep breath, then another, trying to calm my hammering heart. "A lady from family services is meeting me out front," I said, my voice strained and rough. "She'll take us in and make formal introductions."

"Is that her?" Sam asked.

I risked a glance and saw an older lady, thin with straight grey hair, standing outside the café, looking out of place in her pantsuit when everyone else was wearing shorts or running gear. I nodded. "She was in Dovich's office the first time."

"You wanna head inside?"

My stomach knotted, but I opened the car door. Sam quickly followed, and by the time I slowly got out, he was by my side. I shut the door and tried to take a step, but my feet wouldn't move.

"Iz?" Sam asked.

"What if she doesn't like me?" I asked. "What if I disappoint her? What if I don't live up to the expectations she has of me? What if she's a homophobic piece of shit who tells me she's glad she got the better son?"

Sam put his hands to my face and looked me right in the eye. "No. No, no. You are not the disappointment here, Iz. And if she says one thing about you being gay, we stand up and wish her a bitter, miserable fucking life. Then I take you home and call my parents, and we'll have you adopted into my family by dinner time, okay?"

I gave a teary laugh. "Okay."

Then, like he couldn't help himself, he leaned in and gave me a soft kiss on the cheek. "No matter what happens in there today, you will always have me, okay?"

I closed my eyes and let myself absorb his words. "Thank you." I took a deep breath and let it out as slow as possible, and opened my eyes. "Okay, let's do this."

SEVEN

After brief introductions, the family services lady, Brenda, told me that my birth mother and her son were already waiting inside. She asked if I had any questions before we went in, to which I replied, "Oooooh, only about a million."

She waited for me to elaborate, but I just shook my head. "No. Nothing."

"Okay, I'll make the introductions," she explained. "I can stay or leave, whichever you'd both prefer."

I wasn't sure what I wanted.

"How about we see how it goes?" she offered with a smile.

I nodded. "Sounds good."

"Are you ready, Mr Ingham?"

I think I nodded because she opened the door, and I followed her inside. The café itself had huge stacking doors that, on perfect days such as this, could be pushed open. Some tables were inside, some were outside, some in between. We were led over to a far table where two people were seated.

I already knew it was them. It was the woman and man

I'd seen in Dovich's office, and as we approached, they stood up. The woman, my birth mother, was about five foot four, with shoulder length brown hair. She looked… soft, and kind. The guy with her, my parent's birth son, was tall and lean, the same as my father, but his thin pointed nose and pointed chin was exactly like my mother's.

My chest felt like it was in a vice, and butterflies swarmed my stomach. I felt sick, as equal parts excitement and dread rolled through me. Brenda stood side-on, neutral. "Donna and Nick Westbrook, this is Israel Ingham and his support person, Sam."

Staring right at me, Donna nodded and tears ran down her cheeks. She put her hands to her face. "My God, you look just like your daddy."

And out of everything I thought I expected, that wasn't on the list.

I burst into tears, and without hesitating, she wrapped her arms around me and hugged me. I surprised myself by holding on just as tight. And we cried.

It was so surreal, so very remarkable that this woman was a stranger to me, yet we were somehow familiar as well. I couldn't explain it. But it kinda felt natural to hug her. We were strangers, yes. In every sense of the word. DNA aside, we shared an experience, a devastating loss out of our control. Something that no one else could really understand.

She pulled away and wiped her cheeks, her smile wide. "Look at me," she said, "blubbering like this."

"Me too," I said. "I haven't cried my entire life what I've cried in the last two weeks."

"Same as my mum," Nick said. "Just bursts into tears for no reason. Well, not no reason," he cringed. "You know what I mean."

Smiling, I held out my hand for him to shake. He had a firm grip with rough skin that told me he worked with his hands. "I do. Nick, I'm Israel. This is Sam."

Nick shook Sam's hand and Donna hugged him too. "I'm not normally a hugger," she said.

"She hugs everyone," Nick said, and she rolled her eyes at him. It was very clear they were close.

"Please, take a seat," Donna said, still drying her eyes. "I promised I wouldn't get emotional, and I've already lost that battle."

I laughed as I sat down with them. "Ah, me too." I was smiling, grinning even. There were no words to describe how this felt. I knew it was brand new, and I knew there'd be bumpy roads ahead, but as far as starts went, I think we'd done okay.

Sam sat then tapped my leg. "Let me get some coffees."

I nodded and let out a nervous breath. "That'd be great." Sam got everyone's order and left me to it. He was only at the counter, so he wasn't far away. I turned back to Donna and Nick.

"So," Donna hedged. "Where do we start?"

I shrugged. "At the beginning?"

And so she did. As it turned out, both her and my mother had caesarean births, amidst some minor complications, and both babies—me and Nick—were taken out of the birthing rooms and brought into neonatal care, which is where they believe the mix up happened. Shortly afterwards, we were given standard hospital bracelets, but of course, we were given the wrong ones.

Donna got teary again. "I never even held you. An hour or so later, when I was in recovery, the baby they brought back to me was my Nick. I never knew any different. None of us did."

Sam came back over and, with the help of a waitress, slid the coffees onto the table. He sat back down beside me and gave me a reassuring smile. He was obviously happy to be in the background, but even his quiet presence was a fucking pillar.

"It's funny," Donna mused. "Out of all the kids, Nick looks the most different, but still kinda like me. Same hair colour, same eye colour."

I looked at Nick. "You look like my mother. You have her nose and chin." Sam's smile confirmed this, though Nick just nodded slowly, taking it all in. Then I thought about what Donna had said… "All the kids? Are there others?"

Donna laughed. "I have three. Nick, Lachie, and Ashley's the baby."

"She's the spoiled one," Nick added with a fond smile.

I blinked. I couldn't seem to speak. It took a while for me to get air into my lungs. "Are they…?"

Donna's face fell as she realised what I was asking. "Well, yes. I guess they're your full brother and sister."

I took a deep breath, but my eyes burned with tears. I had to bite my lip to stop it from trembling. "I wasn't expecting that," I whispered. I had a brother and a sister? I couldn't believe it. "Do they know about me?"

Nick nodded. "Yeah, of course. They know everything we know." He hesitated for a second, then added, "You look like Lachie. I gotta admit, I wasn't expecting that."

I nodded to let him know I understood. Because I got it, I really did. This whole thing was fucked up. "I don't have any siblings," I said. "I mean, in my family." Sam put his hand on the back of my chair and rubbed his thumb on my back. I gave him a brief smile. "Well, I've got Sam's sisters. And his parents, of course."

"What about your parents?" Donna asked, her head tilted.

"What are they like?" Nick prompted. I could tell he was curious but cautious.

I had to phrase this carefully. I didn't want to cloud Nick's judgement of his birth parents. "We're not very close."

"Oh." Donna's face fell.

I glanced at Nick, quick to clarify. "They're not bad people."

Donna's gaze flicked to Sam for the briefest of moments, and when I looked at him, I saw his jaw was clenched, his smile tight. It was a look Donna obviously didn't miss. So I added, "My father runs a high-tech business, which is where I work also."

"You work with him, and you're still not close?"

I shook my head, just a fraction. "No."

"What did he think about you meeting me? Us?" Nick asked.

"He, uh. He never mentioned it. Well, the truth is, we don't speak that often, and our last conversation wasn't exactly pleasant. And my mother…" I didn't even know what I was trying to say.

The circle Sam rubbed on my back got bigger, and I took strength from his touch.

"I've been somewhat of a disappointment." I had no idea why I was pouring my heart out to these people. Even though I'd barely scraped the surface of the subject of my parents, I had to choose my words carefully. "Sorry, Nick. I'm trying to be very mindful of what I say. I don't want to sway your opinion of them. My parents, your birth parents, are decent people. They have good friends, they donate money to a range of charities, they're generous in that regard."

"Why on earth would you be a disappointment, child?" Donna asked. She looked confused and horrified that any child would even think that. I liked that about her.

"Well," I started. "That list is long."

"Iz has never been a disappointment," Sam said. "Not once. His parents have… different expectations."

Well, that was one way to put it.

"Don't feel you have to hide anything about them," Nick said. "I'm pretty sure I'll want to meet with them at some point, but I have my mum. I don't need or want another one." He said it so simply. "We talked long and hard about this, didn't we Mum?" Donna nodded and Nick continued.

"Whether Mum gave birth to me or not, she's still my mum. Lach and Ash are still my brother and sister. No DNA test's gonna change that."

There was no malice or threat in his statement. It was just a matter of fact. I envied his confidence to speak of love that way.

"You're very close." My voice was gruff.

Donna gave me a sad smile. "When my husband died, the kids' father—your birth father—well, we didn't have much choice. We had to stick together. Ash wasn't even a year old. I had three young kids and not much money. But we were all we needed. We got by okay, didn't we, Nick?"

"We did okay," he said, giving her a smile like it was some inside joke.

"Can I be honest with you?" I asked them both. Fuck, I could barely speak.

Donna nodded. "Of course."

"I don't want anything from you. I don't expect anything." New tears rolled down my cheeks. I didn't even try to hide them. "If you leave here and decide this isn't right for you, then that's okay. I'll understand. This isn't easy for any of us. But if I had to say honestly, if I could get one thing out of this, if it's okay with you, is that I'd like to learn more about me. About where I came from, who I am, and why."

"Oh, child," Donna said. She was crying too. "You're really hurting, aren't you?"

I couldn't answer that. I guessed I didn't need to.

I swallowed hard. "When I first found out about being switched, when Mr Dovich first told us, it was so unbelievable, but deep down I wasn't surprised at all. I've never felt like I belonged." I laughed at how pathetic I sounded. "But I have something to tell you. It's not really how I wanted to say this, but if you decide you don't want anything to do with me because of what I'm about to tell you, then I need to know now. Before we go any further."

I left the "because I don't think I could handle any more rejection" unsaid.

"What is it?" Donna asked.

"I'm gay," I said. Sam slid his hand in mine and held on tight, though I never broke eye contact with Donna.

She surprised me by laughing. She literally laughed. "God, I thought you were gonna tell me you were a bank robber or a Melbourne Storm supporter."

I barked out a laugh. "Uh, no."

Nick looked at me weirdly. "You're not a Brisbane Broncos supporter, are you?"

I chuckled and shook my head. "No. I follow Wests Tigers in the NRL, Sydney Swans in the AFL, and the Waratahs in rugby, of course."

Donna put her hand to her heart. "Your dad was a Tigers fan. Loved the Swans too, he did." She got teary again. "Fancy that, huh." I kept eye contact with her for a long moment.

"Is that why you're a disappointment to your dad?" Nick asked. "'Cause you're gay?"

I swallowed hard. "His disappointment started long before that, but it'd be the main factor now, I guess."

"And you thought we might not approve?" Donna asked.

"I have no clue. I'm not ashamed, and I won't hide who I am, so if that's an issue..."

Donna reached over the table and squeezed my hand. "Oh hun, it doesn't make any difference to me who you fall in love with, be it a man or a woman, or both. It doesn't matter to any of us. Not one bit."

I let her words wash over me, and my heart ached heavy and hurting in my chest. Of course more tears came. I wiped them away with the heels of my hand. "Stupid tears."

"Don't apologise," Donna said kindly, wiping tears of her own.

Nick snorted softly, and he was fighting a smile. "I think it's pretty safe to assume you're related."

Donna laughed, rubbing her son's arm, while of course I just cried some more. Sam rubbed my back, and when I looked at him, he was smiling. It was the kind of smile that told me he was proud of me and happy this meeting had gone well.

"So?" Donna said. "Tell me about you. Where you live, what you do at work, what you do on weekends, what movies you like? Songs, food. That kind of thing."

I got the feeling the meeting was winding down and she wanted to end on a happy note. And so, for the next ten minutes I gave them a brief rundown of my life.

Then it was Donna's turn. I learned that Donna and her family lived in Penrith. She worked in the fabric department at Spotlight, she still had Lachie and Ash at home, and she spent most of her time cooking and cleaning up after them.

"And she loves it," Nick said fondly. "Cried for a week when I moved out."

Then it was Nick's turn. He was a builder by trade and worked for a local construction company, which explained his tanned skin and rough hands. He had just gotten engaged to a girl called Melissa, and his eyes lit up when he spoke of her. They'd moved in together and were planning a wedding. Well, Melissa was planning the wedding; he was doing what he was told.

"I tried telling her it was better to save for a house or something," he said. "But she wants a wedding." He shrugged with a smile. "So she gets one."

It was pretty clear he'd give her whatever she wanted.

"What about you, Sam?" Donna asked. She looked at him expectantly, brightly.

He'd been sitting back observing throughout the whole meeting; he was obviously surprised by this interaction now. "Oh, I uh, I work in the city too. Live not far from my parents," he said. He smiled at Nick. "Not too unlike you. Moved out of home but didn't go too far."

Donna smiled proudly at Nick. "Still has dinner once a week at home, don't you, love?"

Nick looked at me and sighed. "She makes me."

I couldn't help but laugh, and it was a nice way to finish up our first meeting. We'd been there an hour. As good as it had been, it was a lot to take in, and I needed some time and space to decompress. I figured they were the same.

"Well," Donna said. "We should be going along now."

"Yes, so should we," I agreed.

Donna put her handbag on her lap and looked at me. She was obviously trying to get the words right in her head before she spoke. "I wasn't sure what to expect. And I told Lach and Ash that Nick and I would meet you first. You know, before they got their hopes up. I didn't want them to be disappointed. I didn't know if we'd leave here and never speak again, and there was no need for them to get involved if that were to happen. But I'd like for us to meet again, Israel. If that's alright with you?" She smiled kindly. "And maybe you'd consider meeting them?"

"Oh." I wasn't expecting that. "Sure."

"You don't have to," she amended. "If it's too soon. And you don't have to agree to anything just yet. It can be next week. Or next year. It's a lot to take in, isn't it?"

I nodded. "It is. I hadn't expected siblings. I've spent my whole life by myself. Siblings is… Well, it's blown me away. I don't know what they expect, and I don't know what to expect of myself. I can't promise anything to you or them." I let out a shaky breath. "But I'd like to meet them, yes."

"Can we swap phone numbers?" Donna asked. "Is that allowed?" She looked around for Brenda, who was reading a magazine at a nearby table.

"It's fine," I said with a smile. "It's fine with me."

After we'd done that, we stood up and walked outside,

where we hugged our goodbyes. "I refuse to cry," Donna said, her eyes teary again. "This is a happy goodbye."

"It is," I agreed. "No promises, no pressure, but this has been good, yes?"

She nodded, and Nick put his arm around her. "See you soon."

We watched in silence as they walked to a car parked up the road, and when their older model Holden disappeared from view, we walked to Sam's car. I leaned against the door, closed my eyes, and turned my face to the sun. I needed a second.

"You okay?" Sam asked. I could tell by his voice he was close.

I opened my eyes, feeling a tiredness in my bones. "I am. That went okay, didn't it? They're good people, yeah?"

Sam's smile was wide and warm. "She said you look like your dad, but I dunno, Iz. You're a lot like her."

My eyes welled with tears. "Really?"

He put his hand on my arm. "Come on. Let's go home. Yours or mine?"

"Mine."

We got into his car and headed back toward the city.

He let me process in silence, and as we got to the M2, I told him, "I've never looked like anyone before."

He reached over and took my hand. "I know."

He didn't pull his hand away, so I threaded our fingers and held on the whole way home.

EIGHT

Sam hung around all afternoon. He ordered in some Indian food for a late lunch, and he had some emails to catch up on. I did the same, then zoned out in front of the TV while he did what he had to do. So, he hung around; we each did our own thing while he kinda kept an eye on me.

It probably should have bothered me. But the truth was, I loved it. It was a comfort knowing he was there, without being in my face. We'd always been like that, though. We could hang out at each other's places but not have to actually do anything together.

I had so much to process. I had a mental barrage of information and possibilities, and while I knew I had to be reasonable and practical, it was hard not to get a little ahead of myself.

I had a family.

I had a mother, and I had a brother and sister. Though I'd never even seen them, and in all likelihood we had nothing in common, but we shared a mother and father. According to Nick, I looked like Lachie. According to Donna, I looked like my father.

It was surreal to finally have that physical appearance

connection, a genetic bond with other human beings. Yet there was a very real disconnect because these people were strangers.

It was a lot to get my head around.

It was hard to watch them together. Clearly they loved each other very much. The way Nick looked at Donna told me he admired her, and the way she looked at him was the way a mother should look at her son. She adored him, and it showed. They were everything my mother and I were not. Not once had my mother and I shared a laugh. Not once had we looked at each other and laughed at a private joke. They had such a perfect ease around one another, and while I envied it, it was hardest to watch because part of me thought that should have been me. I should've had a mother that loved me.

But the very hardest part, the truly hardest part, was knowing if I had grown up with my real family, they'd have known I was gay and loved me anyway.

That hurt the most.

Sure, I had material things. I had money. Any quantifiable thing I could have wished for. And as Donna had said, they never had much, just enough to get by.

But I'd have given away every damn cent for parents that loved me.

"You okay?" Sam's voice startled me. He handed me a beer and sat on the sofa with me. "You've been staring at the wall for half an hour."

I scrubbed my free hand over my face and sighed. "Just thinking."

"Yeah, figured. Wanna talk about it?"

I took a swig of beer. "I don't know. I don't know what I'm supposed to think or feel."

"There's no right or wrong here, Iz."

"I know. I'm trying not to get my hopes up while convincing myself not to get too close."

"I'm not sure what I can say," Sam said. "Just do what you feel. If it feels right, then go with it. If you decide you don't want to meet the rest of them, then don't."

"I wasn't expecting a brother and sister. I mean, that's a fully complete family."

"There could be uncles and aunties, cousins, grandparents too."

My eyes went wide. "Fuck."

Sam laughed. "Didn't mean to freak you out more than you're already freaking out."

I took a long pull of beer. "Jesus, I didn't even think of that."

He clinked his beer bottle to mine. "One day at a time, Iz. That's all you can do."

"What would you do?" I asked. "If you were me?"

"If I were you and my parents were your parents, I'd go meet the whole fucking Westbrook family."

"You would?"

"Hell yes. I know you, Iz. I know you need this. To find out where you're from, and why nothing up until now ever made sense."

I let out a deep breath and nodded.

"And speaking of family," he added. "Mum wants to know if you're coming for lunch tomorrow?"

Sunday lunches were a sometimes-thing at the Finch household, particularly if the weather was warm. "Will she make the prawn and mango salad?"

He grinned. "I shall put in a request."

"Then I shall be there."

"Well, you may as well sleep at mine tonight. And I better not finish that if I'm driving," he said, sliding his half-empty beer onto the coffee table. "Come on. Let's go."

"Sam," I started.

He stood up. "Don't argue with me. I haven't changed the

sheets on your bed since you were there last so it's not like a big deal or anything. And I'll let you pay for dinner."

"We just ate."

"Then you can buy me breakfast."

"Do I get to pick the movie we watch tonight?"

"Absolutely fucking not."

I laughed, he grabbed my hand, and he pulled me to my feet.

SAM OPENED the front door to his parents' house like it was his own. "Stop what you're doing everyone," he yelled. "The favourite child is here."

Whitney's voice replied from somewhere in the house. "I've been here all morning, loser."

Sam chuckled as I followed him through the large foyer toward the kitchen. When we walked in, we found his sister chopping mushrooms. She threw one at him, which he caught and shoved in his mouth in one fluid movement. She rolled her eyes, but her smile was genuine.

Sam's mother, Ruth, seemed to float out of the walk-in fridge. Her outfit of pants and a linen tunic plumed out, flowing gracefully behind her. She looked like a model from a magazine for women over fifty. She stopped when she saw us, put the tray she was holding down, and ignoring her son, she came straight for me. She put her hands to my face, then patted me over like she was physically checking to see if I was okay. "Oh, my Israel. How are you holding up?"

I smiled fondly at her. "I'm okay, thank you. Sam hasn't let me out of his sight since this whole thing started."

Ruth sighed, then put her hand on Sam's arm. "He's a good boy."

"He is," I agreed. "Though he made me watch *Saw IV* last

night. So before you ask, I'd appreciate all meat cooked well-done today."

Whitney screwed her face up. "That is the nastiest movie ever."

Ruth clearly had no clue what we were talking about, but she wasn't fazed. She just turned back to me, sympathy etched on her beautiful face. "Tell me everything."

Before I could answer, Sam grumbled, "Mum, leave him alone."

Ruth never took her concerned eyes off me. "Samuel, be a darling and take that tray of sliced onions and capsicums out to your father. He's out by the pool getting the BBQ ready."

"*Samuel*," Whitney and I both said in unison, as we always did when his mother called him that.

Sam took two beers out of the fridge, grabbed the tray of sliced capsicum and onions and, after making a face at me behind his mother's back, went out in search of his dad.

I knew I wasn't getting out of Ruth's concern, so I started at the beginning. I gave her the brief, condensed version, to most of which she listened with her hand over her mouth and disbelief in her eyes. Lindsey, Sam's other sister, arrived, and after giving me a hug, caught the rest of my story as well. By the time I was done, Ruth, Whit, and Linds all sat there capti-vated and somewhat horrified that my parents hadn't even called to ask how the meeting went.

Sam walked in, now dressed in only boardies. He took one look at the four of us and sighed.

"Oh good," Ruth said. "Samuel darling, can you take the tray of meat out to your father?"

Without a word, he picked up the tray of steaks and walked in between all of us, snatched up my hand, and dragged me toward the door. "Give the guy a break."

I laughed as he pulled me outside. They had a huge back-yard with a pool, courtyard, and a separate covered outdoor dining area with a built-in BBQ and tables and chairs. He headed straight to his dad and handed him the tray of meat. Mr Finch, or Chris, as he asked me to call him as we got older, always took his duty as CEO of all BBQing very seriously. "Perfect timing," he said, taking the steaks. Then he nodded to me. "Israel! You survived the Spanish Inquisition?"

I smiled at him. "Barely a scratch."

Sam shook his head. "I told them to take it easy on you."

"It's okay. I don't mind." Sam looked at me like I'd lost my mind, so I shrugged. "Means they care."

My words seemed to gnaw at him. I didn't mean anything by it, but he obviously was reminded that there were people in my life who didn't care. I shrugged again, but he seemed agitated, angry even. "Take your shirt off."

I felt my eyebrows almost meet my hairline. "Pardon?"

His dad snorted at my reaction, but Sam was undeterred. "And I suggest if you don't want to see if your phone works at the bottom of the pool, you take it out of your pocket."

I'd forgotten he was shirtless and wearing only boardies, which meant he was ready for a swim. Not that I was complaining. He looked after himself. Not bulky but enough definition to notice. His skin was kinda pale. A light dusting of blond hair covered his chest, his nipples were dark, and I wondered briefly if they felt as soft as they looked.

He waited for me to meet his gaze before giving me an eyebrow flick and a smirk. He cleared his throat. "Shirt. Phone."

I threw my phone onto one of the nearby chairs, followed by my shirt. Only, he waited for me to have my shirt half pulled over my head when he tweaked my nipple. "Ow!"

He ran and jumped into the pool, his laughter cut off by the splash of water. I walked over to the edge, and when he broke the surface and saw me still rubbing my nipple, he laughed some more. I dived cleanly into the water, and when I came up, I splashed him in the face.

That was an invitation to try and drown me, apparently.

Wrestling in the pool was a game we'd played since we were teens. Only this time, I flipped him over and his hold on me slipped on wet skin. So of course, I pushed him down and held him underwater.

"Yeah, fair point. Israel wins that one," his dad called out. I laughed just as Sam grabbed my balls. Not too hard, but hard enough to let me know he won.

I pushed him away and doubled over with a grunt, grabbing my junk. He broke the surface with two hands in the air, cheering his victory.

"Low blow," I feigned in a squeaky voice.

He just laughed and ran his hands through his wet hair, combing it off his forehead. Water shimmered on his skin like diamonds, gliding down his body. His grin, the way he moved through the water, were all things I'd seen ten thousand times. Yet now it all seemed brand new.

Jesus, I was truly losing my mind.

I sank underwater, and needing to clear my head, I swam a few laps. When I pulled up at the shallow end, Sam was there, submerged to his chin, leaning against the wall, watching me.

"Feel better?" he asked.

I shook my head like a wet dog and smiled. "Yep. You?"

He chuckled and gave me a nod. It looked like he wanted to say something more, something he was nervous about, but just as he opened his mouth, his mum called out, "Boys! Lunch is ready."

So we got out of the pool, and I tried not to notice the way his boardies were bunched up around his thighs or the bulge of his groin.

Why was I noticing these things about him now?

I'd never thought of him that way before, and I didn't know what had changed… but something had.

Maybe it was because everything in my life had fallen to shit, and he was my rock. Maybe my brain correlated Sam with safety and warmth and saw something that wasn't there. Maybe my dick was so desperate for action it was interested in anything, and maybe my heart…

My heart…

Well, fuck.

"You okay?" he asked me quietly. I hadn't noticed him standing so close.

I blinked in surprise but covered quickly. "Yeah, yeah. It's all good."

He eyed me curiously but didn't push it. We sat down at the outdoor table with his family, ate an amazing lunch, and they talked an incredible amount of bullshit. But there was so much laughter and underlying love.

I looked around at each of them. Sam, his parents, and his sisters, and how much they all looked alike. I mean, sure. Of course I'd realised before now that Sam, Linds and Whit all looked like their mum and dad. They each had Ruth's blonde hair, her facial structure. But their eyes belonged to Chris. I thought Sam looked more like his dad the older he got, and Whit had Chris's sense of humour, Lindsey had her mum's studious nature.

Genetics was a crazy, wondrous thing.

After lunch, Sam literally rolled into the pool with a splash, and I eased myself in. The cool water felt good on my skin, especially under the hot Australian summer sun. We lazed in the water, completely at ease, but it wasn't long until we climbed out and sunned ourselves on a sun chair beside the pool.

He was lying back with his eyes closed, affording me the luxury of looking at him unbidden. He looked so peaceful, so centred. He was comfortable with who he was, with where he was. He was safe here in his parents' house; free to simply be himself.

His skin looked warm, kissed by the sun, as the beads of water dried where they laid. The line of his forehead, his cheekbone, and jaw were as soft as they were defined. His eyelashes were long, fanning out from his closed eyes, a tiny droplet of water caught in their web.

He was beautiful.

His lips were pink and curved in an ever-present smile. Kissable.

I could remember how he felt against me when we danced the other night. How his lips felt against my ear. How his hips ground against mine, how his hard-on pressed against my own.

My eyes raked down his chest, over the skin of his stomach to his navel and the line of hair that disappeared behind his boardies. With his legs spread out lazily, the material did little to hide the bulge. I could make out the swell of his dick, and I wondered what it would feel like in my hand, my mouth. What it tasted like…

I shot up off the chair and dived into the pool.

Jesus Christ.

I swam lap after lap, praying for some sense to come back to me. Maybe I needed to get laid. I needed to fuck something or suck something. Or I needed to be fucked, and then of course I wondered what Sam would feel like inside me. How he'd come…

I broke the surface, coughing and spluttering, trying to get air into my lungs. Sam jumped off his chair and came to the edge of the pool. I thought he might laugh at me or call me an idiot or take the piss. But he looked alarmed. "Iz, you okay?"

"Just tried to breathe underwater," I said, half joking, half not. Because even though it was ridiculous, it was exactly what I'd just done. I coughed some more.

He certainly wasn't laughing. "Come on," he said, waving me over. "Hop out."

I got to the edge of the water and heaved myself up, so I was sitting on the edge, and tried to catch my breath. I felt guilty for looking at him without him knowing, like some perv. And then for thinking of him sexually, like some deviant.

He was my best friend.

And I was losing my fucking mind. Maybe this whole switched thing was affecting me more than I realised. Maybe meeting Donna and Nick had rattled me more than I thought.

He patted me on the back. "Iz, you're coming home with me tonight."

I didn't want him to babysit me. I didn't want him to pity me. But more than that, I didn't want to be alone. All I could do was nod.

SAM TRIED NOT to watch me. All afternoon, I could tell he was trying to give me space while making sure I was okay. We always had the ability to just be around each other while still doing our own thing. But I could feel his eyes on me, and when I would glance at him, he'd either give me a weird smile or look away and pretend he wasn't looking at me first.

At around five o'clock, when Sam was at his laptop at the dining table and I was on the sofa, my phone rang. "It's Donna," I said out loud. Sam ignored his laptop and turned to face me. With a sudden knot in my stomach, certain she was going to tell me not to contact her again, I answered her call.

"Israel?"

"Yes. Donna?"

"Oh, I'm so glad it's you. I know I said I'd text, so it's not all so overwhelming, and Nick made me promise I'd wait more than twenty-four hours. He thought I might scare you off. You had a lot to take in, and I get that. I really do. But you were upset, and I wanted to check that you were okay." Her words lost steam, and she finished with, "I've been thinking about you all day."

I found myself smiling, relieved she wasn't rejecting me. I didn't really know how much her acceptance meant until I thought I didn't have it. Hope expanded again in my chest as I allowed myself to breathe. "I'm okay, thank you." I didn't exactly feel the need to tell her about my freak out in the pool earlier today. For all I knew, it was my crazy thoughts about Sam that caused me to nearly drown myself, not a delayed reaction to meeting my new family. "I've had a bit on my mind, yes. How are you? And Nick?"

"Oh, we're just fine, love. Now, you can say no if you want, but I was hoping you and Sam might want to come for lunch? Not this weekend, but the weekend after. You know, to meet Lachie and Ash."

"Oh."

"You don't have to," she said quickly. "Just that the others want to meet you, but only if you're okay with that. I told 'em you might wanna get here around eleven, and they can get here at twelve. You know, to give you some breathin' space."

"I'd like that." I was grinning, unable to stop it. "I'll check with Sam, but either way, I'll be there." Sam was staring at me, so I gave him a shrug.

Donna let out an emotional sigh. It sounded like she was crying again. "Well, that'd be lovely. I'd really love that."

"Text me the address," I said softly. "And if you need me to bring anything."

"Will do. But you guys just have to bring yourselves. Don't you worry about a thing."

"Okay then, if you're sure." I kind of got the feeling she enjoyed cooking and fussing over everyone. "Thank you."

"See you soon, love."

"Bye."

When I disconnected the call, I was still smiling. I put my hand to my heart and let out a laugh. "Man, I thought she was gonna tell me she didn't want anything to do with me."

Sam gave me a sad smile. "I would doubt that. She seemed thrilled to meet you."

I nodded. "She wants us to come to her place for lunch in two weeks. To meet Lachlan and Ashley."

"Me too?"

"Well yeah. You don't have to. I can go by myself. I'm sure I'll be fine."

He got up from his seat and walked over to sit on the coffee table in front of me. His eyes never left mine. "Iz, of course I'll be there."

My phone buzzed, and I looked at the screen, expecting it to be Donna's number with her address and details about lunch. But it wasn't. It was my mother. My smile died on my face.

"What's wrong?" Sam asked.

"It's my mother." I held up my phone and let him read the text.

Please call when you have a moment.

I leaned back on the sofa with a sigh. Knowing I couldn't ignore her, I pressed Call.

"Israel," she answered.

"Mother."

"You weren't busy, then," she said. "I didn't want to interrupt anything…"

"It's fine. You can call me whenever you like. You wouldn't be interrupting anyway."

There was a beat of uncomfortable silence. She never knew what to say when I said nice things to her.

"Well, I just wanted to call to see how things went yesterday. You had your meeting, yes? With… them."

I could distinctly remember Mr Dovich telling us Nick's first name. "Them, being Nick. His mother, my birth mother's name is Donna. Yes. I met with them yesterday."

Another beat of silence. "And how were they?"

"Very lovely. Decent people. Hard working. Welcoming."

Again with the silence. "Well, that's good. I hoped it went well for you." She hesitated, then asked, "Will you be seeing more of them?"

"Yes. Actually, I spoke to Donna just now. She's asked us to lunch in two weeks." Then I realised what I'd said and quickly clarified, "Me and Sam. She's asked Sam and I to meet the rest of her family."

"Oh."

"It's not for two weeks. Which is probably a good thing. It's a lot to deal with, and it's probably wise to leave enough time to collect my thoughts."

"Yes. Yes, I guess it is."

"I do think Nick will want to meet you and Dad," I offered. "Maybe not for a little while. But he's curious."

"Is he…?" She cleared her throat. "Is he well?"

"Yes. He seems like a real nice man. He's a builder by trade. And he's just gotten engaged."

"Oh?"

"Yeah. To a girl." I cringed. I didn't mean to sound bitter, but I couldn't help it. My defences were always up with my parents. "I didn't meet her but Donna said she was lovely."

"Well, that's nice."

"He looks like you." I don't know why I said it. I didn't say it to upset her, although I realised belatedly, of course it would. I pressed my thumb and forefinger into my eyes, and when I spoke again, my voice was softer. Kinder. "He has your nose and chin. Though he's a lot like Dad too. He's a nice guy, and he adores Donna."

My mother cleared her throat, and when she spoke, she sounded distant, as though she'd held the phone away from her face. "Well, I'm glad for that."

"There's a brother and sister, Mum," I said. There was no point in withholding this information. She needed to know. "I have a full-brother, and a full-sister."

It sounded like she changed the hand she held her phone with or the ear she had it pressed to. "Oh?"

"I know. It was a shock to me as well."

She sounded distracted, stunned. "Yes, yes. I'd imagine it was."

"I'll meet them when I go for lunch weekend after next. Their names are Lachlan and Ashley." I shrugged at Sam, who was still sitting in front of me, studying me. "Apparently I look like them."

My mother was quiet again. "It's… wow."

"I know." I sighed heavily. Then, telling Sam more than I was telling my mother, I said, "It's confusing and disconcerting, but it's also nice. Comforting, in a way. I don't know. I'm still trying to get my head around it."

"Yes," my mother replied absently.

I think I'd said enough, for tonight anyway. But felt like I needed to add a disclaimer, almost an apology of sorts. Although I was rarely afforded the same in return from her, I wanted to ease her pain. "I'm sure it'll all settle down into some kind of normalcy. I don't know how it will end. If I'll want to continue to meet with them or them me. I just don't know. It's all new and confronting, but I'm willing to let it play out. For now. If they'll be a permanent fixture in my life, I can't say."

"It's okay, Israel," my mother said. "I understand."

Understood what, I wasn't sure. Her tone was unreadable, and I couldn't ascertain if she was agreeing with me or being resigned to being replaced. Either way, I felt guilty. "I should go."

"Yes, okay. Thank you for being honest with me."

That was an absurd thing to say, but I didn't dwell on it. "We'll talk again soon."

"Yes."

The phone clicked off in my ear. I put the phone beside me

on the sofa and let my head loll onto the back of the sofa. I groaned. "God, that was hard."

Sam put his hands on my knees. "You were honest with her, though."

"I feel guilty," I admitted. "Which is ridiculous. And irrational."

"But you still feel guilty."

I nodded. "Like I'm betraying them for wanting to know more about who I am."

His eyes softened. "I wish I could tell you not to feel that way."

"It's stupid, right?" I said with a laugh.

"You shouldn't feel guilty, Iz. You're the last person in the world who should feel guilty."

"I know. I tell myself that, but…"

He rubbed my thighs. "I hate that you're going through this. And I wish your parents were," he searched for the right word, "more receptive."

"That's a diplomatic way to say less arseholeish."

"Well, that too."

I smiled and sighed for what felt like the hundredth time. "Shit, hey?"

"One day at a time, Iz. That's all you can do."

"Thank you. For yesterday, for today. For lunch at your folks' place."

"For when you tried to drown yourself," he said, smiling, but his eyes were questioning.

It wasn't like I could tell him he was the reason I sucked back two lungfuls of water. That I freaked the fuck out because I was fantasising about him. How he'd feel against me, inside me. Or maybe I freaked the fuck out because my once neat and orderly life was a now a fucking mess. Maybe it was because of everything else going on and that I didn't really want to know what Sam's skin felt like, how he smelled after a shower or during sex…

Fuck.

"I might call it a night," I said, my voice thick. "I'm really tired."

I could tell he didn't believe me. "Okay."

"Thank you," I said again. "For everything."

He tapped the outside of my leg. "Any time. You sure you're okay?"

"Yeah, yeah. Just tired." I stood up, finding myself between his legs. His face was in line with my stomach, and I looked down at him, wondering what he'd do if I lifted his chin and kissed him…

When his gaze met mine, I could have sworn he wanted me to do it. His tongue wet his bottom lip and his eyes flickered with something unfamiliar, and the air was suddenly sucked out of the room. My pulse quickened, sending a rush of blood to my groin and my cheeks.

Right then, my phone beeped, startling us out of whatever fucking nonsense just happened between us. I shook my head and snatched up my phone. It was Donna's number. "Donna's address and details about lunch," I mumbled distractedly. It was the perfect opportunity for me to leave. "I'll um, I'll be off to bed then. I'll see you in the morning." I walked to the hall and stopped. He hadn't moved, still sitting on the coffee table, though now he looked confused and hurt. "Thanks again, Sam." He nodded but didn't speak. His smile didn't sit well on his face.

I left him there and climbed into bed. I ignored the ache in my dick, choosing to dwell on the ache in my chest instead.

I was fucking things up with Sam. He was the one and only true rock in my whole life, my one and only constant, and I was ruining everything. I had to pull myself together and separate these emotions with rational clarity, or I'd end up with no one.

I needed to step back, to not be so dependent on him, to not lean on him for everything. If I stood any chance of keeping him as my best friend, I had to put a little distance between us. Although it didn't feel right, by the time I fell asleep, I'd convinced myself it was what had to be done.

NINE

I arrived at work the following morning with a new determination. I needed to stand on my own two feet, like I had my whole life. Until Sam. I couldn't recall the exact time when I'd begun to use him like a crutch. We'd been inseparable since we were fifteen, and he knew my every secret. He'd seen the very worst of me, how my parents' words and cold detachment had hurt me. And shaped me.

He and his family had saved me many times from dark, dark times. And even then, I didn't need him like I did now.

Or maybe I did. Maybe I just didn't realise it until now.

Because I'd sure as hell never thought of him in a sexual way before. I'd never wanted to have him wrap his arms around me and melt against him while he'd tell me everything would be okay. I'd never wanted him to hold my hand or kiss me like I did now.

Even leaving his house and having him drop me off at work, I put my Operation Separation into full effect. I rebuffed his every offer to stay over again, even his offer to call me tonight to check up on me. I had to stand on my own two feet, even if it killed me. I could tell he was unsure of my reaction, my flat-out "no, thank yous." It was hard to be a little standoffish with him, because he was usually bossy and not used to hearing the word "no" very often, and I'm sure he could tell I struggled saying it to him.

It sure would explain his look of confusion as he drove away.

Prue stood when I walked toward her. She handed me my coffee. No good morning or any greeting, for that matter. "Your father is waiting in your office."

I suppressed a sigh and took the offered cup from her. "Thank you. What kind of mood was he in?"

"Well, I offered to send you straight in to see him, but he refused. He seemed… okay, I guess."

I gave her a smile and made a joke out of it. The last thing I needed was to bring my family issues into this family-run business. "Well, I guess I'm still on the Christmas card list. I'll have to try harder next time."

Thankfully she laughed. "Let me know if you need anything. I'll hold all calls until your meeting is over."

"Thank you," I said, walking toward my office. With a deep breath to collect my thoughts and steel my nerves, I opened my door. My father stood at the window, looking out over Sydney's early Monday morning.

"Father," I said.

He afforded me a quick glance. "Israel."

I put my satchel and coffee down on my desk and joined him at the large window. He had his hands in the pockets of his pants and looked every single one of his fifty-two years. His body language told me he was nervous about something. If he were here to lecture me, he'd have his hands clasped behind his back. But he didn't. Which meant I had no clue what to expect him to say.

I aimed for conversational, as awkward as it was. "Looks like it'll be a nice day."

He nodded. "Supposed to be low thirties."

Okay. We were officially talking about the weather. Weird.

He shook his head a little, then said, "The Roche contract is up for review." He prattled on about that for twenty minutes, discussing upgrades and CPI for a new CEO, who was keen to take Roche to the next level, just to prove a point. I nodded and made some mental notes. It wasn't anything I hadn't heard before, and it wasn't the reason my father was in my office talking to me.

We both knew it.

I sat down at my desk and cut right to the chase. "Did Mum tell you about our phone call last night?"

His eyes cut to mine for the briefest moment before he looked back out the window and nodded. "Yes." He frowned. "The meeting went well, I take it?"

"Yeah, I guess. As good as meetings under those circumstances get, I suppose."

"Yes, it's all rather… difficult."

A weird word choice, but I didn't dwell on it. "Donna was lovely. As was Nick." I was going to leave it that but thought *fuck it*. "He reminded me of you."

My father's gaze shot to mine—an involuntary action, an honest reaction—before he looked away.

I smiled. "He looks like Mum, but there was something about him that was all you. His voice, his eyes."

My father said nothing, just kept staring out the window.

"He's a builder by trade," I said, not knowing what information my Mother told him. "Engaged to be married."

Still no reaction.

So while he was listening, I kept on talking. "I think he will want to meet you at some point. I don't know when, and he didn't really say. He needs more time, I think. Would you be interested in meeting them?"

That made him look at me. "Them?"

"Well, I assume Nick would bring Donna. They're like a package deal. Or maybe he'd bring his fiancée. I don't know, but I doubt he'd go alone."

"Oh," he replied quietly. He looked back out the window. "Did you go alone?"

He really had no clue about me. "No. There's no way I could've done that alone. Sam came with me."

He nodded slowly. I waited for him to speak next, and it took awhile. "I'm not sure," he said eventually. "If we should meet. I don't know…" Even though he stood at the window looking out over the city, I could see from his side profile the frown he wore. "I think your mother would like to, so maybe it's inevitable. I just don't know what I have to offer…"

And there it was. The first chink I'd ever seen in the Merrick Ingham armour. He doubted himself, and that was a first. Ever. Gone was the confident businessman façade he normally wore, and in his place was a vulnerable… father.

It was a rare unguarded moment, and I was at a loss for what to say. Comforting him felt… wrong, awkward.

My father turned abruptly, like he'd just remembered where he was. "Right then. I'll have the Roche files sent to you."

"Sure," I replied. I didn't know why, but I couldn't let this conversation—possibly the only conversation we'd ever have on the subject—end like this. "Dad?" He stopped at the door. "I highly doubt Nick will want anything from you other than a hello, and maybe a coffee. I'd say Donna will want to meet you, given you're the biological parents of her son. She'll no doubt cry and thank you." I took a deep breath and let it out slowly. "You only have to meet them to realise she got the right son."

My father looked right at me, then to the floor before he walked out, closing the door behind him.

I didn't mean for my words to sound like that. Or maybe I did. The look of hurt on his face matched the ache in my heart. Yet I couldn't apologise because what I'd said was the truth. Nick was the true child of Donna, regardless of his DNA. They had a mother/son bond that I envied and yearned for. Would Donna have loved me like that if Nick and I hadn't been switched? I'm sure she would have. But there was no point in wishing for what couldn't have been. Fanning the flames of envy for a life I didn't get was foolish and would only cause more harm than good.

And the look on my father's face just now reminded me that I wasn't the only one hurting in all of this. If I'd thought at all that my father's only interest in this was litigious, then I was wrong.

I had my phone out and was texting Sam before I knew what I was even doing. My so-called, newfound attempt to stand on my own two feet hadn't even lasted a fucking hour. Angry with myself, I deleted the message and threw my phone into the top drawer of my desk.

I MADE MYSELF BUSY, and by five o'clock, I had two messages from Sam.

The first was before lunch. *How's your day been?* And the second one just two hours later. *Let me know if you want me to come over tonight.*

Another pang of guilt hit me, this time for ignoring him. I quickly typed out a reply. *Day was busy. Thanks for the offer, but I'm just gonna go home and crash.*

Literally ten seconds later, my phone rang. I smiled at his name on the screen, but then I remembered I was trying to put some distance between us and my dependence on him. I answered, "Hey."

"What's happening?"

"Just leaving work. You?"

"Yeah. Heading home now. Sure you don't want me to come around? It's no big deal."

My chest tightened, because yes, that was exactly what I

wanted. Instead I answered, "Nah, it's okay. You gotta be sick of me by now." I meant it as a joke but my tone fell flat.

"Iz."

"No, seriously. It's fine. I'm just gonna go home. But thank you."

"Okay then. Need some porn recommendations? Because I have a few."

Despite my mood, I laughed. "I'm all good, but thanks."

"Your loss."

I wanted to tell him about my conversation with my father this morning. I wanted to tell him how horrible I felt, and I wanted to admit to him that I was trying really hard to be a big boy and do all this on my own but how I was failing miserably. I wanted to tell him "Yes, please come over tonight, please, please, please."

But I didn't. Instead, I swallowed hard and forced myself to speak. "Thanks Sam. I'll talk to you tomorrow?"

"Sure thing."

AFTER BEING home for no less than thirty minutes, I found the only way to deal with my frustration, guilt, and anger was to throw on some sneakers and run. So I hit the pavement and ran until my legs and lungs burned and my mind was clear.

Then, well before the sun came up and because I couldn't sleep, I ran again. I must have run for miles, and by the time I got home, I was a sweating, panting mess.

I liked the way it burned.

I showered, forced myself to eat something, and was back at work before eight.

Sam texted me after lunch, asking how I was. I ignored it, because the answer wasn't one I wanted to admit. When I got home, I'd just finished putting my running shoes on when he'd texted me again.

If you don't reply, I'll assume you watched some kinky porn and you've now got RSI in your hand. Or you're in the ER with something lodged in your arse, in which case all I want to know is, where are the pics?

I laughed out loud. Knowing I needed to distance myself, this dependency didn't mean I had to ignore him altogether, or so I told myself. I quickly thumbed my reply.

You dirty bastard. LOL Just had a really busy day. You?

Same. Always busy. Gotta say, I'm disappointed my predictions aren't true.

If wanking caused RSI, I'd have been in trouble long before now. And I haven't required medical help getting a dildo out of my arse yet.

I smiled at my phone, waiting for his response. It took a little while, and I'd wondered if I'd gone too far.

JESUS, IZ. I ALMOST CRASHED MY CAR. Then another quickly followed. *You can't say that shit to me.*

I snorted out a laugh. *Don't text and drive.*

Another pause, then, *Want me to come over? I can grab some dinner on the way.*

And just like that, my smile faded away and my wall went back up. With a painful heart clench, I replied, *Nah, thanks anyway. Just heading out for a run. Talk to you tomorrow.*

Without waiting for a response, I threw my phone onto the kitchen bench and headed out the door.

OF COURSE HE'D REPLIED, but I ignored it. And I ignored his other texts at work the next day wanting to know how I was, how my day was going. I knew he was just checking up on me, and it warmed my heart to know that he cared. It also reminded me of how much I relied on him, and it reinforced my decision to try and detach myself from needing him so damn much.

But when I got home after work and went for another 5K run, my mind wasn't clear like it normally was. My legs burned, my lungs too, but my mind was still a mess.

I had a missed call from him, and his last message read, *Iz, are you okay?*

God, I could feel the confusion in his text. I wasn't deliberately trying to hurt him, I just needed some head-clearing space. But I had to answer him: if I left it any longer, he'd kick down my door. But I knew if I spoke to him, with the way my leaden heart ached right now, I'd probably break down and cry. So I thumbed out a text.

Sorry. Today was hell. Just went for a run. Just gonna grab a shower. Hey, I've been meaning to ask how that Mayburn case go?

It was a blatant deflect, and I had no doubt he'd see that. The truth was, I couldn't remember the last time we talked about him and his work. Not that he ever talked about specific details of cases, but he'd tell me what he was working on.

It worked, because his reply was a long time coming, and to the point. *Case was settled a week ago.*

I held my phone and wanted so, so badly to call him. To hear his voice. To say sorry. To tell him I needed him. But I couldn't. I wouldn't.

So I didn't.

Thursday at work dragged by in a monotony of meetings, one after the other, and it was late by the time I had a minute to myself in my office. I checked my phone, expecting a text or two from Sam, that I would only ignore. But there wasn't one.

"Everything okay?" Prue asked cautiously, as she put some files on my desk.

"Everything's fine," I lied. That fake smile, that unreadable mask had become my second skin over the course of my life. I'd been hiding the hurt and loneliness since I was five years old, and I had it mastered. Or so I thought. I put my phone back in my desk drawer, and continued to smile like my heart wasn't breaking.

Prue stood there, not believing me for one second, though clearly unsure of what to say. "Okay."

After she'd gone and I stared out the window at the darkening city skyline, I wondered if I was truly losing my shit. Then I wondered if I really *was* losing my shit, would I know if I was? Prue certainly looked at me like I was. I was sure right this minute Sam thought I'd lost the fucking plot, and I had to wonder how much one person could endure before they snapped.

How fucked up was fucked up enough to seek professional help?

If I spoke to a psychologist, would they pat me on the hand and tell me to "suck it up, there's people much worse off"? Or would they stare at me, gobsmacked, and break out a bottle of liquor and have a few shots with me.

I mentally recounted the steps I'd taken that led me here. It was like a checklist from a Jerry Springer show.

My childhood, where my only fond memories were spent with hired help.

There were my cold and affectionless parents, of course.

Being gay, which didn't help the whole disappointment, embarrassment-to-the-family thing, as clearly stated by my father. Several times.

Not forgetting the whole switched-at-birth thing, which could very well explain the point about why my parents never liked me.

And now, because I wasn't fucking crazy enough, I'd become infatuated with my best friend. And subsequently decided in all my fucked-up wisdom that completely cutting him out of my life was the only way to save our friendship.

With a resigned sigh and a heavy, heavy heart, I opened Google and searched Sydney psychologists. Then, because my list was probably a little too fucked up, I searched psychiatrists as well.

TEN

Friday lunchtime my phone rang. Jamie's name flashed on the screen, and although it wasn't too odd for him to call me, during work hours was almost unheard of.

"Hey, wassup?"

"Hey, Cap," he replied. "Funny you should ask that, because that's what I'm calling to find out."

"What?"

"I just spoke to Sam. Thought I'd try and line up some drinks tonight. He said you're ignoring him, avoiding him, whatever. What the fuck is up with that?"

"I'm not…" I tried to lie.

"Bullshit."

"I'm just dealing with a lot right now."

"I get that. No one doubts that. Fuck, Cap. I can't even imagine what you're dealing with. But Sam? You and him are like Forrest and Jenny."

I snorted. "I think you mean we is like peas and carrots," I imitated Forrest Gump's voice,

"Whatever. My point is, what the actual fuck?"

"I'm not avoiding him."

"Good. So you'll meet us tonight. Eight o'clock at the Oxford."

Which meant we would end up at the Basement, the nightclub under the hotel. "Excellent, because that always ends well."

He laughed. "Don't be late." Without another word, he disconnected the call, and I threw my phone into my desk drawer with a groan.

Fucking hell. Sam had told him I was ignoring him. Avoiding him. Whatever.

My initial reaction was to not turn up. All I wanted to do was crawl into bed and hide under the covers and sleep the weekend away. But the more I thought about it, the more I liked it. Getting shitfaced and finding some random fuck was starting to sound pretty damn good. Actually, it was sounding pretty damn perfect. And by the time eight o'clock came around, I walked into the Oxford Hotel on a mission.

I was freshly showered with my dark I'm-getting-laid-tonight jeans on, a skin-tight black tee, and my long black military boots on, half laced up. It screamed attitude and was the perfect statement for how I felt. I was on edge, mentally and physically, and I was horny as hell.

I wanted—no, I *needed*—to forget.

I saw the guys standing at a tall table and made my way through the early crowd toward them. Connor spotted me first and smiled as he sipped his beer. "Well, Cap. Why don't you start at the 357? Save yourself some time."

357 was a gay sauna/sex club on Crown Street. Four storeys of sex and fun, for all levels on the gay spectrum. I snatched up Connor's beer. "I probably should," I said, taking a long mouthful of his drink.

Millsy and Jamie both looked me up and down. Millsy laughed, but Jamie's eyes darted to Sam's, and of course my gaze followed his. Sam looked good. Fucking hot, if I was being honest. He wore blue jeans, a white button-down designer shirt, and his worn brown boots, and of course he wore it well. But his eyes were hurt and his smile was tight. He wouldn't look directly at me, which I fucking deserved. I felt even worse now and even more determined to drink until I was numb.

Oblivious to the tension between me and Sam, Millsy grinned and pushed my shoulder. "Why don't you just write 'Wanna fuck?' across your shirt?"

"I was thinking of having it tattooed on my chest," I joked. I downed the rest of Connor's beer in one go and held up the empty bottle. "Who wants one?"

Without really waiting for any answers, I made my way to the bar and bought five more beers. I hated this awkwardness, this uncomfortable air between me and Sam, and knowing it was my fault just layered the guilt on even more. When I returned to the table, I knew I had to do something. I slid in beside him and nudged his elbow with mine. It was a piss-poor peace offering, but at least it was a start.

He offered me a small smile but said nothing. Jamie was quick to speak up. "So Cap, how's things with you?"

It was pretty clear by the look on their faces they could see I was strung tight. There was no point in even trying to lie to them. "I've had a really shit week," I said, which was probably the most honest reply I could give without details. "Just really fucking shit. And I gotta say, coming out tonight was just what I needed. So, thank you."

They each held their beers up and clinked theirs to mine. "Cheers to that, my friend," Connor said, and the conversation around the table morphed into work, cricket, and general shit we talked, bitched, and laughed about.

And with every beer, I could feel the knot in my shoulders loosen. Every time they made me laugh, I could feel myself get lighter, and by ten o'clock there was a decent crowd in the bar, and the music was getting louder, people were starting to dance, but Sam and I still hadn't really talked.

The silence between us was the elephant in the room, or more specifically, at our table, and I'd just about had enough alcohol to address it when the music changed.

Tracy Chapman's "Give Me One Reason" started to play. The very song that Sam and I had danced to in his living room. The same song playing when we ground our hips and hard cocks against each other, kissed necks and ears and lips. It was fucking hot.

My cheeks grew hot at the memory, and I dared to look at Sam. He clearly remembered it the same way I did, because a blush covered his cheeks, and he looked at me and smiled.

Connor stared at us both for a long moment before he pointed his beer bottle at us. "What the hell did you two do?" he asked. "You've barely looked at each other the whole night, and this song comes on and you both blush like schoolboys."

So now Millsy and Jamie were both looking at us too. Sam's blush now crept down his neck, and maybe I'd had too much to drink, maybe I hadn't had anywhere near enough, but I said, "It's just a really good song to grind to."

Connor's mouth fell open, Millsy laughed, and Jamie tilted his head, like now something made sense. Sam took a long pull of his beer, slammed it down on the table, and grabbed my arm. He dragged me over to the dance floor. By the time I'd found my feet and straightened to my full height, Sam slid his arms around me and pulled me close.

Really fucking close.

One hand snaked down over my arse and pulled my hips into his. We did that slow-grind dance, fingers scraping against skin, passion just waiting for permission to ignite.

He put his lips to my ear. "Give me one reason to stay here."

He wasn't singing along to the song. He was giving me an ultimatum.

I pulled back so I could see into his eyes and rested my

forehead against his. My lips were barely an inch from his, and the heat in his eyes stripped me bare. I could offer him nothing but the truth.

"Because I can't do this without you."

He slowly closed his eyes, and I wondered for a split second if my answer was right or wrong. But his hand wound up my back, and with the hand still on my arse, he pulled us together, from thigh to chest, and still we swayed to the music. His lips parted, his tongue glistened as it swept across his bottom lip. And I thought he was going to kiss me.

I wanted him to. With everything I was, I wanted him to kiss me.

But he moved his forehead to my cheek as the song ended, and when he chuckled, I pulled back to see what he found so funny.

Connor, Millsy, and Jamie were standing at the table, frozen, all staring with their mouths open. "I think we had an audience," Sam said in my ear. Then he looked at me, wondering what we should do, so I took his hand and led him to the bar. I didn't want to stop touching him, so I pulled Sam against my hip and slid my palm along his waist.

"What can I get ya?" the barman asked.

"Five shots of Chivas Regal, thanks," I answered. So he didn't think they were all for me, I motioned to Jamie, Millsy, and Connor, the three stunned mullets still gaping at our table. Sam and I carried the shot glasses back to them and put them in the middle of the table.

"What the fuck was that about?" Connor motioned to the dance floor. "You two wanna explain what's going on?"

"No," I answered, handing him a shot of scotch. "Now shut up and drink."

No one asked again over the course of the night. Sam and I seemed to be back to good, which I was most thankful for. I made myself a drunken-arse promise not to avoid him again, knowing it wasn't good for either for us.

We ended up in the Basement, and in all the years we'd been going there, I couldn't remember ever leaving the place sober or single.

I had the drunk part well and truly established. But the hooking up part, I had yet to conquer. It probably didn't help that I had a hand on Sam's lower back or in the back pocket of his jeans or that we danced together most of the night.

People normally assumed we were together. Tonight was no different, I reasoned. But no guys were interested. I mean, they were looking, but that was all.

"My jeans have failed," I declared to Sam. I was drunk, but so was he so I had to lean in real close and speak in his ear.

His hands were on my waist. "Failed what?"

"In finding me someone to fuck." Then I amended, "Or to fuck me."

He shot me a drunken, confused look.

"They've never failed me yet," I said, turning around and parading my arse and thighs. "See?"

Sam laughed, and for the three seconds I had my hand off him, some fucking wanker saw it as an opportunity. He sidled on in, drink in hand and a smarmy smirk, getting close to Sam, touching his arm and making him smile.

Sober me might've let it go, even wished him good luck. But drunk me was having none of it.

I moved right in close to Sam, pulled him hard against me, possessively. I glared at the guy. "Don't touch what's mine," I said.

Even shitfaced, I knew Sam wasn't mine. But he was. He was my best friend, my one and fucking only, and if anyone was gonna be putting their hands on him, it better be me.

The guy put his hand up and backed away, disappearing into the crowd.

"Okay, I think you've had enough," Jamie said, putting his

arms around me. "Time for the Captain to go down with the ship."

I still hadn't let go of Sam and didn't really want to let him go either. He fit against me really well, like he was designed just for me. And he didn't seem too keen on letting me go either. Maybe we were as drunk as each other. Maybe he was holding me up. I didn't know. I didn't care. He felt really fucking good.

"I'll take him," Sam said.

"Let me get you guys into a cab," Jamie said. "Fuck knows you'll end up at the Rocket if I leave it up to you."

The Rocket was a pretty hard-core leather bar, where quite often some guy wearing a harness was strapped over a table and ploughed into by anyone who wanted a turn. I looked at Sam. "We should totally go to the Rocket."

He laughed, and his face was so close to mine, it would've been so easy to kiss him… Jamie shoved us toward the door. "Come on. You two are fucking SpongeBob and Patrick when you're drunk, I swear."

Then Connor had his arms around us both, singing the SpongeBob theme song at the top of his lungs.

To which Millsy followed with, "Is nautical nonsense something you wish? Then go home and fuck like a fish." Then they argued about how fish fuck until they shoved us into a taxi, gave the driver directions to my place, and waved us off.

Arseholes.

We kinda laughed the whole way to my place and were still laughing when we pushed through my front door. I made it to the back of my sofa, where I leaned my arse against it and pulled Sam toward me. He fit between my legs and pressed against me. The denim of his jeans and his hard-on felt so damn good.

I'd had my hands on him all night. I certainly didn't want to stop now.

My smile faded into a heated look of desire. I licked my lips, wanting to taste his kiss. The air between us was suddenly electric. I needed it to catch fire.

I pulled his hips harder against me and leaned in, needing to kiss him, consume him. He slid his hand up my neck, scorching every nerve ending he touched. And when I thought he was cupping my jaw, ready to kiss me, he stopped.

He pulled away, not far but far enough. Without a word, he told me "no."

He closed his eyes and shook his head. "Not like this," he murmured. Then with a soft kiss to my cheek, he backed away. He turned and walked down the hall. "Night, Iz."

I sat there, stunned. Not by his rejection, although it stung, but by my actions.

What the fuck was I thinking?

I suddenly felt very sober, even though I was still incredibly drunk. As the room started to spin one way, my mind spun in the other, and even though I could barely focus on anything, something became very clear.

He'd done the right thing. And I was an idiot.

THE NEED TO piss woke me up, quickly followed by the realisation of how dry my mouth was and followed directly by the blunt ache in my skull.

I stumbled to my bathroom, took care of my first issue, then drank straight from the bathroom tap to fix my second problem, and went in search of Advil to take care of the third.

Halfway down the hall, I noticed the spare-room door was ajar and remembered Sam had stayed. Then of course, I remembered splinters of last night—me being all handsy with him, almost kissing him, and him turning me down. God. As if I didn't feel like shit enough.

I half expected to find him gone and was a mix of relieved and disappointed to find his boots tossed on the floor and him still in bed.

"Oh fuck," he mumbled, obviously seeing me in the doorway. His voice was scratchy and pained. "My head hurts. What the fuck were we drinking last night?"

"Beer, scotch, vodka. I think I remember a Jäger Bomb. Or two."

He groaned, a horrid sound. "I fucking hate everything."

I snorted, and a stab of pain shot through my forehead. "Ow."

"Iz?"

"Yeah?"

"Fix me."

Pizza was the only thing that fixed Sam when he was hung over. "I'll order now." Then I realised I didn't even know what time it was. I patted down my pockets because I was still wearing my jeans from the night before. "I don't know where my phone is."

Sam turned his head and opened one eye to look at me. He laughed, then groaned. "Or one boot apparently."

I looked down at myself to find yes, I was wearing one boot. "I thought I was walking funny."

Sam laughed, then groaned again. "Fuck."

I left him to it and walked, unevenly, to the living room. I found my phone on the sofa, but still no other boot. I definitely wore it home…

Checking my phone, I realised it was almost midday. Jesus. I had no clue what time it was when we got home, but we'd slept half the day. I ordered two large pizzas from Sam's favourite wood-fired place, then went in search of some breakfast juice, then poured Sam a glass and delivered it to his bedside table, along with two Advil. He was still in bed, his hair a mess, and looking like he'd been hit with a stun gun. "Pizza'll be thirty minutes."

His only response was to groan.

I went to my room to grab a shower. Before I got to my bathroom, I pulled off my T-shirt but had to sit down for a minute. I plonked my arse on the end of my bed and promptly found my other boot. "Ow," I griped, reaching blindly under the covers to get it.

"What's ow?" Sam asked from my doorway. He looked like shit, wearing his clothes from the night before, but at least he was upright.

I detangled my boot out from my sheets. "That." He laughed and I contemplated throwing it at him but didn't have the energy. I fell back on my bed, apparently lacking the energy to even sit up.

"I'm gonna grab a shower," he said, walking into my room. He headed straight for my walk-in wardrobe and walked out thirty seconds later with some clothes.

"Help yourself," I joked.

"I did."

I heard the water turn on from the bathroom attached to his room and rolled off my bed. The best thing about my apartment was that each bathroom had a separate water supply, so two people could shower at the same time.

By the time I got out, feeling somewhat more human, Sam was already lying on my sofa watching TV. He was wearing an old pair of my jeans and a plain navy T-shirt. Even hung over he still looked good. Actually, the unshaven look really suited him. Then again, the clean-shaven look did too.

"Yes, I'm comfortable," he mumbled. "Don't ask me to move."

I must have been staring at him, so I laughed it off. "Wouldn't dare."

Just then the pizza arrived, and I slid the two boxes onto the coffee table in front of the sofa. I grabbed two glasses, some Coke, and sat on the end of the sofa where he had his feet. Sam kinda sat up, but was still mostly lying down. He inhaled two slices and washed them down with Coke, then fell back into his not-moving position.

When I'd eaten all my stomach would allow, I considered lying down with him as the little spoon but decided against it. Instead, I lay down with my feet at his chest and pulled a cushion under my head.

We were too hung over to speak, too hung over to really watch whatever the hell was on TV, and we certainly didn't bring up what happened last night. We both fell back asleep and woke up when my phone rang.

It was Connor. "Hey," I answered.

"Hey, Cap. You sound like shit."

"Because I feel like shit."

He laughed. "How's Sam?"

"If he feels like how he looks, I'd say shit too."

Sam pinched some hair just above my ankle. "Ow, that fucking hurt."

"It was supposed to," he mumbled.

Connor laughed. "All is well then. I was just calling to see how you were, that's all. We're gonna head down to the Royal later for some tequila shots, maybe some Jäger Bombs."

"Fuck you."

He laughed before hanging up on me. Arsehole.

I threw my phone onto the coffee table and poured myself another glass of warm Coke. I leaned back, and of course squashed Sam's feet, so he lifted his legs and plonked his feet in my lap. "I'm still not moving," he said.

So we stayed like that for a while. Sam snoozed, while I just enjoyed the quiet and easy way it was between us. I'd missed him this last week, and I'd been foolish to think I didn't need him. By how pissed he'd been at me, he obviously didn't like me keeping my distance either. I didn't know what our friendship had become. Whether something had changed, whether it was better or worse. I had so much on my mind these days, I wasn't really sure of anything.

When my bladder wouldn't let me sit there a moment longer, I lifted his feet off my lap and went to take a piss. When I came back out, Sam was up and in the kitchen, putting the boxes of pizza in the fridge. I walked in and popped two more Advil, and when I put my glass of water on the bench, he was staring at me.

Sam leaned against the counter and folded his arms. "Wanna tell me what happened last week?"

"What do you mean?" I tried to play stupid.

"Come on, Iz. I think we're past that, yeah? Something happened last week. With you and me. We were good one day, then you wouldn't talk to me."

My heart hammered and I actually felt a little lightheaded. My mouth was suddenly dry, and I doubted my ability to speak, even if I wanted to.

"Iz, I know this is hard for you. I know you don't like to talk about shit. But it's just me. You can tell me anything."

I let out a shaky breath. He waited for me to speak, and I knew I owed him the truth. "I tried to do this on my own. I rely on you for too much. For everything really. And that's not fair on you. I thought I'd try to stand on my own two feet."

His face fell. "Oh, Iz."

I swallowed hard and continued. "But I really sucked at it. And it has never been more apparent this last week than it has my entire life, that I'm very much alone." He went to say something, but I shook my head. "I am, Sam. I either push people away, or I hold on so tight I crush them, and I know I owe my fucked-up childhood for that. I thought I could handle this whole switched thing on my own, but I really can't. You have no idea how many times I went to call you last week and had to stop myself. I can't keep relying on you to sort my shit out because I'm a fucking mess, Sam."

He frowned and put his hand on my arm.

"I've decided to see a shrink. I made a list at work the

other day, and I was gonna call but it was late and I was too chickenshit, but I need to. I probably should have done it years ago, truthfully. I'm surprised I made it this far without stepping off The Gap."

Sam put his hand around the back of my neck and pulled me against him. "Don't say that. Don't ever say that. Please."

"I wouldn't do it," I whispered into his neck. And I wouldn't.

His grip on me tightened. "Promise me."

"Promise."

He pulled me back and looked me right in the eyes. His eyes shone with tears and fierceness. "You matter to a lot of people, Iz. You matter to me."

"I know. Thank you. And I'm sorry for being a jerk."

He smiled sadly. "You were a jerk, but for good reason, so apology accepted." He put both hands on my shoulders. "But don't ever think you have to do this on your own."

"Well, I think I've proved to everyone that I can't, so…"

He sighed and let his shoulders fall. "Iz, you're the strongest person I know."

I rolled my eyes and ignored his compliment completely. "I don't know what I'm doing."

Sam cupped my face and lifted my chin so I looked at him. "And that's okay. It's perfectly fine not to have a fucking clue. One day at a time, Iz. That's all you can do."

I shrugged one shoulder and gave a bit of a nod. "I think my parents are really struggling with it all. My mum has called me, which is rare enough, but my father tried to talk to me the other day. At work, about non-work things. It was weird. He wanted to know how the meeting with Nick and Donna went. I told him Nick looked like Mum but reminded me of him. And you should have seen his face, Sam. He looked fucking scared. I've never seen him look like that…"

Sam ran his thumb across my eyebrow, along my cheek and jaw. "Does he want to meet him?"

"He kinda blew it off, but I think it's pretty obvious he does." I let out a shaky breath. "At first I thought he was scared that Nick might want his money, but that look on his face… the more I think about it, the more I think he looked scared because now he had another son to be a fucking disappointment to."

Sam frowned and cocked his head. "What do you mean?"

"I don't even know." I let out a humourless laugh. "All these years he's told me *I'm* such a disappointment. But you know what? I think he knows *he's* failed me, and now he's scared shitless to have another son, his real son, telling him he's not a good father. I told him Nick and Donna were very close and despite what the DNA results say, she got the right son." My eyes burned with saltwater. "Because she adores him, and he respects her. I didn't have to spell it out that was *not* how our family was. I knew it, and so did he. He left my office with his tail between his legs, and I wanted to feel good. I wanted to take that as a win, after all these years, but I couldn't. I just felt like shit. More and more guilt, like fucking layers of it."

"Oh Iz." He seemed to need a moment to gather his thoughts or to speak without crying. I wasn't sure. "I'd tell you it's not you who should feel guilty, but we both know it's not how it works. The guilt you feel is so entwined with the fact he's told you you're a disappointment. He made you feel like a failure. So every time you say how you feel to him, it makes you feel like you let him down, which adds to your guilt."

I nodded. He got it. He always did.

"But that shit's on him. Not you. He's the fucking disappointment. He failed you. He should feel guilty. It should eat at him, knowing… the things he's said to you…" Sam shook his head. He was angry and frustrated. Two feelings I knew well. "Who knows? Maybe this was supposed to happen for a reason. Maybe this needed to happen so he realises what a prick he's been to you. There's nothing like having your failings paraded in front of you. But don't feel bad for him."

"I do, though. I fucking do. Despite everything, I do feel bad for him."

Sam smiled at me. "Because you're a good man. You're better than him."

I sighed, long and loud. I never had been comfortable at taking compliments. "Will you stay again tonight?"

"'Course I'm staying. I'm getting back on that couch and I'm not moving. Told you that."

I smiled, what felt like the first genuine smile in a week. "Thank you."

Something flashed in his eyes. A hint of sadness, maybe? He quickly schooled his features and smiled right back at me. "I'm picking the movie. You can make the popcorn. And maybe later, if I feel better, I'll beat your arse at *Call of Duty*."

My FATHER WAS WAITING in my office again on Monday morning, and things with him were officially strange.

"How was your weekend?" he asked, as though it was a foreign language. It ought to be, since he'd never asked me that before.

I considered lying and telling him my weekend had been fine. I doubted he cared for the answer, and honestly, his attempt at small talk made me nervous. But somewhere since the beginning of what I'd now dubbed The Whole Switched Thing, I was done with lying. I was done with façades and wearing skins that weren't my own.

"My weekend was a bit of a mess, actually. I spent Friday night drinking my weight in scotch, vodka, and Jäger Bombs to try and overcompensate for all that's wrong in my life. If hangovers were an Olympic sport, I'd have spent all day Saturday winning gold. Sam spent every waking minute with me because I'm pretty sure he thinks I'm suicidal. Which would be sweet if it weren't so fucking sad. Though we spent yesterday on the pier in the sun watching the Navy yard, which was nice. You know, guys in uniform and all that."

I wasn't going to tell him that Sam and I sat in the park and spent the afternoon laughing and ogling the Navy's finest but figured in for a penny, in for a pound. It's who I was, and I was done pretending.

"Right," my father said quietly. I wondered coldly which part of my spiel bothered him the most: the gay part or the suicide part.

I thought he would've made an excuse and hightailed it out of my office or ignored my monologue altogether and started talking about work.

But he didn't. He sat down across from me, like he couldn't stand up a minute longer. He looked out of place and bone-tired. And really unsure of what to say.

So I spoke instead. "I'm going to make an appointment to see a doctor. A psychologist. I think I need to talk to someone."

My father stared at me, horrified and ashamed. Not of me, for once, but of himself. The distinction was obvious in the way the colour drained from his face. Sam's words flashed through my mind. *There's nothing like having your failings paraded in front of you.* Now, my father was successful at many things. Parenting just wasn't one of them.

I swallowed hard but needed to say this. "I'm not handling this as well as I thought I would."

"It hasn't been easy," he offered. His voice was so quiet I barely heard him. It wasn't a judgement call, merely a statement.

"No. It hasn't."

"I'd like to meet Nick," he blurted out. "But only if it's okay with you."

Only if it's okay with me? What the actual fuck?

"Of course it is. Why do you think you need my permission? Because if we're being completely honest with each other, you've never given a shit about what I've thought before."

My bluntness surprised him. In a boardroom or executive meeting it was expected. About personal matters, not so much.

He straightened up a little and raised his chin. That Merrick Ingham defiance was there, just under the surface, before he sighed and sagged back into his seat. He looked smaller. "I guess I deserved that."

I looked around my office for a hidden camera and wondered if *Punk'd* was still a thing. Because this had just left the realm of weird and was now entering unchartered waters of an alternate universe.

"I wanted to ask if you were okay with me meeting him because..." He squirmed like he was suddenly allergic to his suit. "I didn't want you to think it was a reflection on you."

I replayed his words over in my mind. "Was that a compliment or an insult?" I asked. "Because I'm not sure."

"Israel," he mumbled. "I'm trying to..."

I wanted to ask if he meant a reflection on me being a good son, so I don't need to worry? Or a reflection on me because now he had a real son, I didn't need to worry. But something stopped me from asking. If this was some kind of olive branch from my father, then I'd take it. And something else Sam said came back to me. *You're a better man than him.*

Part of me wanted to be petty and sarcastic, to hurt him any way I could. But if this was a test of who had more empathy, who was a better fucking human being, then I had no other choice.

So be the better man, Israel.

"Dad, of course you should meet him. And Mum. When Nick's ready, you should definitely meet him."

My father nodded, like my approval meant something.

What, I didn't know. "I'm sorry you feel the need to see a psychologist," he said, speaking to the window. I was pretty certain he knew my issues about family were existent long before now. "If you need any time off work…"

"I'll let you know."

"Please do."

I watched in shock as he stood and walked out the door, then took out my phone. I was all set to send Sam a text message, but decided not yet. Instead, I took out the list of psychologists and called the first phone number at the top of the page.

Then I called Sam.

ELEVEN

"My appointment is on Thursday."

"This Thursday?" Sam asked. "Shit, that's fast."

"She's one of the best, apparently, so I guess if you're willing to pay, she'll fit you in."

He hummed his agreement. "Are you okay with going? Like, do you still feel this is a positive step forward?"

I smiled at his professional tone. "You realise you sound different when you're in work mode."

He snorted. "Nice deflection, Iz."

"Yes, I feel okay with it. I mean, I'm not happy about it. I'm not proud of having to put my hand up for help. But I need it. I can see that. I'm not too excited about having my life picked apart at the seams by some over-analytical Freudian type, but it can't hurt, right?"

"For what it's worth, I think you're doing the right thing. Not saying you need it, but being proactive with mental health isn't anything to be ashamed about."

"Do you tell all your clients that?"

"Only those who need to hear it."

I chuckled. "My father asked for my permission to meet with Nick and Donna."

Silence.

I snorted. "I know, right?"

"What the fuck, Iz?"

"I don't know what to make of it." I sighed through puffed out cheeks. "He's really struggling with it. More than he'll ever admit."

It sounded like he scrubbed his hand over his face. "Sounds like it, yeah."

"I can't blame him for not knowing where to tread with this whole mess. But it was like he was trying to apologise or something." I snorted. "He looked like he'd swallowed a cactus."

Sam laughed at that. "He apologised? Seriously?"

"Well, he tried, I think. I'm not sure, to be honest."

"Wow."

"I know."

"Need me to come around tonight?"

"Nah, I'm good. But thank you. I mean it. Thanks, Sam."

"Anytime."

I WENT into my first appointment with psychologist Kathryn Habib at four o'clock on Thursday afternoon. I was oddly excited. Nervous, but looking forward to taking back some control in my life.

Kathryn was younger than I'd assumed she would be. She couldn't have been older than thirty-five. Her long, dark hair was pulled back in a neat ponytail, and her pantsuit was navy, her white shirt crisp. She was petite, beautiful, and reminded me oddly of a secret service agent from some Hollywood movie. After introductions and polite smiles, she asked me to tell her a little bit about myself.

"I'm twenty-six, and I'm a junior executive director in my father's multimillion-dollar business."

"A highly stressful job," she added.

I smiled. "That's the easy part. Professional I can do. Personal is a different story."

She tilted her head. "How so?"

God, where to start? "Well, my childhood was cold, clinical. Literally. I have no memory of being touched or comforted by either parent. I've been a long and consistent disappointment to my mother and father, which is no assumption on my part. Believe me, they told me many times. Well, my father has. My mother said nothing. My best friend is amazed I haven't necked myself yet, and three weeks ago, we found out I was switched at birth."

Kathryn blinked.

I let out a deep breath and wiped my palms on my thighs. "Yeah. It's a shitshow from start to finish."

She put her pen down and focused on me. And for the next two hours, I recounted the parts of my life that led me here. Like my seventh birthday where my driver picked me up from school and took me for ice cream because my mother was too busy. But it wasn't an isolated event, I explained. I had enough of those types of stories to fill a well of heartbreak. I told her how I met Sam at fourteen, and his parents showed me what a family could be. Should be. How I was outed by my school principal and thrown to the wolves. I hadn't expected my father to approve, but his rage and disgust still left a scar that would never heal. And now the cherry on the train-wreck cake that was my life was now my parents, those who were the root of all grief, weren't really my parents at all. How I'd met my birth mother and up until then, I'd never given much credence to the nature versus nurture debate. Now it was a puzzle that I couldn't quite make fit.

I held it together while I told her all of this. I didn't shed one tear. She sat there and listened, paling gradually as she gently pick, pick, picked me apart. The appointment itself was only supposed to go for one hour, but given it was the last appointment of the day, she said she'd rather I stayed a little longer.

"You recount these memories with a factual ease," she concluded.

I nodded solemnly. "It's nothing new to me," I said, as if that explained away a lifetime of hurt. "I've accepted my life for what it is."

I'm sure she was ticking off a list of terms in her head as she studied me: compartmentalised, disengaged, conditioned responses, bereaved.

Is that what the weight in my heart was? Grief for all the love I was robbed of?

"Well, I'm glad you decided to meet with me," she said. She wore a professional mask that belied the concern in her eyes.

"I'm only realising I probably should have done this years ago."

"You're here now."

I felt like I was on the edge of a void. And to think I'd been excited to come here… well, now I was fucking petrified. Scared of falling into a black hole of pain I was not ready for.

"I think it would be wise to look at this as long term. I'm glad I'll be able to help you as you go through the steps of getting to know your birth mother." She smiled. "However, I'd like us to analyse your relationship with your parents, in particular your father."

I nodded, fully expecting that. "Thought we would be."

"You're angry," she said gently. "It's a valid emotion, Israel. A justified reaction to how he's treated you. You should be angry."

I almost laughed. Angry? I wasn't angry. I was fucking livid. Furious. I had the fury of a thousand raging fires in my heart. Most days I had it under control, but she'd brought the edge of the flames too close to the surface. "I hate him." My voice was low and cold, shaking. "Yet I'm driven to try and please him."

Kathryn nodded like it was a textbook response to her, yet I couldn't begin to understand it. "I want to see you twice a week, Israel."

I held it together as I was leaving. I managed to drive home without losing it. The weather had turned to storm, like it matched my very thoughts. The dark clouds hung low, the winds blew rain at all angles, like it understood the emotions coursing through me. I got home and couldn't stand still, couldn't sit, couldn't think. So I pulled on my running clothes and hit the pavement, running in the driving rain farther than I'd ever run.

I welcomed the burn in my lungs. It matched the fire in my heart, the burn in my eyes. My legs could barely carry me, and I was drenched, soaked through from head to toe, yet I couldn't stop running. Pushing myself harder and harder, because somehow the pain I put my body through made the ache in my chest easier to bear.

It was dark by the time I made it home. The storm outside had eased a little, the winds and turmoil had died down, and the rain that fell was now constant and heavy. And whether it was the running or the sympathetic storm, I managed to hold it together.

But when I walked through my front door, Sam was there. He stood in my kitchen looking distraught with his phone to his ear, and when he saw me, he visibly sagged. "He's here," he said to whomever he was talking to. "I'll call you later."

He put his phone down and pointed at me. "Well, you're not fucking dead."

"What?" I couldn't quite catch my breath.

"Your phone, Iz." He picked up my phone from the kitchen counter and held it up. "I called to see how your first appointment went today, but you didn't answer. Six fucking calls unanswered, so I came over here to see if you were okay because I was fucking worried about you, and you'd gone God only knows fucking where without your damn phone. You never go anywhere without your phone, so forgive me for thinking the worst. I called Jamie to see if he'd heard from you because I didn't know what else to fucking do."

He was pissed at me and upset, and I was dripping water onto the floor. Pools leached out from my shoes, and I was shaking. My whole body was vibrating with cold and shock or something. My teeth started to chatter, and I still couldn't catch my breath.

His face crumpled and he fought tears as he looked at me. It was then I realised I was crying. I didn't even know I was. He dragged me to my bathroom and wrapped a towel around me. He rubbed my arms to try and get me warm. "Iz. Talk to me."

I had to stop my teeth chattering before I could speak. "My appointment…"

He took another towel and wiped my face and hair before he looked into my eyes and nodded. "Yeah? What happened?"

"I was okay talking to her. I swear I was. I told her… stuff. About my father and growing up and the things he said to me. She said I have a right to be angry."

"You do."

"But angry doesn't come close, Sam. I am *so* fucking angry," I enunciated slowly through clenched teeth. "I can't even describe it. I told her I hated him. I *hate* him, yet I need to defend him because he's my father and I love him." I let my head fall back, and I groaned through my tears. "Fuck! It's like she put a sternal saw to my chest and cracked me wide open." I put the heel of my hand to my breastbone. "It fucking hurts."

Tears ran down his cheeks, and he pulled me into his

arms. I sobbed with old wounds ripped open, and right there in my bathroom, we held onto each other and cried.

I MUST'VE BEEN SHIVERING because Sam kept rubbing my back and my arms. When the tears stopped, I was left exposed and raw but with an overwhelming sense of shame. "I feel so stupid," I mumbled, laughing at how ridiculous my meltdown was.

Sam pulled me back. "Nothing you feel is stupid, Iz. It's gonna hurt to dig through this shit with your old man. But you did the right thing."

His eyes were still a little red, as was the tip of his nose. It was cute. I glanced at myself in the mirror and recoiled. "Ugh. Dear mother of God. Look at me. I look like a drowned rat. That's been sleep-deprived. With a crack addiction."

Sam barked out a laugh and opened the glass shower door. He turned the taps on. "Get in the shower. Get warm. I'll order food."

He left me in the bathroom, and I peeled off my wet clothes and stood under the water, as hot as I could stand it. It helped unknot my shoulders a little, and knowing Sam was here helped ease the ache in my chest. I shut off the water and dried off then went in search of my favourite sweatpants. I couldn't find them in my wardrobe, even though that's where I swear I saw them last...

Then I heard Sam talking in the kitchen, and I smiled because I knew. I just knew he had them on. I pulled on a new pair I didn't exactly love yet, along with a T-shirt I often slept in, and headed out to find him.

"Yeah, sorry," he said into the phone. "Didn't mean to make you worry. Yeah, yeah, he's here. Okay, talk to you soon." He disconnected the call and gave me a smile. "That was my mum."

"You called her wondering where I was?"

"I called her in a panic because after everyone else hadn't heard from you, I didn't know who else to call."

"Sorry."

He sighed. "Next time, just text me or someone else. I don't care. Just someone. There were a lot of worried people tonight, Iz. Just in case you think no one would care if you disappeared, a lot of people would, okay?"

"Okay," I murmured. "I didn't mean to make anyone worry. I just got home and couldn't keep still, ya know? Like jittery or something. So I went for a run. I've been doing that a lot lately. It helps clear my head." Then I noticed what he was wearing. As I'd suspected, he had on my favourite sweatpants. And my old Big Day Out shirt. "Do you always have to steal my favourite trackies?"

He looked down at himself and grinned. "Yep." Then he pointed to the ones I was wearing. "I left the newer ones for you. What are you complaining about?"

"But these aren't as comfy as those."

"I know. That's why I picked them." He grinned. "I ordered pasta, by the way. Should be delivered soon. Figured the carbs'd do you good."

"Thanks," I said. "And thanks for checking up on me. I really didn't mean to make anyone worry."

"'S okay. You look tired."

"I uh, I haven't been sleeping."

He gave me a sad smile. "It'll all be okay, Iz. Everything will work itself out."

"Yeah, I read that motivational poster at my shrink's office," I deadpanned.

He chuckled. "You know, they say sex is good for insomnia."

I snorted at him. "You offering?"

His cheeks flamed, but before he could answer, the door buzzer rang. I watched him as he pressed the intercom and let the delivery guy through. It was an interesting thing for him to say and an even more interesting reaction.

Like he was joking but not really joking at all.

Or maybe I was just imagining it because I'd been thinking about him that way lately. God, maybe he was right. Maybe I needed to get laid, like fucked-into-oblivion kind of laid, to clear my head.

I couldn't even remember how long it'd been…

"Iz!" Sam snapped his fingers in front of my face. "You in there, buddy?"

I shook my head. "Yeah, sorry. What were you saying?"

"I asked if you wanted to eat at the table or on the sofa?"

"Sofa."

So we ate in front of the TV, watching one of his crap shows on Netflix. I didn't really have an appetite, but I knew I had to eat something. When I'd eaten all I could, which wasn't much, I pushed my container onto the coffee table. And he was right about the carbs. It was exactly what I needed. My belly was full and my eyelids heavy.

Sam put his almost empty container alongside mine, swung his legs up so his feet were behind me, and settled on his side. He patted the sofa in front of him. "Here. Lie down."

We'd lain on sofas together a thousand times, but never as big and little spoons.

"Iz, you can barely stay awake. Just lie the fuck down."

I had to admit, it did look awfully comfortable. So I did as he asked. I lay down in front of him, used his arm as a pillow, and snuggled in. He put his top arm over me, a beautiful weight that was comfort and safety all rolled into one.

I closed my eyes, feeling more at peace than I could remember. He pressed a kiss to the back of my head, and I floated like a feather into a heavy, deep sleep.

I remembered him waking me, telling me to get up. I remembered him holding my hand as he walked me down the hall. I remembered falling to bed, wishing he'd stay with me. Wishing he'd hold me again so I could sleep. Because everything would be better if I could just sleep…

I woke up with a start, sunrise beckoning out the window, and with Sam's arms wrapped tight around me, his chest at my back. I was the little spoon again, which was fast becoming my new favourite thing. His cheek was pressed against the back of my head. His soft breaths caressed my ear.

And his cock lay hot and hard against my arse.

I literally had to stop myself from groaning. And from grinding back on him. From pulling down my pants and letting him slide inside me…

Fuck.

While I still had some modicum of willpower, I eased myself out of his hold and slipped out of bed.

There was no denying it. I didn't have morning wood that would deflate with a piss. I had a full-fledged hard-on. Achingly hard. I went straight for the shower, stripped off, stood under the spray, and quickly took myself in hand.

God, I was so hard, so close to coming already.

Waking up surrounded by Sam, with his full cock pressed against my arse… Fuck. I could almost feel what it would be like pushing inside me, filling me, swelling and spilling inside me.

I worked my own cock, imagining him buried inside me, up to his balls, with his fingers digging into my hips, his teeth scraping my shoulder as he came…

My orgasm took hold, expanding from my bones, shredding every cell as it exploded through me. My cock surged and shot come onto the tiles, and I groaned long and loud.

I remembered Sam was just a room away but couldn't bring myself to care if he'd heard me. I finished my shower and dried off, tying the towel around my waist.

The logical part of my brain knew Sam had slept in my bed. I knew that. But nothing quite prepared me for walking out and seeing him in it, sprawled out and smiling sleepily at me.

My heart skipped a beat, my stomach fluttered, and my mouth went dry.

"That shower must have been *real* good," he said with a knowing smirk.

Right, then. No wondering if he'd heard me groaning when I came. "Fuck you."

He laughed. "Bit late for that. You took care of it in the shower."

Ignoring his comment and the blush I'm sure ran right down my chest, I walked into my walk-in wardrobe where he couldn't see me. I dropped my towel and pulled on some underpants. "Something wrong with your bed?"

"Nope," he answered. "You asked me to sleep with you."

I stuck my head around the doorway. "I what?"

He was still lying in bed, though now he had his arms folded behind his head. "You asked me. You were half-asleep. I was trying to get you into your own bed, and you asked me to stay. You said you'd sleep better with me there."

"I uh…" I swallowed hard. "I don't remember that." That wasn't technically true. I remembered thinking it, just not saying it out loud.

Sam's gaze went from my face, down to my chest, then to my dick. He took his time checking me out, and when his eyes met mine again, he licked his lips. "Nice. Calvin's suit you."

I looked down at myself, and yes, I was just wearing underwear. Not a stitch more. "My apartment. My bedroom, more to the point."

He wasn't fazed. "So did you sleep better?"

"Much. Actually, I haven't slept that good in… a long time."

His answering smile was warm and wide. "Good."

I stepped back into the wardrobe and pulled on my suit

pants, then slid my arms into a business shirt. I walked back out to my bedroom, doing the buttons up as I went.

Sam was now sitting up on the far side of the bed. He looked me up and down again and raised an approving eyebrow before looking out the window. "How are your coffee-making skills, Iz?"

"Stellar."

"Prove it."

I could take a hint. I smiled on my way to the kitchen. "Hope your shower is as good as mine was."

I made him his bloody coffee, then cut up some fruit, served up some yoghurt and granola. Sam walked into the kitchen wearing one of my last-season tan pants, a light-blue business shirt, and a blue blazer.

"Jesus Christ," I griped. "Help yourself to my wardrobe."

"I did. The pants are a little long in the leg."

"Because they're mine. Not yours."

"A bit roomy in the arse."

"My arse isn't big."

He laughed. "Bit tight in the crotch."

"Shut up and eat your breakfast."

He grinned as he sipped his coffee. I had to admit, even with his smartarse comments, it was nice having him here of a morning. Especially this morning. I was still feeling a little raw after last night, but having him around was a balm. I wasn't lying when I said I'd slept better than I could remember, and his presence here this morning was a real comfort.

His stubbornness, not so much.

Because when he dropped me off at work, he said, "I'll meet you back at yours at about seven tonight. I'll need to go home and grab a few things because someone keeps bitching about me wearing his clothes."

I opened my mouth to tell him he didn't have to stay the night if he didn't want to. But he didn't even let me start. "Shut the fuck up. I'm staying whether you like it or not. If we're heading out to Penrith tomorrow morning, I may as well stay at your place."

There was no point in denying it. I wanted him with me, all I could get.

"Thank you."

"But if we're gonna sleep in the same bed again, we should set down some ground rules." He tried to be serious but the slight smirk gave him away. "If you're gonna rub your arse against me, you could at least wear a jockstrap. Or just be naked… Actually, no. I'll go with the jockstrap. And if you're gonna hog the blankets *and* the bed, you better be good *in* bed, if you know what I mean."

"You finished?"

"Nope. You could at least make some room in your wardrobe for a few things of mine. It'd only be polite."

"Anything else?"

"If I think of anything, I'll text you." A car behind us honked.

I looked at Sam and sighed. "You shouldn't have stopped in a clearway, Sam. It's pretty bad form. The poor guy behind us is rather disgruntled. He's probably just trying to get to work, and you just had to be an arsehole and park your car in his way."

He snorted. "Get the fuck out of my car."

I was still chuckling when I walked onto the thirty-seventh floor. Prue greeted me with a smile. "Good morning," I said to her. "My father in?"

"Yes."

"Can you see if he's free sometime this morning?"

"Of course. Anything else?"

"Yes. I'll need to clear my schedule from four o'clock on Mondays and Thursdays."

She was already typing something into our calendar. "For how long?"

"Indefinite at this point."

She tried to hide her surprise, though she kept on typing. "No problem."

"Thought about cashing in on that early-leave pass I offered the other week?"

"Oh." She stopped typing and smiled up at me. "Maybe…"

"It's fine, Prue. If you want to take a Friday afternoon off, just say."

"Well, this afternoon…"

"Yes?"

Her bottom lip pulled down in a frown. "Well, there's a wine and berry festival on the South coast. My friends are leaving at lunchtime. I told them I couldn't go, but—"

"Sounds awesome. You should go!"

She beamed. "I'll bring you back something."

I liked making her happy. It was crazy, but such a small gesture meant a lot to her, and I liked that I'd helped. "And let me know when my father's available."

Which, as it turned out, wasn't until eleven. But to be honest, I was kind of surprised he agreed to see me at all. I was pretty sure he didn't want to know what the shrink had said.

"Israel?" he said, walking in like he had somewhere else to be.

"Dad." I pushed my laptop away so he knew he had my attention.

"What's news with you?"

"My psychologist appointment went well." I wasn't getting into details with him when I wasn't prepared to deal with them myself quite yet. "I've asked Prue to clear my schedule on Mondays and Thursdays from four."

His eyes flashed. "Twice a week?"

"Uh, yeah. I um…" I'm fucked up, thanks to you, mostly, but I have enough issues that would keep Freud himself busy. "We think it might be best, especially while I adapt to having

Donna and Nick in my life." It wasn't an exact lie, and I didn't know why I buffered the reality from him. I was still protecting him instead of making him accountable.

He processed what I told him. "Okay…" He clearly didn't know what else to say.

So I spoke instead. "I won't lie. It was intense. So if some days I need to work from home, I presume that's okay." I wasn't asking permission. No fucking way.

My father rubbed his chin. "Do you need extended leave? You're entitled to—"

"I know what I'm entitled to."

"Right, of course." The look he gave me told me he knew I was talking about more than just annual leave or personal time.

I smiled at his snooty remark. "You can't blame me for wondering what legal footing I had, given we were just handed proof you don't actually owe me anything."

He blinked, and I knew I'd gone too far. Part of me felt bad, part of me wanted him to know. "Israel." He shook his head. "How could you think that?"

"How could I not?" I stared at him. "I distinctly remember a conversation when I was in high school where you told me no gay son of yours would work in your company. Remember that? Sam was there, remember? And you were right all along. I mean, yes, I'm still gay. Always will be. But I'm not your biological son. So technically no gay son of yours does work for you. But that also means you're not under any family obligation to have a gay son working for you, so you could fire me. Or make it exceedingly difficult for me to stay. Either way, I had to know where I stood. Legally, that is. And Sam—"

"Sam." He said his name like he wanted to roll his eyes, only that he thought it'd be beneath him.

"Yes, Sam," I said, probably a little too loudly. "The only person in my life whose loyalty I've never had to question.

He has my back. And still to this day, as always, the only one who does."

My father flinched. "I'm sorry I said that, back then, what I said... I... I'm sorry."

"Are you? Or are you sorry I'm bringing it up?"

He didn't answer.

I refused to back down. I didn't want to buffer him from my hurt anymore. He had to know. "I'm still capable of doing my job. And until that changes, I'll assume it's fine for me to take some leave or to work from home, as needed."

"Of course it is." He looked up at the ceiling like it held all the answers. "You're very capable in your job. Exceptional, even. Israel, I'm sorry you feel this way..."

I wanted to scream at him that I had been *raised to feel* this way. I wanted to throw something at him, but I needed to rein myself in. I needed to try and remain professional, given I'd just told him I was capable of doing my job; I needed to act like it.

With a deep breath, I changed subjects and drew our meeting to a close. "I'm meeting Donna and Nick again tomorrow, and the rest of their family," I reminded him. "I'll see if Nick's thought any more on meeting with you, and I'll do my best to convince him."

He nodded but remained silent. He looked so... defeated. It wasn't a look he wore well or often, and I drew no satisfaction from seeing it now.

A long and awkward silence seeped between us, neither of us knowing what to say or how to move forward from here without losing ground. Thankfully my desk phone buzzed. "Mr Ingham," Prue's voice cut through the air. "Israel, your twelve o'clock is here."

I pushed the button to reply. "Thank you."

My father stood up, looked everywhere but at me, and with no more than a nod, he walked out of my office.

"AND YOU DIDN'T SEE him again all day?" Sam asked as he handed me the takeout container of Thai food. We were sitting in my lounge room in front of the TV watching Twenty20 cricket.

"Nope. Maybe he left right after, I don't know."

"It's weird, isn't it?" he mused. "And there I was thinking him finding out you're not biologically his son would make him shut you out even more. But it's not. I think it's made him realise you don't have to stay. And it sounds to me like he's terrified of losing you."

I chewed my *som tum* thoughtfully. "Maybe."

"And how does that make you feel?"

"Like my mouth's on fire. How fucking spicy did you order this?" I took a sip of my beer to put out the raging inferno in my mouth. "Jesus Christ."

Sam laughed. "You know I like things hot."

"You know I like not having third-degree burns on my tongue." I flattened my tongue onto the side of my cold beer bottle. "Chethus thucking Cwisth."

Sam burst out laughing and fell back on the sofa. "It's not that bad."

"It ain't real good either."

"You're supposed to have banana or milk or yoghurt to stop the burning."

"Is that what they told you at the STI clinic?"

He snorted out a laugh. "There's some bananas in the kitchen." I stared at him, waiting. He had the audacity to look surprised. "What?"

"Just waiting for the deep-throat punchline."

He grinned but shook his head. "No, no. Being totally serious. Something to do with a chemical balance that stops the effect of chili. No deep-throat jokes involved."

My tongue was still burning, so I got up and walked to the

kitchen, only to have Sam laugh and sing from that old kids' show. "One banana, two banana, three banana, four…" which he clearly thought was hilarious.

So I brought out a peeled banana, sat back down next to him, and fucking deep throated it right then and there. I slid it all the way down and didn't gag once. I pulled it out slowly, licking it as I did.

He wasn't laughing any more. His mouth was hanging open.

"Mmm," I said. "You're right. Banana really works."

He was still staring at me, his cheeks pink and his pupils blown out. "Fuck," he breathed.

I clapped him on the back. "Eat your spicy papaya, Sam." I bit into the banana and chewed around my smug grin.

Sam continued to side-eye me most of the night, and every time I'd catch him, I'd just waggle my eyebrows at him. It was pretty obvious what he was thinking when he'd look away and swallow thickly.

When the last ball was bowled in the cricket game, I switched the TV off and declared it a night. He followed me down the hall and stopped at the door to the spare room. "Night, Iz."

I was disappointed he wasn't offering to sleep in my bed again. Not that we'd discussed it, but I'd hoped…

I opened my mouth to ask him if he'd join me, but I stopped myself. Knowing he was here was enough. "Night, Sam."

I changed into some sleep pants, brushed my teeth, and climbed into bed. I tried listening for him in the next room, but he was silent. I tried deep breathing to relax. I tried counting sheep. I tried reading. I tried everything I could think of. I was tired, exhausted even, body, mind, and soul, but sleep still wouldn't come.

Frustrated, I threw the covers back and went down the hall. I cracked the spare room door open. "Sam?"

He sat up, still half-asleep. "What's wrong?"

"Can't sleep."

He fell back onto his pillow and groaned, then threw the blanket down in invitation. I slid into the bed beside him, breathing in his scent. He mumbled something unintelligible, and pulled me into his arms. I froze, wondering if he was aware of what he was doing. His breathing was deep, his arms heavy, so I knew he was already back asleep. Then he mumbled, "…like the banana."

I buried my face into his chest to hide my laugh and settled into a deep, deep sleep.

I WOKE UP ALONE. It took me a second to realise I was asleep in the spare bedroom—the room Sam slept in when he crashed here—though his side of the bed was empty.

I shouldn't have expected him to stay in bed with me. I mean, what did I want him to do? Lie in bed and cuddle?

No matter how blurred the lines were, they weren't *that* blurred.

I didn't even know if he remembered me coming into his room at two o'clock this morning. I didn't even know if he was still here.

Then I heard a clunk, followed by, "Oh, you piece of fucking shit."

Yep. He was still here, and by the sounds of it, he was fighting with my coffee machine.

I got up, took a piss, and found him trying to get the filter handle back into the group head. "Be nice to it," I said.

He stood up and looked at me. "Seriously, buy a new one that takes pods. So much easier."

I snorted and took the filter handle from him. I very slowly, very patiently, slid it into the group head. "I don't want a new machine. I like this one."

"I'm pretty sure it came to Australia on the *Endeavour*."

I slid a cup under the spout. "It's not quite that old."

"Actually, I'm pretty sure Noah had one just like it installed on the ark."

I chuckled at him, then noticed the yoghurt and fruit out on the bench. "Oh look, bananas. Did you dream of bananas last night? Because you were mumbling about them in your sleep."

He blanched. "No."

"You totally did. Want me to deep throat another one? I will."

"If you do, I'm recording it and sending it to everyone we know. Then I'll make a gif and upload it as your *Grindr* avi. You'll have every gay man in the country replying."

I batted my eyelids and pretended to swoon. "You'd do that for me?"

Now he laughed. "Just shut up and make me coffee."

I started to froth the milk and had to speak over the noise of it. "Only because you asked me so nicely."

Sam chopped up some fruit, put some bread in the toaster, and we had a relatively peaceful breakfast. We both checked our emails, got some work done, and before I knew it, it was time to go out to Donna's for lunch.

Showered, dressed in jeans and a T-shirt, I walked out to where Sam was. "How's this? Do I look alright?"

"You look fine," he assured me. "You're nervous, and that's okay. But I'm pretty sure Donna's not the type to judge someone by what they're wearing."

"True."

"In fact, I'd reckon if you were overdressed, they'd notice. They're not the fancy, pretentious types."

"You mean wealthy."

He shot me a look. "No. I mean fancy and pretentious." He tilted his head. "Are you worried that they think you're some rich guy?"

"Well, technically, we kind of are some rich guys," I allowed. "And I'd imagine what they were wearing the last time we met was their 'good' clothes, and Donna's car looked pretty old."

Sam took a deep breath in through his nose. "Iz, they're gonna like you. Okay?"

"What?"

"Your issue isn't about whether you or I think they're good enough. Your issue is whether you think you're good enough."

I brushed down my shirt. "Maybe I should change."

He put his hands over mine to still them. "Israel. Look at me."

He waited until I did.

"They're gonna love you, okay? You know what Donna reminds me of?" He didn't wait for me to answer. "A mother hen. She's gonna fuss over all her brood, making sure everyone's fed and happy. You're one of her brood, Iz. So don't go stressing over something that won't happen. No one is gonna care what you wear. They just want to meet you. The long-lost brother."

Oh, Jesus.

"Brother." I said the word slowly.

Sam smiled at me. "You have an hour or so driving time to get used to that word, Captain."

"Uh, for the love of God, please don't tell them about my nickname."

He walked to the front door and held it open for me, and proceeded to sing the theme song to SpongeBob, very deliberately off-key.

I walked past him, out the door. "Shut up, Sam-I-Am."

He pulled the door shut and followed me down the corridor. "Dr Seuss is awesome!"

He didn't really think Dr Seuss was awesome. He just said it so if we thought he thought it was cool, we'd stop saying it.

It was a reverse psychology that kind of worked. And because he'd then quote every line he could remember until we eventually stopped calling him Sam-I-Am just to shut him up…

"Don't even think about reciting Dr Seuss the whole way there," I warned, getting into his car.

He clearly took that as a challenge. "But from there to here, or here and there, them funny things are everywhere."

I groaned, and he grinned.

"If you never did you should."

"Oh, please don't."

"Things are fun, and fun is good."

I rolled my eyes. "I can't take you here or there, I can't take you anywhere. Near or far, just drive the fucking car."

Sam laughed. "You're quite good at this. Although your ad lib could use some work, and I don't think he dropped the f-bomb in kids' books."

I stared at him. "I do not give one fuck, two fucks, red fucks, blue fucks."

He burst out laughing. "You win. Though I've seen that on Tumblr."

Truth be told, so had I. "What were you looking for on Tumblr? Anything in particular?"

Sam waggled his eyebrows at me. "One dick, two dicks, red dicks, blue dicks."

I found myself laughing, despite my best attempts not to. "You're really not funny. And if the dicks are red or blue, they need to take their cock rings off. Or get bigger ones."

He grinned. "Any personal experience with that?"

I looked ahead and deliberately avoided his question. "Just shut up and drive."

An hour and fifteen minutes later, we pulled up at the address Donna had given me. The house was a small, 1970s red-brick home. It looked like it could've been a commission house at one point, though the garden was well kept, the lawns mowed and tidy. It was very clear Donna was house-proud.

Sam gave me a minute of silence. Then he asked, "What are you thinking, Iz? You wanna go in?"

I nodded. "I could have grown up here. This could have been the house where I spent summers as a kid, playing outside."

Sam glanced up the street with a far off look in his eyes. "Long way to ride your bike to my place from here."

I smiled at him. We both knew if I'd had the life I was born into, we would never have met. Even if that seemed impossible. "Come on. Let's go inside."

TWELVE

Donna welcomed me, then Sam, with a great big hug. "I promised no tears today," she said, wiping her eyes.

Nick stood in the living room, and when his mother was done hugging us both to death, he shook our hands with a grin. "Nice to meet you again." He then motioned to the woman standing beside him. "This is my fiancée, Melissa. Mel, this is Israel and Sam."

Melissa was a thin, blonde woman, about twenty-four years old. She had a round face, kind eyes, and wide smile. "Nice to finally meet you."

After introductions were done, while I took a deep breath, wondering where on earth to start, Sam said, "Something sure smells good."

Donna beamed. "I've been baking. Come on through to the kitchen. I'll make us a cuppa."

The house was definitely a 70s build, with brown carpets and an arch that led to a small kitchen with fake-wood-laminated cupboards and a green countertop. There was a table in the corner, photos on the wall, and a homey feel that made my heart ache.

"Tea or coffee?" Donna asked.

"Coffee," Sam and I answered in unison. We sat at the table, along with Nick and Melissa, who asked us about our drive out and whether we found the place okay. I relaxed a little, still wishing I was better at small talk, but I felt comfortable with them.

I didn't know them well, if at all, really. But they'd welcomed Sam and me into their home with open arms and kind smiles, and that said a lot about who they were. Donna put some coffee cups in front of us. "I told Ash and Lachie to give us a bit of time. I sent them to the shops to grab a few things. They'll be back in half an hour or so. Then we can eat, unless you're hungry now. I can dish up lunch now if you'd rather."

I smiled up at her. It was nice to be fussed over, kind of how Sam's mother used to fuss over us when we'd spend weekends at his place swimming in the pool. "It's fine. Perfect, actually."

Donna sat down, smiling but clearly nervous. "How've you been since we saw you last? Still trying to get your head around everything?"

I nodded. "Yeah. And you?"

"Same, but good."

I let out a slow breath. "And Ash and Lachie? They're okay with meeting me?"

"Oh yes," Donna said with a laugh. "Very excited."

I sipped my coffee, which was just the basic supermarket-bought, instant stuff. And it was actually pretty good. "Coffee okay?" Donna asked.

"Perfect, thank you." I looked over at the photos on the fridge, then smiled at Donna. "You have a really lovely home."

"Oh, thank you," she said. She beamed with pride. "It's not much, but its mine. Lots of wonderful memories inside these walls."

I wasn't sure if this was the right time or if there was ever a right time to say this, but ours were hardly normal circum-stances. "I don't assume to know anything about your life or what you've been through, so forgive me for saying this. When we met the first time, you mentioned tough times, financially, and I... I never had that. I guess as a kid, I had all the material things I ever needed: a big house, all the toys and gadgets. My nannies would buy me whatever I wanted. But I never had this." I motioned around the table and got choked up and blinked back tears. "I never had a family home. And I can tell you, it makes you the richest person I know."

"Money don't mean shit," Nick replied. "I mean, it'd be nice and all, but it's not what's important."

I nodded, and the tears I'd been fighting spilled down my cheeks. "I know." I scrubbed my face and laughed at myself. "I told myself no more tears today too."

Donna snorted, teary eyed. "We make a good pair."

"I'm not normally so emotional," I said. Sam put his hand on my knee under the table, and I gave him a bit of a smile. "Well, up until a month ago I would have said I wasn't. But this whole switched thing has changed my life. I decided to see a therapist to deal with... everything."

"Oh, love," Donna said. Her eyes filled with sadness and sympathy.

"No, it's a good thing," I told her. I felt stupid for being an emotional fucking wreck five minutes into our meeting. Poor Melissa must have thought I was a basket case. "It's a good thing."

"Sonya at work's been seeing a shrink for years," Melissa said. "Said it's the best thing she's ever done. Lord knows, with everything she's been through, but there ain't nothing wrong with it."

I had absolutely no clue who Sonya was or what she'd been through, but this was Melissa's way of telling me and everyone else in the room that seeing a shrink wasn't a bad thing. I gave her a smile. "Thanks. Yeah, I probably should have gone years ago."

The oven timer went off, startling me. Jesus, I was jumpy. Sam squeezed my knee again, and Donna rubbed my shoulder as she stood up to tend to whatever was in the oven. "I better get that. You boys catch up," she said. She then busied herself getting trays out and plates ready, in what I realised was an attempt at giving me and Nick some time to talk.

I collected my thoughts and started again. "Thank you for agreeing to meet me and inviting me into your home."

He smiled at me. "Nah, it's fine. Bit of a shock, innit? This whole mess."

"Uh, yeah. Though not really. I never felt like I belonged, so it also kinda made sense. That probably doesn't make sense," I said with a laugh. "I mean, as a kid I always wished I had a different family." Sam squeezed my leg again.

Nick stared at me for a while. "I can't imagine that."

I didn't want this to be a pity party for me. I wasn't the only one who was hurt in this. "I'm sorry about your dad. It must have been very difficult."

"You look just like him," Nick said, looking over my face.

Jesus. There it was again, guilt for something I wasn't responsible for. "Sorry."

He laughed. "Don't apologise. This isn't anyone's fault. Well, not anyone in this room's fault."

"Still. It must be hard for you too. That I look like your dad. I mean, he was your father and..." I didn't know what else to say.

"He was your father too."

And again with the tears. Fuck. I laughed at how stupid my tears were. "I haven't cried this much in my life."

Sam squeezed my knee so hard it hurt. I looked at him, and he didn't speak. He just scooted his chair closer to mine and let go of my leg so he could rub my back instead. It was such a simple touch that soothed me like a balm.

"Do you want to see photos?" Nick asked. "Of my dad. Our dad, I mean. Shit. Hey, that's weird."

I smiled with him and wiped my cheeks. "Yeah, I'd like that."

I followed him into the small family room. The furniture looked dated but well cared for, the carpet was worn, and there were trinkets around the room that screamed *family home*. It was a far cry from the house I grew up in, but it was lived in and well loved. The whole house felt like a home.

The mantel was lined with photos, a picture timeline, a growth chart of the people who lived here. Nick picked up the first one and smiled at it fondly, like it was an old, old friend. "This is him. His name was Richard."

Richard Westbrook.

He handed the frame to me, and I couldn't believe my eyes. The man in the photo was me. I mean, the photo itself was clearly from the 80s or early 90s, if the fashion was anything to go by, but the man in the photo could have been me. Dark hair, pale skin; he even had dark stubble in the photo. I had his dark eyes. Our tall and lean builds were the same.

I now understood why Donna had burst into tears when she saw me. She'd nodded like she knew I was her son without any introduction. Because I was the spitting image of her late husband.

My father.

"Oh wow."

Nick nodded. "Told ya. You look just like him."

I showed the photo to Sam, and he grinned at me. "Jesus. That could be you."

All I could do was nod. I took a shaky breath and swallowed hard. "I've never looked like anyone before."

Nick clapped his hand on my shoulder, but it was Sam's hand on my back, rubbing circles with his thumb, that kept me from losing my shit altogether. His gentle touch was a reminder that I wasn't alone. Because not only had I never looked like anyone before. I'd never belonged anywhere before either. I'd never had a family connection before. I didn't need to say that out loud. Everyone seemed to understand.

Especially Sam. Always Sam.

Donna was there now. "I have whole albums," she said gently. "I can show you them all if you like? Maybe later?"

I looked at her. "I'd like that."

A car pulled up out the front of the house, and we could see through the large front window as two people got out. A younger girl and a guy, who I could only assume were Ashley and Lachlan.

"Well, quiet time's over," Nick said.

Mel pushed him playfully. "Be nice to your sister."

Donna looked at me, her eyes wide with hope. "You ready, love?"

Too bad if I wasn't, because they were almost at the door. "As I'll ever be."

The door swung open, and the girl walked through first. She looked about seventeen, had shoulder-length, dark-brown, curly hair, and a huge smile. She was clearly very excited; her eyes focused in on me like a heat-seeking missile. "You must be Israel!"

Oh boy. I could see why Nick said the quiet time was over. She was loud, cheerful, and bouncing with energy. I held out my hand. "Yes. And you must be Ashley."

"Call me Ash. Everyone else does."

Then it was Lachlan's turn. He was maybe twenty-two, and I didn't really need to explain what he looked like, because he looked just like me, though he had cautious eyes.

He was quieter than Ashley, but he smiled, nonetheless, and extended his hand. "Lachlan."

"Israel."

"Holy shit," Nick said, looking between us. "Lach, if you wanna know what you're gonna look like in a few years, this is it."

I laughed, because fuck. I didn't know what else to do. I looked to Sam, who was staring at Lachlan. "Yeah, wow."

I made introductions, everyone shook hands, and then I noticed Donna. She was standing under the archway into the kitchen with tears running down her face. Everyone else seemed to notice at the same time. "Ah, Jesus," Lach groaned. "Mum!"

She waved him off. "Oh shush, you. I can't help it." Then she blotted her face with a tissue. She obviously cried all the time, at every little thing. "Righteo, who wants lunch?"

So the seven of us sat around Donna's kitchen table and ate lunch. There were no more tears, only smiles, and a lot of good food. All home-cooked, hand-made, and delicious. I didn't realise I was so hungry, but I cleaned my plate, then had seconds.

We talked about family histories, whether I'd inherited any allergies or illnesses, which I was grateful to admit I hadn't. Nick asked if my parents were in good health and even asked about my grandparents.

"I've never met my father's parents," I told them. "He doesn't talk of them, and I've never asked. My mother's family are in England. I met them once when I was about five. I have no cousins that I know of." I smiled at the five faces staring blankly at me. "It's always been just me."

Having no family was obviously a foreign concept to them. They started to talk about first cousins and second cousins, aunts and uncles, and I was well and truly lost. It was easy to get caught up in their happiness, though.

Hard too.

I excused myself to use the bathroom and took a moment to splash some water on my face. I just needed a few seconds to breathe. When I thought I'd left Sam alone for too long, I opened the door and walked back down the hall, but I heard them talking about me, and I stopped.

Sam had his head down. "Iz thanks me for showing up, he thanks me for being a friend. He thanks me for things that people don't think twice about. It breaks my heart because he's so grateful to have people in his life who won't hurt him. Those people, I won't call them his parents, have messed him up more than even he realises."

"I know," I whispered from the doorway.

Sam looked at me with sorry in his eyes. "Iz, I didn't mean—"

"It's okay," I reassured him. "Because it's true. I'm pretty messed up, I know that. I grew up in a museum, not a home. I was closer to my nannies than I ever was to my parents. Hell, I think growing up, I actually spoke to Mr Boddington more than I ever did my father." I looked at the solemn faces staring back at me. "He was the gardener."

I swallowed hard, and I refused to cry. "When I had my appendix out, I was in hospital for three days. My mother visited once, my father not at all. They sent my nanny and a driver to come get me." I rocked back on my heels. "I was eight."

Donna wiped her eyes. "Mr Dovich said they referred to your blood type from when you had that operation as a boy. I wondered why your parents never picked up your blood type on your medical files..."

"I doubt they ever read them. Because they never cared."

There was an awkward silence around the table, because really, there wasn't much to say. Sam frowned at me, then spoke to Lachie. "Wanna check my car out?"

He smiled. "Can I?"

"Sure."

"Can I take it for a spin?"

"No!" Donna answered. "Absolutely not."

Sam shrugged. "Maybe next time." It was a blatant ploy to give me some alone time with Donna. I gave him a smile, and he patted my shoulder as he left. "Ash, you too?"

Ashley glanced at Donna, who nodded. Mel went with them, and the four of them walked out through the front of the house. I smiled at Nick and Donna, but my gaze fell back on Nick: the guy who should have lived my life.

I studied him for a second, trying to ignore how much he looked like a mix of both my parents. "I'm sorry. I'm trying not to speak ill of my mother and father. We won't pretend that Sam likes them," I said with a smile. "You can meet them if you want and make up your own mind. I'll say this, though," I said seriously. "Something's changed with them, my father in particular, these last few weeks. Like he's trying to reach out to me, or he's trying to apologise but doesn't know how. I don't know. We've had a few discussions these last two weeks, which have been… well, honest and a little confronting. Mostly for him. I've said some things that needed saying, and he took them pretty well." I sighed and shrugged. "I think he's trying to make amends. I don't know."

"Do you want him to?" Donna asked.

I took a moment to answer. Part of me wanted to push against my father, reject any offering of peace, and hurt him like he hurt me. But more than anything, I wanted his approval. I wanted his love. Did I really want to make amends with him? "Yes. Yes, I think so. Though it will probably take some time. I don't think Sam will ever forgive him."

Donna smiled and nodded to the door Sam had walked out of. "He's a lovely young man."

"He's the best. I wouldn't have survived my teenage years

without him, I'm sure." I smiled sadly and let out a long breath. "His family is pretty great too."

"How long have you two been together?"

I shot my gaze to Donna. "I'm not… we're not… it's not like that."

She blinked in surprise. "Really?"

"Uh, yeah. We're just friends." It was a gross understatement. He was so much more to me than that. But as far as labels went…

Donna clucked her tongue. "There are things in life you can't hide, child. And love is one of them. I can see it between you."

I shook my head. "No, it's not like that. I mean, not for him. I mean, I love him, but…"

God, what was I admitting? That I *loved* him? Of course I did. But *love* love? Like romantically? Oh fuck…

"Like Sam said. Not everyone who loves you will hurt you, Israel. Let yourself be loved by him."

I stared at her, unable to speak.

She pointed to the front door. "I can tell you, that boy out there, your very best friend, is head over heels in love with you. He looks at you…" She shook her head in wonder. "Like really looks at you, Israel. You have to know that."

I opened my mouth, then closed it. Words failed me.

Nick laughed. "Don't even try to deny it. She knows. She told me the same damn thing when I met Mel. Mum said she was the girl I was gonna marry as soon as she laid eyes on her." He shrugged. "And she was right."

"Sam's not in love with me," I reasoned. "He's my best friend. Since we were in year seven at school. He's been with me through everything, good and bad. He's my rock, ya know? If I need him, he's there. And I do the same for him. It's how it's always been."

"Is he seeing someone?" Donna asked.

"No."

"Have you ever seen him smitten with anyone?"

"Well, no. He's dated a little bit, but nothing serious."

"Like you."

"Yeah. I guess."

"And why do you think that is?"

"I don't know. It's just the way it's always been."

"Maybe it's because the only person he can ever see himself with, is you."

"I don't think that's why..." I said, though there was no conviction in my voice.

"But you wish it was."

And for that I had no reply.

"When you think of something funny, who's the one person you want to tell?"

"Well, Sam, because he finds that shit hilarious."

She smiled. "And when you're having a crap day, who's the one person you want to see?"

I didn't need to answer that.

"And when you want to go out or do something fun, who's the one person you call?"

I didn't need to answer that either.

"And when you sat in that office with Mr Dovich and everything you ever knew fell to shit, who was the one person you wanted?"

I looked down at my hands but said nothing.

Donna and Nick seemed to have some silent conversation before she reached over and patted my hand. "It's okay, Israel. I'm sorry if I brought up something that's hard for you. It's just when I first saw you together, I assumed you were a couple."

"A lot of people do."

She smiled, and I ignored the *thought so* look in her eyes.

"You know, that's how I knew Richard was the one for me. It's all in the eyes. We'd been dating a little while, and he was so charming. He took me to the Royal Easter Show and we went on rollercoasters and spent the day laughing. He was a gentleman." She looked at me with a wicked gleam in her eye. "But when he dropped me home and kissed me good-night, I could see it in his eyes. He was in love with me. It wasn't in the words he said, it wasn't in his actions. It was in his eyes. Honey, it always is.

"When you're alone with him, look at him. I mean really look at him. Look into his eyes and ask yourself what you see staring back at you."

"Mum," Nick warned gently. "Leave it alone."

"It's okay," I said, trying to smile. I looked right at him. "You're lucky to have a mother who cares so much, that talks about—" Love, emotions, anything. "—that stuff."

He smiled at her. "I know."

Donna patted my hand. "Sorry, love. I'm just shocked to hear you're not actually a couple, that's all. I just assumed you'd been together for years."

Sam's laughter rang out from the front yard, and it made me smile. It seemed to break the solemn mood, and I checked my watch for the time. As much as I'd enjoyed my time here, I could use some breathing room.

Nick seemed to understand. "So, what do you think of your brother and sister? You gonna leave here and never look back?"

I barked out a laugh. "Ah, no. Actually, it's pretty cool. It's a lot to get used to, I'll admit, but they're great people. I'd like to get to know them better."

Donna smiled proudly. "They'd love that. We all would."

On that note, I stood up and thanked Donna for everything. She hugged me, kissed my cheek, and told me I could come back anytime, no invitation necessary. Nick walked with me out to the car, and I could tell he wanted to ask me something. He was just unsure of how to start.

I smiled at him. "Just say it, Nick."

He chuckled and leant against the front porch railing. "Do

you think I should meet your parents? My parents?" He shook his head. "Whatever."

I smiled with him, because we were the only ones who really understood what a mindfuck it was. "I can't make that decision for you. But for me, I felt like I had to meet your mum, my birth mother, to move forward. I felt stuck, in limbo or something. I don't know how to explain it. But I had to know. Whether it worked out for the better or if we'd meet once and never speak again, I just had to know. I needed to do it so I could move forward." I sighed. "But we had very different upbringings. I needed to know about where I came from to help me understand why I felt so detached from my parents. You're the opposite; your family's pretty fucking cool."

He smiled and nodded over towards where Mel, Ash, and Lachie were still talking to Sam. "They're a pain in my arse."

I laughed because it was easy to see he adored them. "Then meet them for curiosity's sake and nothing more. But it's you who needs to be ready for that."

He took a deep breath and nodded before he held out his hand for me to shake. "Thanks, mate."

I shook his hand. "Any time."

"Hey," Sam called out. "How about we take a few photos?"

"Good idea," I said. We called Donna out and all stood together, smiling at Sam as he snapped a few shots.

My first family photo.

With another round of goodbyes, Sam and I got into his car. As we drove away, Nick had Ash in a headlock and she was trying to tickle him, and Donna was lecturing them as she waved goodbye to us.

"Good day?" Sam asked as we headed down the street.

"Yeah. I think so. What about you?"

"They're real good people, Iz. And I know you didn't grow up in that house, but Jesus, you're so like them. Not just in looks, because fucking hell you look like them, but your attitude and the kind of person you are." He shook his head like he couldn't believe it. "You fit in with them."

I smiled and leaned my head on the headrest. "It's weird, huh?"

"Yes and no. It should be surprising, but it's not," he answered. Then he shook his head again. "My God, you and Lachie look alike."

"Yeah, I wasn't expecting that. I mean, they'd said I looked like my dad. I guess biology would mean that I'd look like my brother too." I blew out a deep breath. "Is it weird that Nick feels more like a brother to me than Lachie or Ash? I mean, I know we share this whole switched at birth thing and we're different on so many levels, but we're a lot alike. I dunno. It's weird."

Sam smiled at me. "It is weird. You know what's weirder? That if you hadn't been switched and he'd been you and I met him in high school, I reckon I'd still be friends with him."

"Maybe. But he wouldn't go to the park with you to scope out the Navy boys. He's straight, remember?"

Sam chuckled. "The Navy has women too, you know."

I snorted at that. "Well no. I never paid that much attention."

He laughed but fell silent for a while. "Well, you're in a better frame of mind after this meeting with them."

"I feel better."

"Don't need me to hold your hand this time?"

I couldn't tell if he was joking or not, but I smiled at him and held up my hand. "You can hold my hand if you want."

He rolled his eyes but took my hand in his anyway. He entwined our fingers and rested our joined hands on his leg. He never said another word, though I'd catch him smiling, and I couldn't help but think of what Donna had said.

That boy out there, your very best friend, is head over heels in love with you. He looks at you, like really looks at you, Israel. You have to know that.

It's in his eyes. It always is.

God, could she be right? Did he really think of me that way? Did he love me as a best friend, or was it more? My heart pounded at the possibility, thrilled that maybe, just maybe, Donna was right. I was also scared shitless, petrified, that she might be…

"You okay?" Sam asked. I was so lost in thought, I hadn't even realised where we were. We were parked out the front of my apartment, sitting in his car, still holding hands. "Iz?"

"Yeah." I cleared my throat. "Yeah, I'm good."

He frowned. "Well, I could do work from your place…"

I had no clue what conversation I'd missed, but he obviously had some work to catch up on. "Nah, it's cool. You do what you've gotta do. I have a tonne of shit to get done too. I'll text you later."

"You sure?"

"Yeah, absolutely."

"It's just the Greenburg case, but it won't wait. I've had five emails since we were at lunch."

"Sam, it's fine. You can't put your job on hold for me. I can be at home by myself for a night. Honestly, it's fine."

He looked torn. "I'll call around later. I'll bring dinner."

"Sam. I'll be fine. I'll text you later."

He nodded and gave me a reluctant smile. "Okay." There was something in his eyes that resembled pain and uncertainty, and I hated that I was the reason for it. He leaned over the centre console and gave me a soft kiss on the cheek. For all our hugs and hand-holding, kissing—any kind of kissing—was new.

I might have gasped a little, and he pulled back suddenly. His cheeks tinged pink, and he leaned back in his seat. "I'll just be at home. Call me anytime."

I grabbed his hand and squeezed, making him stop. "Thank you. For today. For everything."

He looked at me, then, like really looked at me. He stared into my eyes, and even though I couldn't look away from his face, I could see the rapid rise and fall of his chest. "You don't have to thank me," he said softly.

I recalled his words earlier today, about how I thanked him repeatedly for all the little things he did, and how it broke his heart. But the truth was, I'd always be thankful to the people who've never hurt me. "I'll never not be grateful."

Now he leaned his head back on the headrest and looked at me. And it was there, in his eyes. I saw it.

Look into his eyes and ask yourself what you see staring back at you.

Jesus. I think Donna was right.

I flew out of the car in a panic, then tried to cover it up by thumping the turret of the car. "Catch ya later," I called out, not stopping until I was inside my apartment. I closed the front door behind me and leaned against it, trying to catch my breath.

I spent the rest of the afternoon tidying and cleaning, doing laundry and everything else to try and take my mind off it.

By five o'clock, my apartment was spotless, I'd answered all my work emails, and my mind was running in circles, and I couldn't get my heart rate down. I'd never had a panic attack before, but I had to wonder if this was close.

I couldn't stop thinking about him, about what Donna had said, about the way he held my hand and kissed my cheek. Jesus fuck, the way he looked at me.

So I did the only thing I knew to do. I threw on some running clothes and my sneakers, and hit the pavement. I ran, and I kept fucking running, trying to clear my head. But the more I ran, the more I thought. And without any conscious thought, without realising where I was going, I found myself at Sam's front door.

I had no keys, no phone, and not a great deal of fucking sense either, because before my brain could stop my heart, I knocked.

Sam opened the door, shocked to see me. "Iz? What are you doing here?"

I was a sweaty mess, out of breath, and had clearly lost my mind. "I need to know, Sam. I need to know now."

THIRTEEN

I motioned between us. "This. Us. Whatever the fuck it is."

He looked behind him, then back at me. "Iz, now's probably not the best time—"

Once the dam had broken, I couldn't contain it. "I can't leave it. It's driving me crazy. And I know I have so much going on right now… Maybe I am crazy, maybe I'm wrong, but I don't think so. I think you want more to whatever this thing is between us. You look at me like you want to kiss me, like you want to take me to bed and fuck me, and I want you to. Jesus Sam, I can't stop thinking about you."

He stood there, his mouth open, and looked at me like I'd lost my freakin' mind. He lifted his hand and kind of pointed behind him, then closed his mouth. "Um, Iz…"

And I understood, like a sinking stone understands the darkest waters. I was wrong. I'd misread everything. I was so very wrong. He didn't want me at all. He didn't love me, and I'd risked everything.

And lost.

I felt physically sick. My heart had gone from hammering

to breaking in one horrifying moment. I shook my head and took a step backwards. "Oh."

Sam blinked and realisation washed over his face. "No!"

"It's okay. I'm sorry. I'm sorry." I stumbled back another step.

He grabbed my shirt, taking a fistful of material, and pulled me forward. I fell against him, our noses touching. His eyes were wild and desperate. His mouth was open. His breaths were hard and fast.

He let go of my shirt and gripped my face, then crushed his mouth to mine. He kissed me so fucking hard there was no mistaking his passion, his need. He tilted his face and slid his tongue along mine, moaning at the contact. He let go of my face and slid his arms around my neck. I pulled him tight against me, and the hard press of his cock against mine spurred me on. I pushed him back through the door, never breaking our kiss. I walked him backwards until his arse hit the back of the sofa. He groaned, or maybe I did...

"Fuck."

I froze, because neither Sam nor I had said that.

Breaking the kiss, but keeping my mouth an inch from Sam's and with him pushed back over the sofa, I looked up and around the room.

Millsy sat on one sofa with a beer bottle stopped halfway to his mouth and Connor stood near the kitchen, both of them stunned mannequins. Jamie leaned back on his sofa and grinned. It must have been him who spoke, because he hummed and bit his lip. "Don't stop on our accounts."

I stood straight up, pulling Sam with me, and tucked him in behind me, protectively. I don't know why. I just did.

Jamie laughed. "No seriously, that was fucking hot."

I turned to face Sam, and he was blushing with swollen lips. His kiss-drunk eyes were trained on me. "I tried to tell you," he murmured. "That now probably wasn't the best time..."

"We'll just be going," Connor said. He was smirking at us now. "Catch ya's both later. Much later."

Millsy got to his feet. "I told you there was something going on between 'em." He kicked Jamie's foot. "Come on, get up. You can't just sit there and watch, you fucking pervert."

Jamie laughed and stood up. "I fucking *could* just sit there and watch." Millsy pushed him toward the front door. "Twelve years of sexual frustration between them two is gonna make for some fucking hot sex."

One of them laughed as the door clicked shut and their chatter died away.

"Well, that wasn't embarrassing," I mumbled.

Sam laughed, a deep blush colouring his cheeks. "At least we don't have to tell them."

"True." I put my hand to his face. The heated passion from moments before was gone, and in its place, a deep-seated longing. I traced my thumb along his cheekbone and down to his bottom lip, hardly able to believe I was touching him like this. I leaned in and kissed him again, softer this time, tender and sweet.

He hummed, and his eyes fluttered closed as he let me deepen the kiss. The touch of his tongue, the taste of him, sent pulses of desire through my blood. My heart kicked up a notch. Butterflies spiked in my belly. I was kissing Sam, and by the way he held onto me, I knew he wanted this. His fingers dug into my back, his desperation climbing with each pass of his tongue in my mouth. And with each of his whimpers and ragged breaths, my cock throbbed.

"Fuck," I murmured into his kiss. I pulled my lips from his but kept his body right where it was. "I need a second. Or I'm gonna embarrass myself."

His chest heaved against mine; his breath at my neck was short and sharp. He chuckled but stepped back. His blue eyes were clear and dark, imploring and playful. "We're gonna talk, Iz. All night if we have to."

I nodded.

"But first, shower." He took my hand and led me to his ensuite bathroom. I did my very best to ignore his big bed, though my heart rate spiked and my balls ached at the thought of ending up there. I palmed my dick to try and ease the urge: I was already close to coming.

I was also a sweaty mess. Sam dropped my hand and turned the shower taps on. "Yeah, sorry. I tried to run to clear my head of thoughts of you. But after about 10K, I wound up here." I glanced at the mirror and saw my shirt was soaked through, my hair was damp, and lines of sweat ran down my neck. "I didn't realise I was this bad."

Sam pulled at the hem of my shirt and lifted it over my head, then oh so slowly leaned in and licked a line of sweat from my chest to my neck.

"Fuck, Sam."

He pushed me back against the bathroom counter and kissed me. Like really fucking kissed me. I could taste the salt of my sweat on his tongue, and he pulled back almost savagely. I had to stroke myself through the material of my running shorts. His nostrils flared, and his voice was low and husky. "Get undressed."

Jesus.

Fuck.

Me.

I toed out of my runners and ripped my socks off in record time, then slid my shorts down over my hips and let them fall down my legs. I stood there, naked and exposed in front of him, my cock hard and precome leaking from the tip, and he watched me with heat and fire in his eyes. Without breaking eye contact, he undid the button on his jeans.

Oh.

I wasn't showering alone.

My cock twitched, and he smirked. "Fuck you're hot, Iz." He pulled his shirt over his head, and my eyes raked over his chest, back up to his beautiful face. "Get in the shower."

I did as he ordered. And he did order me. I had no idea he was so demanding, and I had no idea that I found it so insanely fucking hot.

The water was scalding and I hissed as I let it spray over my back. I didn't dare change the temperature. I let my head fall back, lost momentarily in how every nerve in my body sang: hot water on my skin, an erection ready to explode, the scent of his soap in his shower, and the taste of him on my tongue. It was overwhelming.

Then his hands were on my back, caressing gently, his teeth nipped my shoulder, and his hard cock pressed against the crack of my arse. I moaned like a whore without meaning to, without shame. I was so turned on, so strung out, I instinctively lifted my arse for him and rolled my hips. A silent invitation for him to take me, no lube, no condom, just fucking fuck me.

Sam growled and spun me to the side and pushed my back hard against the tiles. His stare pinned me where I was, and he crushed his mouth to mine. God, he kissed me so hard my eyes rolled back in my head. He wrapped his hands around our cocks, sliding them together, rubbing us in time with his tongue thrusting in my mouth.

And I was gone.

Pleasure ripped through me, blinding hot and bursting. I groaned and cried out, though he only kissed me harder. I had his tongue in my mouth when I came. My cock swelled against his, spurting come between us, over his hand, as wave after wave of my orgasm crashed through me.

Sam grunted into my mouth and bucked his hips, his hand tightened around my sensitive flesh, and he shot ribbons of come between us. He panted in my mouth, let go of our cocks, and sagged against me. I wrapped my arms tighter around him and held onto him while he caught his breath.

He burrowed his face into my neck, and I manoeuvred the shower nozzle so it sprayed over us without moving from being pressed against the tiles. The hot water was heavenly, washing away the mess between us, and Sam kissed my neck, over my jaw, until he found my mouth.

He put his hands to my face and kissed me slower, sweeter, until we needed to breathe. He kept his eyes closed and rested his forehead against my cheek. "That was really fucking hot."

"Uh, that was hotter than fucking hot."

He smirked and let his head fall back, allowing the water to wash over his head and face. Then he soaped me up and washed me off, taking perfect care of me. "You ready to get out?"

I nodded. Was I ready to get out of the shower and start talking? Was I ready to put my heart on display and tell him everything? "Yeah."

He turned the water off, and stepping out of the shower, he handed me a towel. I watched his naked form, appreciating him in full view. He ran the towel over his hair, making it stand up all over the place, then tied it off around his waist. "Need something to wear?"

"Depends."

Sam smirked. "Let's start with clothes."

Wrapping the towel around myself, I followed him to his large and extensive wardrobe. He went straight to a pile of folded sweats and handed me a pair. "No undies?"

He stared at me and shook his head.

Fuck. Even one look and I was in trouble. My spent cock stirred. I pulled on the sweatpants underneath my towel, then pulled the towel away. Sam ogled my crotch, then his dark eyes met mine before he laughed. "Jesus. I don't know how we're gonna get any talking done. I want to push you back on that bed already." My cock twitched, which he noticed, and he replied with a raised eyebrow. "Something you're not terribly opposed to, I take it?"

I blushed and tried to laugh it off. "Not opposed to that at all."

He pulled his towel away, without an ounce of modesty, just stood there, daring me to look at his dick.

Of course I did. He was perfect; smooth, uncut, semi-hard, and hanging heavy.

My mouth watered. "Sam..."

If he ordered me to drop to my knees and suck him dry, I would.

He swallowed hard and let out a deep breath. "Iz, we should talk. And if you keep looking at my dick like that, your mouth'll be busy for a while."

I licked my lips.

He laughed and pulled on some sweatpants. The outline of his dick was still visible, so I wasn't completely at a loss. But he put his fingers under my chin and made me look into his eyes. "Talk first. You can suck my dick later." A shiver ran through me, something he didn't miss. "Jesus," he whispered. Then he pushed me toward the door. "Okay, talking first. In the living room. Separate sofas."

I sat on the three-seater, and Sam collected two water bottles from the kitchen. He walked back to me, handed me one, then sat down beside me. "I thought we were sitting on separate sofas."

He smiled. "Not a chance." He took a mouthful of water. "Okay, Iz. What changed and when?"

Okay then, jumping straight in then. "Donna said something to me today. She thought we were a couple, and I said we weren't. She asked me how long I've been in love with you, and I said forever."

Sam stared at me.

I laughed at his reaction, but mostly at myself. "Scared the shit outta myself when I said it. She said you looked at me, like really looked at me. Like you saw the real me or some shit, and she said it was pretty obvious you felt the same way about me."

I studied the water bottle instead of looking at him. "And I know I'm dealing with a lot right now. I know my head is all over the place, and when I spewed my heart all over you when you opened the door, I thought you were gonna tell me no. God, I almost died."

He reached over and took my hand. "I knew you thought I was saying no, that's why I grabbed you. I was trying to tell you that the guys were sitting in the living room. They just rocked up for the free beer, as per usual, on their way to the pub." He let out a long breath. "The look on your face, Iz. God, you went pale, and I panicked. I should have offered to talk, but kissing you was easier."

I snorted at that but looked at him seriously. "I'm not wrong, am I?'

His smile was one sided and sexy as hell. "You're not wrong. And neither is Donna."

...she said it was pretty obvious you felt the same way about me.

"I've wanted to tell you for a while," he added. "But then all this happened with your family, and you needed a friend. God, some days you were barely hanging on and I didn't want to add to your problems." He lifted our hands to his lips and kissed my knuckles. "I just wanted to be there for you, however you needed me to be."

I nodded. "I didn't say anything sooner because, if you turned me down, I'd have no one and that scared me so fucking much. I didn't want to risk losing you. I couldn't. But then today happened, and the way you looked at me, the way you held my hand and kissed my cheek..." I let out a shaky breath. "I couldn't stop thinking about it. I tried running because it clears my head, but it didn't clear my mind. I fucking ran here."

Sam chuckled, and sitting side on to me, he leaned his shoulder against the back of the sofa. "I'm really glad you did."

"So, are we doing this?" I asked, then cringed. "Not to be demanding or whatever, but I need to know what this is. In my head. If you just want to be casual, then tell me. If you want to be together, then tell me. Right now, I don't think blurred lines are good for me. As long as I know what you expect, then I'm fine."

His reply was immediate. "Together. Boyfriends. Exclusive. I've wanted you for years, Israel Ingham. I won't share you."

My breath caught, and I had to swallow so I could speak. "Good. I won't share you either."

"While we're talking about things and being honest," he continued, "I only have sex with condoms. Well, I have only, up until now. If we're going to be wholly exclusive, then I'm open to being tested so we don't have to."

"I've only used condoms too. Ever."

He tilted his head. "In the shower just now, you offered me your arse. I was so fucking close, Iz."

I think I blushed all the way down to my toes. "Oh, I uh…" God, I wanted to die. I laughed off my embarrassment. "I've never done that before, with anyone. I was so turned on, I would have let you. But only you."

His nostrils flared and his jaw bulged. He traced the back of his index finger along my cheek. "Look at this blush," he whispered. His words, his touch, his scrutiny sent another wave of heat across my face and down my neck. "God, Iz. How am I supposed to control myself around you?"

My gaze shot to his. My heart was pounding. I'd never been left speechless before. I'd never been pinned by his molten stare before. I'd never been so turned on before…

He licked his lips. "I want you so bad. I've wanted you for

years, and now I've tasted your mouth, your skin, I'm pretty sure I won't ever want to stop."

Fuck. I squirmed in my seat, leaned into his hand, and finally met his eyes. "Then don't."

He quickly pushed me back on the sofa so I was half lying down with my head on the armrest. He crawled up my body, like he wanted to devour me, and rolled his hips into mine. He leaned down til his nose touched mine; the heat in his eyes stole my breath.

"Was that an open invitation, Iz?" he asked. He smirked and teased my lips with an almost kiss.

I hooked my feet around the backs of his legs so he couldn't move, and rocked my hips so our cocks pressed together. I held his face in both hands. "Don't tease me, Sam." I brought his mouth to mine for a deep kiss. Passion soon took hold in his desperate touch, his deep and consuming kiss, and how his hips rolled and bucked. He kissed me like that for a minute, an hour, I had no idea. I lost all track of time as he skimmed his hands over every inch of skin he could touch, as his tongue delved into my mouth.

I groaned as a spike of need ripped through me, and Sam surprised me by pulling back. He leaned back on his haunches, his breaths rough, his lips red and swollen. He took a moment to look me over, clearly enjoying the view of me lying beneath him. He slowly kissed my chest, then sucked my nipple between his teeth. I gasped and gripped his hair, making him chuckle, then he slid down lower, trailing his tongue over my abs, my navel, then lower still...

Oh, fuck.

"This okay?" he asked gruffly.

"God yes."

He pulled down the front of my sweatpants, letting my erection spring free. The head of my cock tapped my belly, spilling a line of precome into my navel.

"So beautiful," Sam murmured before he lapped at the

clear liquid eagerly, then licked my cockhead before taking me into his mouth.

My back arched at the sensation of being engulfed by him. I tugged on his hair to tell him it was too much, too soon, but he looked up at me with those blue eyes and wrapped his lips around my shaft.

I sagged back down and put one hand over my eyes. "Fuck Sam, you're gonna make me come." I wanted him to stop, to slow down, but at the same time, I didn't want him to stop what he was doing. "Yeah, like that."

He hummed and sucked harder, swirling his tongue around the head, and I couldn't look away any longer. I watched as he worked me over, taking me deep, sucking me hard, pumping my base, and tugging on my balls.

"Oh fuck, I'm gonna come," I warned him. But he didn't pull off me. He just sucked me harder and harder until I couldn't hold it back anymore. I came down his throat and he moaned around me. Wave after wave of bliss rolled through me, and he drank me completely dry.

I slumped back onto the armrest of the sofa, spent and lightheaded. Dizzy, even. I chuckled at his smug expression and closed my eyes.

I felt him tuck my dick in, and then he pressed soft kisses back up my stomach and chest. I felt his thumb on my chin, so I opened my eyes in time to watch him pull my mouth open, and he kissed me. Lazy, sensuous tongue, letting me taste myself.

"Mmm, your turn," I mumbled.

"'S okay," he offered.

I raised an eyebrow at him. My orgasm-induced brain fog had lifted some. "Like fucking hell it's okay." I tried to use my stern voice. "Get up here and let me taste you."

Sam grinned and crawled up so his knees were in my armpits, his crotch in my face. His cock was straining against his sweatpants, and I slowly pulled it free. "Oh, hell yes," I whispered and breathed in his scent. I lifted his glorious cock and licked his balls first, causing him to squirm.

"Jesus, oh fuck," he choked out.

Then I licked his shaft, from base to tip, and sucked the head between my lips. Then, like I did with the banana, I slowly took every inch of him into my throat. He groaned hoarsely, a sound I'd never heard from him before, and he started to shake.

He was trying not to come, and I wasn't having any of that.

So I pulled off a bit and put my hands on his hips and urged him to fuck my mouth. He was soon thrusting in and going a little deeper with each pass.

"Iz, oh my fuck—"

His words died as I took him in deep and swallowed around him. He put both hands on my head and his cock swelled and he moaned as he pulsed down my throat. His hips shook, his hands trembled in my hair as he shot his load. "Oh fuck. Oh fuck. Oh fuck," he said over and over.

When he pulled out of my mouth, he was still shaking, and he crumpled onto me like one of those collapsible puppet dolls. It made me chuckle, and I kissed the side of his head. "You okay in there?"

His voice was gruff. "Holy fucking Christ on a cracker, Iz."

I laughed, making him jostle on my chest a bit. He pushed his legs down and shuffled down until he was lying with his head on my chest. I could feel his heartbeat against me, and it almost lulled me to sleep. But I didn't want to miss a second, so I drew lazy circles on his back while he dozed, wondering how on earth, in this very moment, my life could be so incredibly perfect.

Despite everything else being a clusterfucking mess, this right here, just me and him, was perfect.

"Don't overthink anything, Iz," Sam mumbled.

"What?"

He leaned his head in one hand and looked at me. "You overthink things. You always have. Don't overthink this. Please."

I was gonna call bullshit, but he was right. I did overthink things, and of course he knew this. "For once, I'm not. Wanna know what I was actually thinking about?"

"Yep."

"How utterly perfect this moment was. Just you and me, no outside crap. Without my parents, without the whole switched thing. Nothing, just you lying on top of me. I could feel your heartbeat on my chest, and that was pretty amazing. And all the reasons I gave you for not telling you sooner how I felt now seem stupid because, fuck, why did it take us so long to get here?"

Sam smiled in such a way that his eyes sparkled. He pressed a kiss over my heart and put his head back on my chest, sighing deeply. "We're here now, Iz. That's all that matters. And I like the sound of your heartbeat too."

I leaned up and kissed the top of his head.

"You can keep scratching my back."

I chuckled but went back to drawing patterns on his back. "Bossy shit."

He snorted. "You've known me how many years?"

"Thirteen."

"And my bossiness is a surprise now?"

I chuckled. "Nope."

"I think you secretly like it when I get demanding," he said flippantly. "Like in the shower and the walk-in robe. One order and you were panting for it."

I gasped and pushed him off me, but all he could do was laugh. So I tweaked his nipple and he yelped. We wrestled for a bit, but somehow ended on our sides on the sofa, facing each other, kissing. "Want me to give you orders?" I asked.

He was grinning. "Give it your best shot."

"Get in the kitchen and get me food."

He rolled his eyes. "That was so fucking lame." But he rolled off the couch and headed toward the kitchen. I smiled as I watched him go, loving the fact that, despite things changing between us, we were still us. I sat up on the sofa, feeling more relaxed than I could remember. Yes, the two mind-blowing bouts of sex contributed to that, and it was kinda hard to describe because this was all so new, but it felt like something that had been misaligned for so long had finally been set right.

Sam came back with a bowl of grapes and some salted pretzels and plonked himself right next to me. He handed the bowl to me and leaned against my shoulder. "Oh crap," he said. "You wanna know what I just thought of?"

"What's that?"

"We have to tell my parents." He sighed.

I felt an instant stab of self-doubt. "Is that a bad thing? They like me, don't they?"

Sam smiled. "Of course they do. My mum is gonna go ballistic. She'll wanna host a welcome to the family party, and my sisters..." He rolled his eyes. "Oh man, they're gonna be all over this. I can see it now. They'll post pictures all over social media of us together when we were kids and pictures of us now with the heading 'OMG how adorkable,' and I'll have to issue DMCAs to get them taken down. And oh, one good thing is that now my mum can call you directly to ask you to come for dinner. So there's that, I guess."

I laughed. "Yeah, they're gonna be a bit excited. When should we tell them?"

"Not for a bit. Let us just enjoy it before they start submitting photos to Sydney's Cutest Couples in the *Telegraph*."

I popped a grape in my mouth. "Good idea."

"Though, Connor, Millsy, and Jamie have already probably posted something online somewhere. Fuckers."

I snorted. "True."

"What about your parents?"

"My parents won't care. Literally. I'll have to tell Donna, though," I said. "It was her words that got me thinking."

"I'll send her a thank you card."

I laughed and kissed the side of his head. "What's our plans for tonight?" It was getting dark outside and I wasn't sure if he'd want to go out. It was a Saturday night after all…

Sam didn't miss a beat. "Well, I was thinking I'd take you to my bed and fuck you. And all day tomorrow too. Cause if you're gonna go to work on Monday and your father doesn't care that you're now dating Sydney's most eligible bachelor, then the smile you won't be able to get off your face should be enough to annoy him at least."

I burst out laughing. "It would be the least we could do."

He chuckled along with me. "I know, right?"

"Sydney's most eligible bachelor? Really?"

"Yep. That was the part you picked up on? No comment about the 'fucking you for twenty-four hours' part?"

"I already told you not to tease me, Sam."

He laughed. "Dinner first. I'll even let you pick the movie."

"Really? You've never let me pick the movie before."

His eyes flashed with warmth. "You've never been my boyfriend before."

"Boyfriend sounds…"

"Weird? Permanent?"

"I was going to say good."

He jumped off the couch, then leaned down and kissed me soundly. "That is the correct answer."

He walked back into the kitchen, and I called out after him. "What are you doing?"

"Making a start on dinner."

I followed him and slid the bowl of grapes onto the bench. "What are we having?"

"I can make grilled chicken and salad. How does that sound?"

"Perfect."

It was weird, moving around the kitchen with him like we'd done a hundred times, but now it was different. When I chopped up a capsicum, he put his hands on my hips and kissed the back of my neck. And when he was grilling the chicken, he made some lame joke about protein, and all I wanted to do was nudge my nose into his hair. And just yesterday, all I could have done was dreamed of doing it... then I remembered that I could do it if I wanted.

So I did.

I stood behind him, put my arms around him, nudged the back of his head with my nose, and told him he was a dickhead.

He chuckled and turned around in my arms so he could kiss me. The sound of chicken sizzling got louder and louder and he pulled away with a frustrated growl. "This is why I got up from the couch and started cooking dinner. Because I needed to put some distance between us. Now that I've had you, it's all I want." He turned the chicken like it was its fault. "It's *all* I want."

I chuckled and kissed the side of his neck. "I'm not opposed to that."

He groaned louder. "You're not helping. At this rate, we'll never have a conversation or eat food again."

I scraped my teeth over his neck. "How long till the chicken's done?"

He turned sharply, his eyes dark and his lips parted. "I'm trying to be good here, Iz. I'm all for the physical side to this. Like I *really* am. But I don't want to lose us either. We have to find a balance."

"I get it," I said, kissing his cheek. I took a step back and waggled my eyebrows. "I'll let you feed me while we talk, then I'll let you fuck me."

He waved the kitchen tongs at me. "You don't play fair."

I grinned victoriously. "Am I setting the table? Or are we eating in front of the TV?"

———

I UNDERSTOOD what he meant about finding a balance, and all jokes aside, I agreed wholeheartedly with him. So we ate dinner, cuddled on the couch, and watched a movie—well, I watched it because I picked it, and it was awesome. He twirled tiny circles in the hair at the back of my neck the entire time, which was also kind of awesome. And whether it was the 10K I ran earlier, or the two orgasms since then, or the immense relief of finally telling Sam how I felt and having him return my affections, but by ten o'clock I was drifting off to sleep on the sofa.

Sam kissed the shell of my ear. "Am I that boring that you're falling asleep?"

"You tickling the back of my neck is relaxing," I mumbled. "I also ran 10K this afternoon, and you made me come twice. And you fed me."

Sam chuckled and he sighed as his arms tightened around me. "Wanna come a third time?"

"Thought you said we had to find a balance."

He skimmed his hand over my hip. "We do. But it's been hours…"

I snorted. "Hours? Well, before today, it had been months for me."

"Me too," he said with a groan. "Which I blame you for, by the way."

"How was it my fault?"

"Because I didn't want anyone else."

I shuffled in his arms so I faced him instead of the TV. "Then I think if we've waited months, years even, then the balance is well and truly in need of fixing."

He put his hand to my face. His lips were barely an inch from mine. "Iz, I want to take you to bed. I want to have you, in ways I've only dreamed of. I want to be inside you, and I want to make you mine."

I swallowed hard. Fucking hell.

He almost kissed me. "Tell me now if you have any doubts…"

I looked into his eyes so he could see the truth. "Never in my life have I ever doubted you."

He covered my mouth with his and tenderly touched his tongue to mine. Then before we could get carried away, he rolled over the top of me and got to his feet. He turned the TV off, took my hand, and led me to his bedroom.

The light was on in his bathroom, the door slightly ajar, letting in a sliver of light in the otherwise darkened room. He turned to face me and pulled me close. My nerves coiled tight and butterflies swarmed my throat. Every cell was on fire with anticipation, desire, and need.

Sam slid his hands under the waistband of my sweatpants and pushed them over my arse. My cock sprang free and the pants pooled at my feet. "Fuck you're hot," he murmured.

I reached into his pants and took hold of his erection, giving him a hard pump, before pushing his sweatpants down to his thighs. I was about to tell him how beautiful he was, but he grabbed my chin and kissed me.

When we were both breathless, he broke the kiss. "Get on the bed."

A thrill shot through me. Bossy Sam as a friend had been a pain in my arse some days, but Bossy Sam in the bedroom was fucking hot. "How do you want me?"

He closed his eyes and took a deep breath in through his nose. "Fuck, Iz. On your back."

I sat on the bed and scooted into the middle, while he retrieved a foil packet and a bottle of lube. My heart rate spiked when he threw them on the bed beside me.

His silhouette looked beautiful in the darkened room. Broad shoulders tapering down to his slim waist, his hard cock pointing right at me.

It was hard to believe this was Sam.

My Sam.

I was naked on his bed, and he was just about to fuck me.

I was going to let him inside me. After all these years, this was really happening.

He put one knee on the bed, then the other, and he crawled over to me. He gripped my leg closest to him and pulled it wider, making room for him between my thighs. His panting breaths were the only thing I could hear, apart from my hammering heart. I leaned back on my elbows so I could watch his every move. Because I couldn't take my eyes off him…

On all fours, he stalked up my body until I was lying down completely, and with no other parts of our bodies touching, he crushed his mouth to mine. It was a bruising kiss, deep and demanding, and it made my whole body sing.

Like he knew I was getting desperate for touch, Sam broke the kiss and backed off to kneel between my thighs. I gripped my own cock and slid my hand along the shaft. I needed the friction and I liked the idea of putting on a little show for him.

"Jesus, you keep doing that and I'll come before I even get a condom on."

I smiled but never stopped my hand. "Then hurry the fuck up."

His eyes flashed with daring, his grin widened. He bit his bottom lip, rolled the condom down his cock, then took the bottle of lube. He flipped the lid and slicked himself, then it was my turn. "Leave your cock alone," he ordered, rubbing lubed fingers across my hole. "I want you to come when I'm inside you."

I groaned and reluctantly did as he told me. I raked my

hands up my stomach and squeezed my nipple instead, just as he slipped a finger inside me.

"Oh!" I cried out as a jolt of pleasure ripped through me.

Sam laughed, though it was a pained sound. "God, this is gonna be over real quick if you keep that up." He gave his dick a hard squeeze to stay his own pleasure, then started to pump his finger inside me. Then two. He watched me writhe as he stretched me, pleasured me, and when he tried to get a third finger in me, I stopped him.

"I'm fucking ready Sam," I growled, my frustration at a breaking point.

Sam pulled his hand away and gripped the back of my knee instead. He pushed it up toward my chest and leaned over me, kissing me softly, teasing me with his tongue. I could feel the heat and weight of his cock rubbing against me, so close, but nowhere near close enough.

I took his face in my hands and brought his nose close to mine. I was aiming for angry and demanding, but all I could manage was pleading. "Please Sam. Please. I need you inside me. Wanna feel you."

With his other hand, he positioned the blunt head of his cock at my hole, and he kissed me as he entered me. Slow and teasing, with his tongue and his cock. Every second, every inch, every touch. His huge cock breached me, burned and buried inside me.

I gasped. Or cried. I wasn't sure.

Sam quickly put his hands to my face, making me stare into his eyes as he pushed all the way in. Then he kissed me, and he stayed still inside me, giving me time to adjust. But I didn't need or want time. I wanted him to move.

I rocked my hips and he started to thrust into me. Slow and deep, perfect.

"You okay?" he asked, brushing his lips against mine.

I nodded. "Feels so good."

His eyes fluttered closed and his neck strained as he pushed himself deeper. "Take hold of your cock," he murmured, his voice tight. "Make yourself come. I'm not gonna last much longer."

I did as he told me, bringing myself closer to climax with every pull. Sam thrust harder and I got closer and closer, and he kissed me, plunging his tongue inside me as I came.

"Fuck!" I cried, arching into him and pulling his hips into mine, needing his cock as deep as it could go.

My orgasm rocketed through me, pleasure in every cell. Sam slid his arms underneath me, holding me and pinning me onto his shaft as he swelled and shot deep inside me, filling the condom.

Sam never stopped kissing me. I felt wholly worshipped and owned, and I'd never, ever, made love like this before. He pulled out of me slowly, discarded the condom, and wrapped himself around me. He held me to his chest, and our hearts beat as one.

If he wanted to make me his, he did. He owned me, body and soul.

He always had.

I woke up to the feeling of being watched. It took me a second to remember where I was, and when I turned my head, I found Sam lying there, all sleep-mussed and gorgeous, smiling at me.

"Sleep well?"

I hummed. "Like the dead."

His smile became a grin. He sat up and pounced on me like a playful kitten. His blue eyes shone bright, his hair flip-flopped, and he looked the picture of pure happiness.

I laughed at him. "You always wake up so bright eyed and bushy tailed?"

He straddled my stomach and held my hands and slowly shook his head. "Just today. I could get used to waking up with you."

"Pretty cool, huh?"

"You wanna know the best part?" he asked. "I was watching you sleep this morning, like a total creeper, and I figured out what it is."

"What's that?"

"There's nothing about you I don't know. The best parts, the worst parts; we're through all that. I was watching you, thinking 'That's my best friend,' except things just got a whole lot better." He shrugged. "It's like *Monopoly*. We passed Go, collected $200, skipped all the shitty property, and landed straight on Mayfair."

I laughed. "Is that right?"

"Yep. And you wanna know the other best part?"

"I'm starting to think no, no I don't."

He grinned and told me anyway. "You already know what I like to eat for breakfast and you can get up and make it for me." He sprang off the bed like a cat and walked to the door. "Come on Iz, I'm hungry."

He was wearing boxer briefs, where I was still naked. I pulled down the sheet, giving him a good eyeful of my morning wood. "How hungry?"

He stopped, and his smile became a devious smirk. "Starving. But"—he put up his hand—"I have plans for us today. Plans that involve a lot of sex, so you need to eat a proper breakfast first. You're gonna need all the energy you can get."

"Is that right?"

"Yep. Then after lunch, when you've had enough of my dick in your arse, I was thinking we could go tell my parents."

"I thought you said you wanted to wait."

"I did, but I think I've waited long enough. Is that okay?"

"Which part? The me-making-you-breakfast part? Or the sex-all-day part? Or telling your folks?"

"All of it."

"Sounds like a perfect way to spend a Sunday to me."

I DID MAKE his breakfast for him, and he made good on his promise of sex all day. Though he was wrong about one thing: I would never have enough of his dick in my arse. Ever. Sex with Sam was intense and powerful, emotional, and it was truly a physical expression of how we felt.

I couldn't get enough of him, or him me. It was in the way he gripped me, held me, clawed at my skin, and in the way he bit my jaw.

Afterwards, when we were a crumpled, sweaty mess on his bed, he roughly turned my face and he studied my jaw. "Shit. I didn't mean to do that."

"Didn't mean to do what?" I asked. Feeling along the scruff, there was a tender spot about halfway along my jaw. "Oh. Then maybe next time you shouldn't bite me."

He laughed at that. "Maybe next time you shouldn't be so fucking hot I lose my mind."

It made me snort. I remembered very clearly when he was inside me, with my knees up near our chests, he held my face and kissed me, frantically kissing down my jaw to my neck as he hit my prostate, making me buck underneath him. I came in a frenzy of bliss, making him spill inside me. He held onto me, almost crushing me in his embrace, and his teeth scraped over my jaw.

It was quite possibly the hottest thing I've ever experienced.

He looked horrified and sorry, gently massaging the mark with his thumb. "God, Iz. I think it's started to bruise already."

I could only laugh. "You know, if it were anyone else that marked me, I'd be pissed. But is it kinda weird that I like that you did?" I rubbed the mark on my jaw. "You can mark me wherever you want."

He fell back onto the bed with a groan. "You really shouldn't say shit like that to me."

"Why? You like it?"

His gaze shot to mine, and there was something in his eyes. His voice was low and rough. "Yes."

I deliberately stretched out on my stomach and bent one leg at the knee. I hummed as I rubbed my arse. Even though we'd only just finished having sex, I still wanted more. "My arse is already yours, but if you want to mark it…"

Sam rolled on top of me. His spent cock fit snug between my arsecheeks, his hands on my hips, and he kissed my shoulder. "Haven't you had enough yet?"

"Nuh uh," I moaned my answer. "Never."

He growled in frustration and rolled off me, bringing me over with him so we were both on our backs with my head on his shoulder. He grabbed his phone from the bedside table.

"What are you doing?"

He snapped a few selfies of us together, then inspected which was the most decent. It was pretty obvious we were in bed, and by our hair, what we'd just been doing. He didn't seem too impressed with any of those, so he took another picture of him kissing my cheek. It was actually a pretty cute photo: I was smiling as he kissed me, and you could see more of our naked chests.

"That's better," he said, typing something into his phone.

"Are you setting that as your screensaver?"

"Nope." He showed me the screen. It was a text to his mum with *So this is now a permanent thing* as the subject line.

He hit Send before I could stop him. "My God, Sam, you can't send photos like that. We're naked in bed, for fuck's sake."

He chuckled. "That's precisely why I chose that pic."

Right on cue, his phone rang with *Mum* flashing on the screen. He answered the call on speakerphone. "Oh my God, Sammy, tell me you're not joking. You and Israel? You're a permanent thing? Please tell me it's true."

He laughed. "Hi, Mum. Yes it is, and you're on speakerphone. Iz is right here."

"Hi, Mrs Finch," I said. I instinctively pulled the sheet up to cover us, even though it was just a phone call. It was still weird to be talking to Sam's mum while completely naked in bed with her son. Sam just laughed.

"Oh my God." She sniffed. "I'm so happy!"

"We were going to come around this afternoon, is that okay?"

"Oh, we have plans already. Can we go out for dinner another night? To celebrate. Oh my God," she said again, like she couldn't believe it. "After all these years, you two finally got your shit together."

"Mum!"

I laughed this time. "Yes, finally. After all these years."

"Oh, Israel," she said quietly. "You have no idea how happy this makes me." She sniffled again, like she was crying actual tears.

"I'll call you about dinner plans during the week sometime," Sam said.

"Oh, okay, yes," she replied. "Can I tell people, or is it hush-hush?"

Sam looked at me, I shrugged, and he replied, "Tell whoever you want. Mum, I gotta go. Talk soon. Love you."

He tossed the phone onto the floor and kissed me. "What did you just do?" I asked.

"I multitasked."

I laughed. "How?"

"I just told my mother about us," he said, pulling down

the sheet. "She'll tell everyone we know, and I just freed up our entire afternoon." He pulled on my shoulder, manoeuvring me onto my stomach. He spread my thighs apart with his knees, and he kissed down my spine to the cleft of my arse. "Because I have some marking to do."

FOURTEEN

"Good morning," Prue greeted me cheerfully on Monday morning.

"Morning."

She eyed me funnily. "Good weekend?"

I bit the inside of my cheek so I wouldn't smile like a clown. "Yes. And yours? How was the festival?"

"Oh, it was so great," she answered. She handed me a small jar of what looked like some kind of jam. "Strawberry jam, fresh made. A little gift for you, for letting me leave early."

"Oh." I took the jar. It was such a simple gift, and it was weird that it meant a lot. "Thank you."

"You're welcome."

"No meeting with my father?"

"Not that he's scheduled."

And this day just kept getting better and better.

Then Prue noticed the purplish line on my jaw. It was a straight line, about two centimetres, that went straight down and over my jawbone. Before she could ask, I touched it and said, "A war wound from the gym."

"Oh." She seemed placated by that, then reminded me, "You have a teleconference with Fesco Intel at nine."

"Perfect."

And my Monday was going pretty good for a Monday, until I got a text message from Nick. With a sigh, I went to my father's office. I knocked and stuck my head inside. He was busy signing off on something, and when he saw it was me, he put his pen down.

"Israel, please come in." I took a seat across from him, and his cool demeanour was back in place, though there was a hint of nervousness in his eyes. "What can I do for you?"

I held up my phone. "I just got a text from Nick."

"Oh?"

"He wants to meet you." Then I read the message verbatim. "'Hey, Israel. Hope you don't mind the interruption at work. Been thinking about what you said. I think I'd like to meet your mother and father. Can you ask when it would suit them?'"

My father blinked, then blew out a breath. "Oh. Right. Okay then." He frowned, then looked at me. "What did you say to him? He said he'd been thinking about what you said."

I looked my father square in the eye and told him the truth. "I told him I couldn't make that decision for him. Only he could. My reasons for meeting my birth family were different to his. I needed to know where I came from. He doesn't. Not really. His family's pretty great."

He seemed to consider that. "You met with them all," he stated. "How did that go?"

"It was awesome." I smiled. God, was it just two days ago? It felt like so much longer than that. Then, because I had my phone in my hand, I thought I may as well show him a photo. "I have photos, if you want to see?"

"Oh." He swallowed hard. "Yes, of course."

I found the photos, and in particular, the one that Sam took of all of us in front of Donna's house. I handed my phone over. "That's Nick, next to me. Then Donna and my sister, Ashley, and my brother, Lachlan. It's crazy how much we look alike."

My father stared at the photo, and I had no idea what was going through his mind. His expression was unreadable. Was he looking at Nick, his birth-son? Did he see himself? Was he looking at Lachie and how much he looked like me? Or was he looking at me in that photo, standing and smiling with people who not only looked like me, but were more of a family than he could ever be?

"Yes," he said quietly. He handed my phone back with a tight smile. "I'll check my schedule and with your mother, and let you know when we're free to meet him."

Okay then. His voice sounded strained, distant even, which was weird, even for him. "It'll have to be on a week-end, because he works in Penrith. Unless you want to meet him for dinner out there one night, I guess." Not that I could imagine that in a million years. My father thought any suburb west of Bondi was beneath him.

He gave a hard nod. "I'll let you know." He turned his attention back to the papers in front of him, which was his way of saying he was done talking to me.

I'd come in here with hopes that we might have a civil conversation from start to finish, but it seemed we couldn't even manage that. He was back to signing his papers like I wasn't even there. I stood up and figured now was as good a time as any to bring this up. "Just so you know, Sam and I are now together. Not that I expect you to care, but we're very happy."

My father looked up at me then, the pen in his hand momentarily forgotten. "Sam Finch?" The look on his face, the distaste in his tone, made my blood boil.

I bit back my anger, though my nostrils flared, and a hurt that only my father could inflict bloomed in my chest. I turned on my heel and walked toward the door. "I don't know why I even bothered to tell you." I opened the door with more force than was necessary and stalked to my office.

I had no idea why I continued to let him get to me the way he did, but man, he could get under my skin. Prue followed me in with a job file in her hand. I took one look at her and groaned. "That man is a colossal pain in my arse. And believe me, after this weekend, that's a pretty big call."

Prue stared. "Pardon?"

"My father," I continued. I should've stopped. I should've taken a breath, but I couldn't help it. "Not that he's even my real father. Fuck."

Prue was now wide-eyed, holding the job file like it was a safety net.

I sat up straighter in my seat. "Sorry, that was incredibly unprofessional. I apologise." I shook my head and took in a deep breath to compose myself. "Sorry."

"It's perfectly fine, Mr Ingham," she said politely. "I could never work with my parents. I'm sure the police would be involved by morning tea on the first day."

I looked at her, then barked out a laugh. "So, I'm not the only one."

"Definitely not."

I closed my eyes slowly and let out a breath. "And please ignore what I said about him not being my real father. I didn't mean that. I was angry, and that was uncalled for and again, very unprofessional of me." I didn't even want to get into the fact I'd blurted out that any pain in my arse after this weekend was a big call…

"Mr Ingham," she started.

"Please call me Israel."

She nodded. "Israel, please understand, whatever you say in this office, to me or otherwise, is in the strictest confidence."

"Thank you."

She put the file on my desk and blushed. "And, if you need, you will have my utmost discretion."

Oh god, the sore-arse comment.

I sighed. "Take a seat, Prue."

She blanched but sat awkwardly across from me.

"You're not in any trouble," I reassured her. "I just wanted to fill you in on what's going on with me."

"Okaaaay," she said warily.

So I laid it out to her straight. "I had a fucked up childhood, there's no other way to describe it. I'm also very gay, which is just one of the many disappointments on a long list of disappointments I am to my father. Who, by the way, we only recently discovered, is not my father. As it turns out, I was switched at birth with another baby. Hospital mistake. Whatever. Doesn't change anything, really. Well, it kind of changes everything, but you know what I mean... Anyway, this whole clusterfuck is the reason I'm now seeing a shrink twice a week." I checked my watch. "Which I need to leave for soon."

Prue blinked, then blinked again. "Okay then."

"Okay then?"

She nodded. "Yes, okay then. That explains the heated discussions you've been having with Mr Ingham. It explains why you needed to clear your schedule twice a week after four, and it could very well explain the pain-in-the-arse comment."

I choked out a laugh. "Right. I was hoping you missed that part."

She smiled and her whole face softened. "Israel, I don't care if you're gay, straight, or anything in between. I care that you're a good and fair boss. And you are. If you need me to tell Mr Ingham you're out of the office when you just don't want to see him, you only have to ask. If you need me to tell him you're meeting with clients when you're really just taking ten minutes to breathe, then I will do that too."

I sighed, more relieved than I realised. "Thank you."

"You're welcome."

"I'm sorry I didn't tell you sooner."

"It's fine. Thank you for telling me now." She smiled and put the file she was holding onto my desk. "Okay then. So that's the data you requested on the Fesco job. But it will have to wait until tomorrow."

I checked my watch. She was right. If I wanted to get to my appointment with Dr Habib, I had to leave. "Thank you, Prue. I mean that."

I left the office feeling positive, and after a quick chat with Sam while I drove to my shrink appointment to tell him I told my father about us, I felt like I was taking back some modicum of control. Even sitting in the waiting room, I felt pretty good.

That was until my father sent me a text message. *Please tell Nicholas I won't be meeting with him at this time.*

I read the message, then I read it again.

"Mr Ingham."

I blinked, feeling strangely calm before an ocean of anger. "Israel?"

I looked up at the sound of my name. "Yes."

"Doctor Habib will see you now."

SAM WAS WAITING for me when I got home. He was nervous but mostly concerned. "What happened?"

I'd called him when I left my doctor's appointment, not giving him any details. Just asking him to be there.

He put his hands to my face. "How'd the appointment go?"

"I had a good day today," I started with. "I had a fucking awesome weekend, thanks to you. And I got to work, feeling pretty good. Then I got a text from Nick saying yes, he's finally agreed to meet my father, could I ask him when would suit. So, I'm thinking this is all great, right?"

Sam nodded, his brow furrowed. "Yeah."

"So I went in, spoke to Dad. He was weird about it, like he has been lately. He said he'd let me know when a good time was, then pretended I wasn't there. Same old, same old, right?"

"And that's when you told him about us?"

I nodded. "Yep. To which he was less than thrilled with. Which, believe me, is more to do with me being gay than it has to do with you being my boyfriend. But then I get to my appointment, and I'm just about to walk in and I get a text from my father saying no dice. He won't meet with Nick."

"He what?"

"He won't be meeting with Nick at this time," I replied. "Can you fucking believe that? And he expects me to tell him?" I groaned. "Man, I was so fucking mad when I walked in to my appointment. I should have bailed. I should've walked the fuck out and said not today. But no, she said my anger toward my father was good. Better than being unresponsive. That's what she said. My father was indifferent, cold. I am not."

Sam had one hand on my chest, one on my face. "You're nothing like him."

"I'm not. But I am. Some part of me still holds on—wishes—for his approval."

"Oh, Iz." Sam frowned and pulled me in for a hug. "What did the doctor say?"

"She said that I need to meet this. Like how I needed to meet my birth mother to move forward. Whether she accepted or rejected me, I couldn't stay stuck. I needed to progress, right? She said I need to meet my father head on. I need to confront this, so I can live my fucking life."

Sam nodded. "Do you think that will end well?"

"I don't know. I no longer care. I need to do this, Sam. I

can't stay stuck here, with him holding all the strings, anymore. If I lose my job, then I'll get another one. I'm good at what I do. I'm sure I can walk into any of my father's competitors and get a start. And if I lose him? And my mother?" I shrugged. "It's kinda hard to lose what I never had."

He cupped my face and kissed me softly. "Whatever you decide," he murmured. "Whatever you want to do, I'm with you, okay?"

I nodded. "Thank you for being here."

"Any time. Always."

I kissed him this time. "I like the sound of that."

We stood in the kitchen, with his arms around me, and I just took a moment to gather my thoughts.

After a while, Sam pulled back and asked, "So? When are we gonna have it out with daddy dearest?"

"You don't have to come with me."

He raised one eyebrow at me. "Don't think for one second I'm not going with you."

I smiled and sighed. "Thank you. Though I do prefer your bossy side in the bedroom."

Sam finally smiled, but only briefly. "When did you want to speak to him? Your father, that is?"

"I don't know. I'd like to go now. But part of me thinks I shouldn't when I'm angry. I don't want to give him any ammunition to use against me, but ya know, maybe he should see how pissed off I am about how he's treated me. I'd rather not have this out at work, because I keep telling him I can be professional, but if he were to start with me, I don't think I'll be able to hold back."

"If you wanna go now, then let's go now."

I looked at him for a long few seconds, trying to decide if I was ready for this to all come to a head right now. With a nervous breath, I nodded. "Let's go."

"You wanna call first? See if he's home?"

"Nope. It'll only give him time to make up some bullshit excuse."

Sam picked up his keys. "Okay then. I'll drive."

We pulled up out the front of the house where I grew up. There were some lights on, so I assumed someone was home. The gardens were immaculate, as always, and I wondered who the gardener was these days. I wondered if my father actually knew the first name of the person who tended to his gardens…

"You okay, Iz?" Sam took my hand over the centre console. "If you don't want to go in, that's okay. We can do it another day."

"Nah, it's fine. Just thinking, ya know?"

Sam nodded slowly. "Whatever happens in there, Iz, we'll get through it. Okay? You and me. I'm not going anywhere. Whatever changes after this, you have to know that you and me are good."

I squeezed his hand. "Thank you."

He smiled and looked at the house through the windscreen. "You ready?"

I nodded and got out of the car. I waited for Sam to join me so we could walk down the path to the front door together. With a sense of foreboding, my stomach in knots, and my heart in my throat, I said, "I can't stay stuck in limbo anymore."

And I knocked on the door.

After a moment, I heard soft footfalls on the other side of the door get closer before my father opened it. He was clearly surprised to see us. "Israel? Samuel? What are you doing here?"

We'd clearly caught him unawares. He had socked feet,

his tie was gone and business shirt was undone a button or two, and he held a tea towel in his hand.

"May we come in?" I asked.

Remembering his manners, he stepped aside. "Yes, of course."

Sam and I stepped into the marble foyer and waited while he closed the door and led us back to whichever room he was in before we arrived. From the tea towel in his hand, I guessed it was the kitchen, and I was right.

There were no other sounds in the house. "Mum not here?"

"No," he said, walking to the microwave. Using the tea towel, he pulled out a TV dinner and slid it onto the bench. "She had something or other on."

And for the first time in my entire life, I saw my father in a different light. He wasn't the CEO of a multimillion dollar, multinational company. He wasn't the high and mighty, emotionless man that I grew up knowing.

He was standing in his state of the art kitchen that I could never recall him or my mother using, in a mansion that was purely for status only. He looked tired, old, smaller than I remembered, and he looked very, very lonely.

"Can we talk?" I asked.

"Of course," he said. "I didn't get a chance to eat all day and found this in the freezer. I couldn't have been bothered to order in, so I thought, what the hell? So you'll have to excuse my manners, but I'm famished. Mind if I eat while we talk?"

Despite what he said, I got the distinct feeling he ate a lot of frozen dinners by himself.

And if I came here expecting war, defences up, and full body armour on, I didn't find it.

"That's fine," I answered.

He led the way to the lounge room, which surprised me. The TV was already on, the volume down low, but he muted it anyway. I expected him to use the dining room, but he plonked himself on the sofa, slid his poor excuse for a dinner onto the coffee table, and again, I got the feeling he did this often. The coffee table never used to be that close to the lounge…

"Something on your mind, Israel?" he asked, taking a forkful of whatever goulash-type thing he was eating.

"Uh, yeah. Did you want us to order in dinner for you?" Not the question I came here prepared to ask, and food was the last thing I felt like, but jeez…

My father looked up at Sam and I. "Are you boys hungry?"

I shook my head. "No."

"I'm fine, Mr Ingham," Sam said beside me. I didn't have to even look at him to gauge his reaction. I knew Sam'd be thinking the same as me.

My father stabbed his meal unhappily. "I don't mind. I have a few reports to read over after, so I thought I'd just eat something quick." He ate a bit more, and I sat on the three-seater sofa with Sam beside me.

He was clearly waiting for me to say whatever it was I'd come here to say, so I steeled myself. "I got your message about not wanting to meet Nick."

My father chewed thoughtfully. "Thought that's what this might be about."

"Only partly." My mouth was suddenly dry. "If you don't want to meet him for whatever your reasons, then that's fine. But you'll need to tell him. I won't do that for you."

He frowned. "Fair enough."

"Can I ask you something?"

His gaze shot to mine, and the defences that were absent before flashed in his eyes. "Sure."

And for all the things I could have asked him… Did they even want children? Did he just not want a gay son? Did he realise all those things he'd said to me when I was growing up still hurt? Is that what he wanted all along?

But instead, the question I asked him, surprised even me.

"Why don't you ever talk about your parents?"

FIFTEEN

My father paled, slowly put his fork down, and pushed his half-eaten dinner away. "Is that what you came here to ask me?"

"One of the things, yes."

I didn't know why, but something about my father's relationship with his own parents must have shaped him into the father he became. I didn't know why I never saw the connection sooner, but from his reaction, I knew my guess was spot on.

He licked his lips and scrubbed his hand over his face. He stared at the TV for a while, and when I thought he just wasn't going to answer, he did. "I never saw eye to eye with my father." He cleared his throat. "He wanted me to become a dentist, like him. But I couldn't think of anything worse. He wouldn't listen. At all. He enrolled me at the Faculty of Dentistry, gave me money for tuition. Instead, I used that money to take a chance on iCon and… well, to say he was livid would be a gross understatement."

"Did you speak at all after that?"

"A few times. Once at my mother's funeral, and once when I invited him to the Annual Business Awards when I won for Fastest Growing New Business. I thought he might like to know, but no. Apparently not. And once when you were born."

So my father was a disappointment to his own father. It was obviously something that still bothered him, and whether or not he had tried to avoid making the same mistakes with me, he'd done the exact same bloody thing. I would have laughed at the irony if it weren't so fucking tragic.

"Is he still alive?" I asked.

My father shook his head. "No. He died twenty years ago."

I would have been six. "I don't remember that."

"You wouldn't," my father replied. "The day you were born, the only words of wisdom he bestowed on me were that he hoped I wouldn't be the disappointment to you as I was to him." My father laughed, a bitter, humourless sound.

Jesus Christ.

I swallowed hard. "So, all those times you called me a disappointment, was that aimed at me, you, or him?"

My father's gaze shot to mine. His voice was just a whisper. "You were never a disappointment."

"Then why did you tell me I was?"

"Because I was angry."

"At who?"

"At myself."

"What for?" I asked. "What were you so angry about that you'd tell a fifteen-year-old kid he was a waste of your time?"

My father paled. "You remember that?"

"I remember everything you ever said to me."

"That had been a particularly bad day," he mumbled, shaking his head. "I'd been in court all day. I stood to lose the rights on a contract. Their parent corporation had gone into receivership...," he trailed away.

"So I was a waste of your time because of that?"

He shook his head slowly. He looked pitiful and power-less, yet I couldn't bring myself to stop. "Your main focus in life became iCon because you didn't want to fail in front of your father, despite what that meant for your son."

He didn't reply, just took my words like punches.

"And you made a scared and lonely kid feel worse, for what? To make yourself feel better? And where was Mum throughout this whole thing? You know, there are parts of my childhood, when I was really little, that I don't even remember her being around."

He looked far away, as if seeing something in his distant memory. "Your mother was a good woman, Israel. Full of life and laughter, she was like sunshine on a rainy day."

"Was?"

"She suffered after you were born. Postnatal depression, they called it. We tried all the different doctors, all the different medications, treatments…" He sighed heavily. "But it never got better, and then it became clinical depression… She was never the same. Even now she's not the woman I once knew."

I sat there staring at him, trying to get my head around the bomb he'd just dropped on me.

I could understand the dynamics of his relationship with his father and how that must have messed him up, but to hear my mother had mental health issues blindsided me.

My father smiled as he obviousl remembered something. "You wanna know why you were called Israel? She wanted a dozen kids, all named after places around the world. She had a list: London, Paris, India, Brooklyn, but it had to be Israel first. She'd seen a travel show on television and just wanted to go."

I swallowed hard. To hear him talk of her and me in an affectionate manner made me teary. Sam took my hand and squeezed it. "Did she ever go?" I asked. "To Israel?"

He shook his head. "Not after… No."

"You should take her," I suggested. "Sounds like she'd love it."

No one spoke for a while. The silence wasn't exactly looming. It was just that we both had so much to think about. It felt good to address the demons but it was also draining, and my father looked exhausted.

"I'd like for us to talk again," I said. "We need to do this. My shrink, Kathryn, asked me if I wanted to have you guys in my life or if I wanted to move on. She wanted to know which path needed addressing, which is fair enough, I guess. I told her I did want you in my life. Of course I did. But I needed to face some of these issues, these barriers in my life."

My father licked his lips and nodded sadly. "I'm sorry I failed you."

"Dad," I said. "As a businessman, you're outstanding. I've seen you head meetings that were breathtaking in their audacity, and you'd walk away the winner every time. But I have to say this... As a father, you failed."

He met my eyes. He looked utterly defeated. "You never would sugar coat anything," he said eventually. "It's what makes you so good at your job."

I thought that was a compliment. I wasn't sure. "No I won't sugar coat it. I'm done. I'm done pretending. I'm done lying about how I feel. I'm done ignoring how fucked up in the head I am."

He looked at me like I was about to deliver a final blow.

"But Dad," I said. "I'm not walking away. And I know I'm not perfect in this either. But we need to meet in the middle."

He nodded, and for the first time tonight, there was a flicker of hope in his eyes. "I'd like that."

I stood up, and Sam did as well. "And just so you know," I added, "you're welcome to come around to my place for dinner any time. I'll cook us a steak or something. We don't have to talk much if you don't want—we can put the cricket on the telly and watch that—but it's better than eating a frozen dinner by yourself."

He smiled up at me. "Sounds good."

"We'll see ourselves out," I told him. I didn't expect to hug it out. We were nowhere near ready for that. "See you at the office tomorrow."

We left him sitting alone in his too-big, too-quiet house, and I barely got to the car before Sam stopped me. He pulled me into his arms and held me tight.

"I'm so proud of you," he whispered.

And then the tears came.

WE LAY on the sofa in front of the TV. Sam was the big spoon, his arm lazily draped over my stomach, my head on his chest. He made me eat, though I didn't really feel like it. I was so tired. There was an exhaustion in my bones, and it wasn't long before he made me get up and took me to bed.

We stripped down to our underwear and climbed into bed. He pulled me close, so his bicep was my pillow, and he traced the outline of my face in the moonlight.

"How are you feeling?" he asked gently. "About what you said to your old man."

"Good. I guess. I needed to say those things, and he needed to hear them. I gave him a bit to think about."

Sam kissed my forehead. "And he gave you the same."

"Yeah, he did." I sighed. "I had no clue about my mother having postpartum depression. None."

"It makes it all rather sad, doesn't it?"

I nodded. "Yeah. Clinical depression is serious, and I can't believe I was never told. Maybe I should've seen it; but she was always so distant. I mean, I know we never talked about *anything* in my family, let alone such personal things, but it would've been better if I'd known the truth rather than think my own mother just didn't love me."

His arms tightened around me, and he kissed the top of my head.

"My father looked really old. He's always been a wall, ya know? Infallible. Impenetrable. But tonight, he was… I don't even know. He looked smaller, and old. He looked lonely and really fucking sad."

Sam hummed. "He did. It was kinda unnerving, wasn't it? To see him like that. I know exactly what you mean."

"I knew you would. Thank you for being there with me for that. It wasn't easy."

Sam pulled up the blankets and sighed. "I'm proud of you."

I gave him a bit of a squeeze. "Thank you. That means a lot."

He chuckled. "Oh, Iz. One of these days you might actually not thank me for the littlest of things."

I leaned up so I could look into his eyes. "I won't ever not be grateful for you."

He lifted his head and softly kissed me. "I love you, Iz."

It made my heart skip a beat and butterflies swarmed my throat. I put my hand to his cheek. I didn't think my heart would hold out long enough for me to speak. "I love you too."

He kissed me a little softer, sweeter, and pulled away so he could nudge his nose to mine. He tucked my head in under his chin, tightened his arm around me, and sighed contentedly.

After such a taxing day, I fell asleep, warm and safe in the arms of the man I loved.

WHEN I GOT to work the next day, I'd almost forgotten the conversation I'd had with my father the day before.

Well, after waking up with Sam's mouth on my dick, then returning the favour, laughing in the shower with him, then feeding each other breakfast, it was hard to remember the less-than-pleasant shit in my life.

Things with Sam were pretty damn perfect.

I was literally having the best fun with my best friend, and having the best sex of my life, all with the same person. Perfect didn't even begin to describe it. Which was why it wasn't until I got into the office that I remembered. With a sinking stomach, I remembered that I'd dealt my father a pretty rough blow last night.

"Morning," Prue said in greeting. "Your father was in earlier. He's had to duck out, but he did say he'd like to meet with you after lunch. If you have time."

If I have time? What the hell? He's never asked if it suited me before.

"I didn't want to confirm until I'd spoken to you, but your schedule is free after lunch."

"Yes, of course. It's fine." I gave her my best smile. "Can I borrow you this morning?"

"Uh, sure."

"It's just the Fesco job. I could use an extra pair of hands."

Prue brightened, clearly thrilled at learning something new and the extra responsibility. "I'll grab us a coffee and bring them straight in."

"Perfect."

"Did he, uh, did my father say where he was going?"

"No."

"Did he mention what he wanted to speak to me about?"

She shook her head. "No."

"It doesn't matter. Come on then, network projections await."

WITH PRUE'S HELP, I got through more work in a few hours than I would have the whole day. She had a keen eye for detail and a memory like a vault. I threatened her with more analysis work if she wasn't careful, which she laughed at but offered to do whatever I put on her desk.

I was grateful for her, and I was glad I'd made the choice of conversing with her on a more personal level. I felt like I had a friend in the office now, which made a nice change. I had lunch ordered, and we ate at my desk while we continued with our work. She offered me snippets of her weekend away with friends in between comments about data and findings.

Time got away from us, and it wasn't until there was a knock at my door that I remembered my father had requested to see me.

He stuck his head through cautiously and cleared his throat. "Is now a good time?" he asked.

Prue quickly tidied up her sandwich wrapper and juice bottle, then started on the pile of reports.

"It's fine," I said, probably more to Prue than to my father. "Prue's been outstanding help today."

She blushed and nodded graciously, straightening the perfectly straight pile of papers. "It was nothing. But I'll take these and continue from my desk. Thanks again for lunch."

"No worries. Thanks for your help."

My father held the door for her and smiled her way, but I doubt she saw. She had her head down as she walked past him with the manila folders clutched to her chest.

My father stepped inside and the door closed behind him. Only then did he walk to my desk and sit in the chair opposite me. This was the man I knew; impeccable suit, chin high, eyes of steel.

It was a far cry from the man I saw heating up a frozen dinner in his kitchen.

"I wanted to speak to you about what you said last night. I just need to say it without interruption, please. Or I won't be able to finish," he said. He leaned back in his chair and sighed, and just like that, the smaller man from the night before was back. "What you said stung. I won't lie. It stung because there was truth in it. And because it came from you."

I blinked, and I think my mouth fell open.

Who the fuck was this man? And what did he do with my father?

"You're right," he went on. "I did fail as a father to you, first and foremost. But I also failed as a son to my own father. Everything you said to me was everything I wished I had said to him, but I was never brave enough. I should have fought harder, I should have knocked on his door and sat him down and told him how I felt, but I never—" His voice cracked with emotion. He cleared his throat. "I was not as strong as you."

My eyes burned with tears. "Dad…"

He put his hand up and smiled, teary eyed as well. "Please let me finish." He took a deep breath. "The reason I told you I wouldn't see Nick is because… well, I'd failed you. I didn't want to fail another son."

I wanted to tell him he hadn't. I wanted to ease his pain, but the truth was he had. I shouldn't have to apologise for that.

"Nick doesn't want anything from you," I offered instead. "He just wants to meet you and Mum. Maybe he's curious, maybe he just wants to see where he came from. I don't know. But he has his family. Donna, Lachlan, and Ashley. No DNA test will change that for him." I wasn't trying to intentionally make him feel worse, though I needed to speak the truth, and he needed to hear it. "The only way you can fail him is if you never meet him."

He nodded slowly. "Yeah I know. I want to... I really do..."

"But you're scared."

His eyes shot to mine, and I knew I was right. "It's okay to be scared. I was nervous as hell meeting Donna. I kept thinking, 'What if she rejects me too?'"

I realised as soon as I'd said it, how it sounded, what it meant.

My father didn't miss it either. "Too?"

I stared right at him. "Yes. I'd already been rejected by the people who raised me; I didn't fancy it a second time around with the woman who gave birth to me."

He held my gaze until he couldn't look me in the eye any longer. He stared at his hands instead. "I never rejected you... well, I never meant to. I'm sorry I never... I'm sorry for a lot of things." He looked up at me then. "I really am."

"I know you are. I can see that." It was the truth. I think he was genuinely sorry. I just don't know what he wanted me to do with that. "And I appreciate you coming to speak to me. That took guts. And I appreciate you saying sorry. But I have a lot of... issues that I'm working on. I want to forgive you. And I think one day I'll get there. But it will take time, and small steps." He had to know twenty-six years of hurt weren't going away overnight.

He nodded quickly. "Fair enough."

"But I think we covered a great deal of ground today."

He finally smiled. "I think so too." His smile faltered and he looked out the window for a moment, and I knew then that he had something else to say.

"I spoke to your mother last night when she got home. I sat her down and told her things needed to change. In a good way, don't get me wrong. I told her I knew she was miserable, and that was partly my fault. I've spent the last twenty-eight years of my life with iCon being my number one priority, and it was about time that changed. It was just a shame it took being told off by my own son to realise that." He shook his head. "God, I've made a mess of things, haven't I?"

"It's not too late," I offered. "Is it? With Mum?"

He smiled like I've seldom seen. "I asked her if she'd go to the theatre with me this weekend. She said she'd like that." He made a quiet sound of disbelief. "Crazy, huh?"

I found myself smiling at him. "Sounds good."

"Well, small steps, like you said. I'm going to suggest she see someone, professionally, I mean. Maybe I should go with her, I don't know…"

"It can't hurt."

"And she has her book club meetings on Wednesdays," he said. "So I was wondering if your invitation to join you for dinner still stands?"

To say I was shocked was an understatement. "Of course," I said quickly.

"Sam too, if he wants," he added. "I mean, I don't have a problem with that… or with him, or you being…" He did this weird wave thing with his hands.

"Boyfriends?"

"Yeah."

I tried not to laugh. "I'll ask him, but I think he's busy. Not sure."

"Okay then." He wiped his palms on his thighs and sighed with a smile. I'm pretty sure this meeting went better than he expected because he looked pleased with himself. "Well, um…" He stood up.

He was so awkward with small talk, so I let him off the hook. "Be at my place any time from seven on Wednesday. No need to bring anything, just yourself."

My father nodded, and I wondered whether he'd ever been to someone's house for a BBQ. Fancy dinners at exclusive restaurants, yes, a thousand times. But a simple home-grilled steak and a beer, probably not.

I watched him leave and I must have stared at the door for about ten minutes. I didn't want to jinx anything, but I slowly took out my phone, still watching the door. Part of me expected him to burst back through the door and say, "Just kidding," but he never did. I typed out a quick text to Sam.

You are never going to guess what just happened? I think my little convo with my father last night sunk in. Like seriously, holy shit.

Ten seconds later, my phone rang. "Tell me what happened."

I laughed. "Is that how you greet all your boyfriends?"

"Only the ones who are fuckhot in bed."

"Just as well."

There was a smile in his voice. "So? What happened?"

I relayed the entire conversation, and all he could say when I was done was "holy shit."

"I know, right? It's like he's human or something."

Sam laughed at that. "Wow. Like he's really doing a one-eighty, isn't he?"

"He's trying to."

"That's good, right?"

"Yeah, for sure. I meant what I said about small steps though. If he thinks I'll forgive and forget the last twenty-six years, he doesn't know me at all."

Sam snorted.

"But I'm prepared to try. And so is he. So that's a start, right?"

"God yes."

"I still can't quite believe it, to be honest." I heard him speak to someone in his office. "Sorry to call you at work. I just had to tell someone."

"It's fine, Iz. But yeah, I do have to go. Hey, getting back to your earlier comment about a particular boyfriend who's fuckhot in bed, what are you doing tonight?"

I snorted. "You. I'll be at yours at seven." I didn't wait for him to reply, I simply disconnected the call and slid my phone onto my desk.

I was still smiling when he met me at his front door and pulled me inside.

SIXTEEN

SAM SHUT THE FRONT DOOR BEHIND ME AND PUSHED ME UP against the wall. He used his entire body weight to hold me in place, and I could feel how turned on he was already. He bit down on my earlobe. "Plan on doing me, do you?"

My breath hitched. "Yes."

"You don't sound very convincing."

He scraped his teeth down my neck, and it took me a minute to gather my thoughts. When I could speak properly, I reached up and took his face in my hands, pulling him back a bit. "I'll fuck you anytime you want," I told him. His nostrils flared and his chest heaved, so I knew he wasn't opposed to the idea. "But first I want you in me."

He crushed his mouth to mine and hoisted one of my thighs over his hip. He pushed me harder against the wall as he kissed me, grinding his hard cock against me. So unforgiving, so fucking hot.

"Bedroom," he mumbled, breaking the kiss. "Before I have you right here."

My knees nearly buckled, but I somehow managed to push him back. "Don't tempt me," I warned him. Because I was turned on, if he wanted me right here and now, no condom, no lube, I wouldn't stop him.

He hissed out a breath, snatched up my hand, and led me to his bedroom. He wasted no time in stripping me, yanking my shirt over my head and pulling at the fly on my jeans. I stilled his hands. "Desperate, huh?"

"I've been thinking about you doing me since one o'clock," he said, his voice low and sexy. "I almost jerked off earlier but thought I'd save it for you."

"Good," I said, matter of factly. Then, while he watched, I slowly put one knee on his bed and leaned over it, offering him my arse and exposing myself to him completely.

"Jesus," he whispered. I heard the rustle of foil, then the snap of a lube bottle lid, and I waited for his cool, slick fingers to breach me. He was desperate in his touch, on edge already.

"Need you inside me when you come," I told him, moaning as he inserted his second finger.

He withdrew from me, then pressed his cock against me and impaled me in one deep push. I gripped the bedcovers, and he gripped my hips and bent over me, driving me forward while his cock pinned me where he wanted me. The stretch and burn was counterbalanced by the soft kisses he pressed to the back of my neck.

There was a sweet tenderness in the way he fucked me. He was merciless in the way he drilled me, slamming into me, deeper than ever before, but he was soft and loving in the way he held me, planting kisses up my spine.

He was showing me that he owned me and that he loved me.

I'd never felt anything like it before, this possessiveness, this adoration.

He slammed into me one final time before stilling. He grunted and growled as he came inside me and collapsed onto my back. His ragged breaths were short and sharp, we were a sweaty mess, and I didn't ever want to move.

I threaded my fingers with his and chuckled underneath him. "Feel better?"

He slowly pulled out of me and rested his forehead on my back. "Sorry."

"Don't apologise. You can have me like that anytime. That was fucking hot."

He chuckled and kissed my spine. Eventually he stood up straight and pulled me with him. He turned me around and kissed me so tenderly, so reverently, it stole my breath.

He put his forehead to mine. "You okay?"

"Better than okay."

He ran his hand over my hip and down the front of my thigh. "You didn't come."

"No. You can take care of that later. I need to eat. I'm starving."

Sam chuckled. "Quick shower first, then I will make you anything in the world you want."

He led me into his bathroom, tossed the used condom in the bin, started the shower, and stood underneath the spray. He held out his hand, which I took, and he pulled me into the tiled cubicle with him. He quickly washed himself, then turned his attention to me with such gentle affection. Then he lifted my chin into the stream of water and pressed his lips to mine. "I'll go start dinner. What do you feel like?"

"Anything."

He stepped out of the shower, wrapped a towel around his waist, and left me to it. I finished washing myself, careful with my tender arse, and shut off the water. I dried off, stole a pair of Sam's boxers, and met him in the kitchen.

He looked over my naked chest and still-wet hair, and he appeared to like what he saw. He licked his lips and swallowed hard. He was wearing some sleep pants, no shirt, and I *definitely* liked what I saw. "What am I eating?"

Only then did he seem to remember the knife in his hand. "Oh. Um. I only had a small amount of ground beef, so it's going to be more vegetables than meat, but it's my mum's spag bol."

I grinned and kissed his naked shoulder. "I always loved your mum's spaghetti bolognese."

He smiled brightly. "That's why I'm making it."

So he cooked, I helped, much like we had for the last decade. Only this time there was a gentle touch or two, and we sat at either end of the couch with our feet and legs touching, laughing as we ate.

My phone beeped with a message, so I reached out and snatched it off the coffee table. "It's from my father," I said, reading his name on the screen.

Can you please tell Nick that yes, we'd like to meet him. Or give me his details and I'll do it. Thanks.

I turned the phone around and showed Sam. "He must have spoken to my mother, because he's talking *we.*"

"Sure," I said as I typed the word. "I'll forward you his number. He'll be happy to hear from you." I hit Send, then sent him Nick's mobile phone number. I smirked at Sam and shrugged one shoulder. "Well, shit."

Sam laughed and slid his empty bowl onto the coffee table. "He even said please and thank you."

"I told you, it's like he's actually human." I put my empty bowl on the floor. "You know, I should probably let Nick know to expect something..." I said, already typing a quick text.

I spoke out loud while I typed so I wouldn't have to repeat it to Sam. "Hey Nick. Spoke to my father. Just a heads up that he'll be in touch. He wants to meet you."

I hit Send, then considered adding something else. "Go easy on him. He's trying."

Sam watched me for a moment, smiling, but he said nothing.

"What?"

"Nothing."

"Bullshit."

He laughed. "The one downside of finally hooking up with you is that I can't lie. You know me too well." He sighed contentedly. "I like seeing you happy, that's all."

"Happy?" I thought about that. "Happy with you, yes. Happy that things with Donna and Nick and Lachie and Ash seem to be going well, yes. Happy with the new developments with my old man? I think cautiously optimistic would be more apt."

"Still. It's good to see you happy."

I sat up and crawled between his legs, lying with my back on his chest. "Now I'm happy."

He wrapped his arms around me and nudged his nose to the back of my head. "Hey, did you ever tell Donna that she set this whole thing in motion?"

I snorted. "You mean, what she said to make me pull my head out of my arse."

He chuckled, his chest vibrating under me. "Well, me too. If you hadn't turned up on my doorstep all sweaty and sexy as hell, rambling—"

"I wasn't rambling!"

"You totally were. I had to kiss you to shut you up."

"What a crock of shit. You told me no, and I was back-pedaling down the hall when you kissed me. There was no rambling."

He laughed. "Maybe. But you definitely shoved me backwards on the couch with your tongue down my throat in front of the guys."

I snorted. "Jamie didn't seem to mind."

Sam barked out a laugh. "He called me the next day and wanted to know if we'd broken some kind of sex record."

I laughed too. "He's such a dickhead."

"He is. But I told him hell yes we did."

"We should organise another night out with them," I suggested. "I don't want them to think we're shafting them."

"No. If anyone does any shafting around here, it'll be you and me."

"That's the lamest joke you've ever made." I still had my phone in my hand, so I switched it on and held it out to take a photo of us. We were shirtless, but it was pretty obvious we were on a sofa in a living room. It was just of our faces, though you could tell I was lying on his chest. I showed him the photo. "I'm going to send this to Donna, is that okay?"

"Sure."

I typed out a message to go with it. *I have you to thank for this. What you said to me the other day rang true for both of us. I really appreciate the push.*

I sent the photo and settled in against Sam to watch some crap show he was watching. Nick replied saying yes, he'd had a text from my father. They were going to work out a time to meet, and he thanked me. Donna replied with a brief phone call, so very happy for us both, and I was pretty sure she was crying those happy tears again. We promised to see each other again soon. Sam and I then made plans with Millsy, Jamie, and Connor to catch up on Friday night, then we went to bed where Sam remedied the fact that I didn't reach orgasm when we had sex earlier.

I fell asleep happier than I'd remembered ever being.

I was nervous about having my father over for dinner on Wednesday. Sam agreed that it would be best if I did this alone. This meeting was my home-ground advantage. It would only make my father more uncomfortable if he were outnumbered.

So, it was just going to be me and him.

And when I opened the door to him, right on seven o'clock, he looked as nervous as I felt. "Come in," I said, standing to one side. "I'm just heating the grill."

He brought with him a six-pack of Crownies, which was not the beer I drank, but I took it graciously. It was a nice gesture, and if he was making an effort, then so would I. I kept two beers out and put the others in the fridge. "I got this grill last summer. Sam had one and swore by it. It's like having a BBQ in your kitchen."

We made awkward small talk—and it was awkward—but this was progress. We found safer topics, such as work, which, as it turned out, we could both talk about for a while. It was common ground for us, and we discussed it all through our dinner of steak and salad. It was a simple dinner, but I got the feeling it was more than just about the food for him. I mean, it had to beat a frozen dinner for one, but he seemed to savour every bite. And maybe he savoured the conversation as well. When he was done, he put his knife and fork down and sighed contentedly.

The conversation seemed to stall for a moment, and I wondered if he thought now that dinner was over, he should leave. Did he want a reason to stay?

"The ice hockey playoffs are on ESPN tonight," I offered.

He smiled, relieved. "Sounds good."

So we watched ice hockey in relative silence, him on one sofa, me on the other. It was weird, slightly awkward, but somewhat comforting as well. When he fought a yawn, he stood up. "I should probably go," he said. "It's getting late and my days of all-nighters are well behind me."

I got up and walked him to the door. "Yeah, I don't bounce back like I used to, and I'm only twenty-six."

He smiled. "I really enjoyed tonight. We should do it again some time."

"For sure. I'd like that."

He beamed, then reined it in a bit. "Maybe you could come over one night for dinner with me and your mum. I'm sure she'd like that. Bring Sam if you want."

Okay, so the olive branch was fast becoming the whole damn tree. "Deal."

We left it that and said goodnight. I cleaned up the kitchen before grabbing my phone. I had three missed messages from Sam.

How'd dinner go?

Everything okay? You haven't tried to kill each other yet?

And the third and final one: *If you need help hiding the body...*

I laughed and hit Call. "Oh my God, you're still alive," he answered.

"Of course. I had my phone on silent, sorry."

"So how did it go?"

"Pretty good. Awkward at first. We talked about work, then we watched ice hockey and he left."

"He just left now?"

"Yep."

"Well shit. That's about three hours longer than I thought."

"I know, right? We didn't talk much, just kinda hung out. I dunno. It was weird."

"He was there for four hours and you didn't talk much?"

"Nope. Like I said, it was weird. Awkward at times but kind of new and comforting. I don't know what to make of any of that and figure I'll hand my findings over to my shrink and let her sort it out for me."

Sam laughed at that. "Well, your timing to call me was perfect."

"Why's that?"

"Because I just got into bed," he said, his voice low. "And I'm naked."

"Oh, really?"

"Yep. How about you do the same? It's kinda late, and it'll help you sleep."

I picked up the remote control, switched the TV off and

headed down the hall to my room, turning lights off as I went. "Gimme ten seconds to get undressed."

"Make it five."

I was naked in three.

On Thursday after my appointment with Kathryn, Sam was waiting for me at my place. He was wearing his gym clothes but didn't look post-workout. "Thought we could go for a run," he said, obviously answering my questioning look.

"Really?"

"Yep, and you can tell me how your appointment with your doctor went."

"While we run?"

"Yep."

"Why?"

"Because boyfriends who work out together, have more sex together."

I snorted. "Pretty sure that's not how the saying goes."

"It could. If we take it upon ourselves to up the quota."

"What's the real reason?"

"Well, you said running clears your mind. I thought after your session this afternoon you might need it. And I haven't been to the gym in a while and I was going to go tonight but then I wouldn't have been able to see you, so I figured I'd kill two birds with one stone and do exercise while spending time with you."

"Your time management skills are stellar."

"But wait, there's more!" he said in his best infomercial voice. "I've also ordered Japanese food to be delivered in ninety minutes. That gives us time to run, have a quick shower, by which time dinner will arrive. We can then eat said dinner, then spend hours doing... other things."

"Have I told you lately that you're a bossy shit?"

He grinned. "And you love it when I'm in charge, don't deny it."

"Wouldn't even if I could."

"Then go get changed." Then he made a face. "Please."

I barked out a laugh as I toed out of my shoes. "Did that feel as awkward as it sounded?"

He rolled his eyes. "Shut up and get changed."

Ten minutes later we were jogging side by side down Mrs Macquaries Road into the Botanical Gardens. We hadn't got too far when Sam asked, "So, how'd your appointment go?"

"Pretty good. I told her everything that happened with my father. How he's having a go at being human."

"What'd she say?"

"I told her how it was awkward and nice at the same time. She said me wanting him to try doesn't mean I forgive him. I told her I knew that. Then she said I still have years of unresolved anger to work through, which I'm also fully aware of. She thinks it's positive that I'm willing to try, but I should set boundaries so I'm comfortable and set the pace."

"Makes sense."

"She told me not to feel responsible for my father's guilt at failing as a parent."

He glanced at me as we ran. "Do you?"

"I'm not responsible for his guilt. Well, when I was younger, I felt responsible because I always thought he didn't love me. I felt like it was all my fault. But not about the guilt. I dunno. Maybe I do. That's the thing about therapy. Shit sneaks up on ya."

"I'm glad you're talking to her. She sounds like she knows what she's on about."

"She said I need to confront my mother."

He shot me a wary look. "Is that a good idea?"

"I think I need to."

"But if she has mental health issues…"

"I know. But I still need to talk to her about it. And let's face it, there's never a good time to bring shit like this up."

We jogged for a little while in silence, and when we got to The Point, Sam stopped and leaned on the railing overlooking the water to catch his breath. "No, there's not. I'll come with you when you speak to her, if you want. It's not going to be easy."

"Thanks." I shoved his shoulder. "You can't be out of breath yet. We still have miles to run."

He groaned pathetically but straightened up. "Next time I have the great idea of running with you, slap some sense into me."

"Oh, I can do better than that."

"Don't look at me like that, Iz. I can't run with a hard on."

I laughed and took off ahead of him. "We run down to the Opera House, up past the Conservatorium, and the first one back home gets to pick who tops tonight."

I could hear him laughing and swearing at me as I raced away. There was no way he was gonna beat me.

WE STOOD IN MY KITCHEN, sweaty as hell and sipping water. "You cheated."

He smirked victoriously. "You should be clearer in your subclauses."

"There were no subclauses."

"And therein lies your downfall. There were no such clauses to specify the participants had to take the path. The defendant clearly stated the winner only had to go to the Opera House and up past the Conservatorium, then home. You never said one had to run on the path toward home."

"You cut through the middle of the park. Therefore you cheated."

"Objection, your Honour. *Cheated* is such an unlikable term."

"Quit your lawyer bullshit with me."

Sam laughed. "The court finds the plaintiff not guilty of all charges, therefore the chooser of who tops and who bottoms tonight rests with them."

I rolled my eyes and took a long drink of water. "Like it was ever gonna be a choice. I'm showering in my bathroom. Your cheating arse can take the ensuite off your bedroom."

He looked truly offended. "You don't wanna shower with me? *My* bedroom? What does that mean? I thought we'd sleep in yours…"

He stopped talking when I started to smile. "Of course you're sleeping with me. But you ordered dinner to arrive any minute. I was saving us time in the shower, because if you join me, we won't be eating dinner any time soon."

He checked his watch. "Shit. I didn't know running a marathon would take so long."

It was hardly a marathon, but whatever. I headed toward my bathroom and called out, "How are you gonna play power top if you're too tired?"

He yelled back. "Who said I wanted to top tonight?"

I almost tripped over my feet. Maybe he heard me sputter something, because I sure as hell heard him laugh. I had the quickest, coldest shower I could stand, and Sam was still in the shower when dinner was delivered.

He strolled out wearing my old, comfy sleep pants and a smile. "Mmm, food."

I planted a kiss on his lips and handed him his plate. "You ordered my favourite."

"Of course I did. I know what you like, I know what you hate, and I know what you tolerate even though you'd rather not eat it but you do because you don't want to be rude."

"Really? And what's that?"

"Tuna bake. My mum would serve it and you'd say nothing, swallow it down like gravel, and still say thank you. You don't like falafel, but when Connor brings it, you eat it."

"His grandmother makes it."

"My point is, you suffer through things you don't like to make other people happy." He put his hand on my stomach and kissed me softly. "And I ordered you the *gyūdon* because you love it. You don't have to tell me these things. I know you."

I looked at him for a long moment, seeing the warmth in his eyes. "You do."

He took a mouthful of his *laksa* and his eyes went wide. "Holy shit that's spicy."

I snorted. "So, maybe you won't be bottoming tonight."

Sam burst out laughing. "Ah, the joys of gay sex." Then he sipped his water. "No, but seriously, my mouth is on fire."

I went to the fridge, grabbed the milk, and poured him a glass. "Here, drink that." Then I grabbed him another fork. "Share mine."

With the cutest smile ever, he took the fork like I'd handed him my heart. "Thank you."

I bit my bottom lip, ignoring how giddy he made me feel. "Any time."

He ducked his head shyly, which was very unlike him, but when he looked up, there was something new in his eyes. And with every mouthful of dinner, his gaze got more intense. I'd always thought the term *eye fucking* was a ridiculous notion of giving some random guy a drunken look on a dance floor. But no, this was different.

There was heat and promise in every glance, desire like a physical entity stood between us. It was like he was seeing inside me, like he craved every inch of my skin. I put down my fork. "If you keep looking at me like that, I'll…"

He breathed out the words, "You'll what?"

"Let you do whatever you want to me."

He dropped his fork onto the plate, snatched up my hand,

and led me to my room. Five long and torturous minutes later, after I told him I was more than ready, begged him to take his fingers out of me and just fuck me already, he did exactly that.

FRIDAY AT WORK WAS INTERESTING.

I called my mother and asked if she'd be home on the weekend, telling her I'd come around. She said of course, Saturday would be best, so we made a lunch date. But she sounded despondent or distracted, so we didn't talk long.

It saddened me greatly that she'd suffered alone for so long. And even though I needed to talk to her about how I felt, I needed to tread carefully.

Not long after I'd spoken to her, my dad knocked on my door. He did have genuine work questions at first, which we worked through together, easily enough, but then when that was done and silence loomed between us but he still didn't leave, I knew he wanted to chat.

"I talked to Mum earlier," I said, figuring it would be easier on both of us if I started the conversation.

"Oh?"

"Yeah, I want to come around and talk to her. I spoke to my therapist yesterday, and she thinks it might be good for both of us."

His brow furrowed. "I know you said you need to address certain subjects, but I don't want to see her upset."

"Neither do I. That's not my intention at all. I just want to talk, have lunch. Bring Sam and officially introduce him as my boyfriend. That kind of thing."

"Oh." He seemed relieved?

"I'm not going to upset her," I said again, trying not to be defensive. "I'm trying to mend bridges here, not burn them."

"Sorry," he said quickly. "I didn't mean it like that." Then he sighed. "Small steps, huh? I'm trying. You'll have to bear with me, I'm afraid."

"I know, Dad. I have no intention of deliberately being hurtful or spiteful to her, but I can't wear this guilt any more. And pretending nothing's wrong won't fix anything."

He looked out the window for a while and smiled to himself. "When did you get so smart?"

I didn't answer that. I was pretty sure my answer of "when I was twelve and was more of an adult than you" wouldn't help the situation. Instead, I answered, "You'll just have to trust me when I say I'm trying to make things right."

"Of course. And I do." He stood up. "I better let you get back to it. Oh, and I saw the Blackhawks are playing next Wednesday night."

I smiled. "Sounds good. Steak again?"

He beamed. "Perfect." And walked out my door.

SEVENTEEN

Going out for drinks with friends for the first time with Sam, as boyfriends, was also weird. We walked through the doors of the Oxford Hotel like we had a hundred times before, only this time Sam took my hand.

"That okay?" he asked.

"Yeah, of course." The truth was, I loved it.

And so did the guys. Millsy wolf-whistled, Jamie laughed, and Connor wanted to know if we were late because of sex reasons.

Sam didn't miss a beat. He slid his arm around me and pulled me in tight. "He sucks dick like a Dyson. Believe me, you're lucky we're here at all."

They all laughed, we bought a round of drinks for everyone, we talked, we laughed some more. It was all like old times, except this time, Sam had his hand in my back pocket, or I had mine in his. Sometimes he'd kiss me, all smiling and happy, much to the chagrin of the guys.

"For the love of God," Connor griped. "Can you two not touch each other for two minutes?"

I shook my head. "Nope."

Millsy pushed Sam in the direction of the bar. "Go do something useful."

Sam took the hint and went toward the bar, while I stood at the table and grinned like an idiot. "Yeah, yeah," Jamie said, rolling his eyes. "You're both getting an incredible amount of sex. We get it."

I laughed and held up my half-empty bottle in a cheers motion. Until Connor nodded toward the bar, toward Sam. "Seems like you got some competition."

I turned to see what he was talking about and saw Sam at the bar. Some random guy was talking to him, trying his hardest.

"Nah," I said, turning back around to face the guys. "No chance."

Millsy scoffed. "You that confident?"

"In Sam? Absolutely," I answered.

Connor nodded back toward where Sam was. "In Sam, yes. The other guy, not so much." He got a serious look on his face. "Sam doesn't like that."

I spun around this time to see Sam push the other guy's hand away. I put my beer down and was halfway across the floor when I heard Jamie laugh behind me. I walked straight up to Sam and slid my arm around him and stared at this fucking loser who wouldn't take no for an answer. "Is there a problem here?"

Sam leaned into me. "I was just explaining personal space to this guy here."

"He didn't seem to be getting the message," I said flatly.

The guy put his hands up. "Peace out. Take a compliment, dude."

"Shut the fuck up and move on, arsehole," I bit back. "Or I'll give you a compliment fair in the fucking mouth."

I was irrationally pissed off, not at Sam, just pissed that someone might try and take what's mine. The guy finally backed off, and Sam burst out laughing. "Damn, Iz," Sam said in my ear. "Didn't think you were the possessive type?"

I pushed him against the bar with my hips. "I've never had anything to lose before."

His eyes darkened and he licked his lips. "You're never gonna lose me."

"Good."

"You guys want a drink?" the barman interrupted us.

Sam turned and ordered another round of drinks while he kept one hand on my waist. When the barman went to grab our order, Sam smirked at me. "So? Wanna show me how possessive you can get?" I laughed him off, but he put his hand over my arse and pulled me hard against him. "I mean it."

The barman brought our drinks, and when we took them back to our table, Millsy, Connor, and Jamie were laughing at us, shaking their heads. I handed Jamie his beer. "Well, you sorted that guy out," he joked.

"He shouldn't touch what doesn't belong to him," I replied.

"Oh, God help us." Connor rolled his eyes.

"Let's go downstairs," Millsy said. "And see if SpongeBob SquarePants here can get his Mike Tyson on."

I would have told him to fuck off, but Sam laughed and kissed my cheek. "Dancing with you sounds good."

So we ventured downstairs and into a sea of dancing, grinding bodies. It didn't take Sam long to drag me into the middle of the dance floor and meld our hips together. He slid one hand onto my arse and kept me in place, his lips at my ear. "I've had a good time with the guys, but I really think we should go home."

"Why's that?"

"Because if you think I belong to you, maybe you should take me home and prove it."

I brought our lips together and kissed him, hard. If there

was anyone in the club that didn't know who Sam belonged to, they did now. When he pulled away, breathless, I took his hand, waved goodbye to Connor—I didn't see Millsy or Jamie—and I dragged Sam outside.

Thankfully the cab ride back to mine was quick. Now, I was usually a bottom and I fucking loved it. I loved being manhandled. I loved the weight of a guy on top of me, inside me. But if Sam wanted me to take charge, then I was more than happy to oblige.

Seeing that guy earlier with his hand on Sam and seeing Sam push him away triggered something in me. Sam always had guys fawning over him. He looked like a younger Brad Pitt, carried himself with confidence, and had a natural charisma that drew people in.

But it was different now. Now he was mine.

Once inside, I walked straight to my room, knowing he'd follow. I threw my keys and wallet onto the dresser and turned to Sam. "I didn't like that guy touching you."

He licked his lips. "I noticed."

I took a step toward him. "I've never felt jealousy before. Not like that."

He smirked, but his voice was low and husky. "He was harmless."

I cornered him against the wall. "No one touches you but me." His pupils were blown out, and his breath was shallow. He was definitely turned on. I put my hand to his jaw and slid my thumb over his bottom lip. "No one kisses you but me." Then I slid my other hand down his stomach, over the bulge in the front of his jeans. "No one fucks you but me."

He gasped, so I kissed him, ploughing my tongue into his mouth, and when he whimpered, I pulled away. "You want me to fuck you?"

His lips were swollen and glistening, his eyes heavy lidded, and he nodded.

I pulled his shirt over his head and popped the button on

his jeans, then with my lips barely touching his, I slowly undid his fly. I slid my hand inside and gripped his cock through his briefs.

His breath stuttered. "Fuck, Iz."

I let go of him and stepped back. "You need to be naked," I demanded in a whisper. He did as I told him to do, pulling his boots off first, then slid his jeans and briefs down and ripped his socks off. He shifted his weight and didn't seem to know what to do with his hands. "On the bed. Face down."

He seemed to hesitate for just one second before he moved onto the bed. I quickly stripped and crawled up over his body. I whispered behind his ear. "I'm gonna rim you first, then I'll fuck you. Is that okay?"

Sam laughed, a desperate sound. "God, yes."

I kissed down his spine until I reached his arse. I spread his cheeks and swiped my tongue along his hole. He cried out and gripped the pillow at his head, but he left his arse high for me. He was all tang and sweetness and desperate for more.

So I gave him everything he wanted. I fucked him with my tongue, stretching him until he couldn't stand it anymore. Until he was begging me for my cock.

"Roll over," I ordered.

He scrambled onto his back and I rolled a condom on. I slicked myself with lube, then applied more to him, slipping my fingers inside him.

He quickly pumped his own cock, precome leaking from his slit. "Goddamn it, Iz. Just fucking do it."

I placed my cockhead at his hole and tested the resistance, which only made him growl in frustration. So I leaned over him, with one hand by the side of his head, and the other guiding my cock inside him.

He gasped, he blinked, he stopped breathing.

I kissed his lips. "Breathe, Sam."

He nodded and sucked back a breath.

I pushed farther inside him. He was so tight, so hot I didn't think I'd last a minute. I concentrated on his reactions instead.

"Oh fuck," he hissed.

I stilled. "You okay?"

He nodded quickly. "Keep going."

I ghosted my lips over his, kissing him softly. "No one has you like this but me," I murmured, rolling my hips to inch farther inside him. "No one will ever be inside you but me."

Sam nodded and sucked in another breath, but he gripped my back with his hands, digging his fingers into my skin. I'd be sure to have marks.

I pulled out a little and slid back in, sparking a fire inside me that would soon explode. So I leaned back onto my knees, enough to keep rocking my hips and slowly thrust inside him, but so I could take his cock in my hand.

I worked his shaft in time with my thrusts. I must have aimed just right, swiping his prostate at each turn because he arched his back, his eyes going wide. "Fuck! Yes! Right there!"

I kept going until his hands started to shake and hips started to move, and I knew he was close. So I went harder, deeper, chasing my own pleasure with his, and then his whole body went rigid and his mouth opened without sound as he came.

I kept fucking him as he spilled come onto my hand and onto his stomach. When his body sagged, I leaned over him, and with every inch of me inside him, I came. The orgasm that tore through me was blinding, obliterating all my senses, leaving only pleasure in its wake.

When I floated back to reality, I was still on top of Sam, still inside him, and he was stroking my hair. "You alive?"

"I think so."

He chuckled. "Well that was the hottest fucking thing ever."

I pulled out of him slowly and leaned back so I could look into his eyes. "That was incredible."

"If that was you staking a claim, I think we can all consider me well and truly owned."

"Let me know if you ever need reminding."

He grinned. "Challenge accepted."

I chuckled. "And you can own me every time in between."

He smiled serenely and let out a deep sigh. He didn't have to say it was perfect. It was one of those things that passed between us, like things often did. We didn't always need words. It used to be just a look or a smile, but now it was gentle touches and kisses to the side of my head.

MEETING with my mother to talk about how my life, up until now, had been one hurt after the other was so different than it had been with my father. I used to harbour anger toward her. For years I'd been so pissed off that a mother would treat her child the way she had treated me.

But after my father had told me that my mother had suffered terribly with postpartum depression and subsequently, clinical depression, everything changed. My view of her changed. I was more hurt that I hadn't known. And yes, I probably should've seen the signs. But as a kid, when my own mother was so cold and distant, I put the blame solely on myself. It had to be me, because little kids don't know any different. All I could remember was being five years old and wishing I was better at everything so my mother would love me.

As a teenager, I was so used to her despondency, I never questioned it. Still, I thought it was me. What else was I to believe when I'd speak and she'd have a tired, humourless smile on her face? I felt patronised. Like I was a stupid kid and she knew it. Like she could barely tolerate me and we both knew it.

My entire life, in my head, I'd been the problem. I was the common denominator, in the fact that neither parent could bear to be around me.

It never occurred to me that my father's fear of failure would keep him too stricken to try. It never occurred to me that my mother had mental health issues.

Both very different reasons for the way they treated me. My father treated me much the same as his father had treated him. I still blamed him for his behaviour toward me all those years, though it was something we were working on. It'd be something I'd have to work on for a long while, I presumed.

My mother on the other hand… My anger had turned to sorrow. Heartbreak for a world of pain she had suffered on her own. I was still hurt that I'd never been told, I couldn't deny that. A five-year old kid understands "Mummy isn't feeling well" better than twenty-six years of self-loathing.

But right here and now, to salvage any possible future relationship with my parents, I had to take the hard road. So with a deep breath and Sam's firm hold of my hand, I walked into my parents' house.

My father met us at the front door. "Hi, boys," he said, standing aside to let us in.

"Mum's here?"

He nodded. "She's out in the back garden. I've told her," he said. "About what we talked about, how you're seeing a therapist. How you two are together now. I just thought it was best she wasn't too surprised."

I squeezed Sam's hand. My father's seeming acceptance of Sam and I being together was a surprise. "Okay."

We followed him through the house and out to the back-yard. My mother sat at a patio table in the shade with a book, which she closed when she saw us walk out.

"Israel, Samuel," she said pleasantly. "Please take a seat."

We did as she asked, as did my father. "You wanted to speak to me?"

I nodded. "Yeah, Mum. I haven't... we haven't really talked." I couldn't say *since*, because the truth was, it was closer to never. "I thought it was about time we started."

She patted down her hair. "Yes. I spoke to you on the phone that time, but I know you get busy at work. I hate to be a bother..."

"You're not a bother. If you want to call me, no matter the time, you can call me."

My father smiled at that; something about my metaphorical white flag pleased him.

"You two are dating?" My mother asked, looking between Sam and I.

"Yes, Mum," I answered. I smiled at Sam. "We are."

"That's nice," Mum replied. There was no malice or sarcasm, and when I looked into her eyes, I saw such a profound, deep, and hollow sadness. I could never recall a smile that reached her eyes. Jesus. I didn't know why that hit me right then or why it hit so hard, but it steamrolled me.

Sam squeezed my leg under the table. He no doubt saw what I saw, how horribly sad my mother was. It broke my heart.

"Mum," I said gently. "Dad told me you didn't have the easiest time when you came home with a newborn."

She said nothing for a moment, then sighed. "No, I didn't." She gave me another one of those hollow smiles. "I haven't had the easiest time since. It's part of me now. It's who I am. I know it wasn't easy for you..."

"No it wasn't," I said gently. I didn't want to cry. Truly I didn't. But a lump formed in my throat and my eyes burned with the effort to stem the tears.

"You met Mrs Westbrook?" Mum asked.

"I have. And her son Nick. And her other children."

"Is she a good mother?"

"Mum," I mumbled. I shook my head.

"It's okay, Israel," she said with a serene smile. My mother looked out over the garden. "Life is often cruel," she said cryptically.

"It can be," I agreed. "But we can choose. We can either burn bridges or we can build them."

Mum looked at me and nodded slowly. "This is very true." She sipped a bottle of water. "Can I ask about her?"

"Donna? Mrs Westbrook?"

My mother nodded but quickly looked back over the garden like she didn't want to see the answer to the question she was about to ask. "You like her?"

"Yes. She's very kind and generous." I stopped short at saying maternal, or very motherly, because that would be a barb to an already wounded heart. It wasn't my mother's fault she struggled with motherhood, but I had to tell the truth. "She loves Nick with all her heart. If you want to know if she raised him well, then yes, she did a great job."

"Oh, it's not that," she whispered.

I got it then. Reading between the lines, I saw what she wouldn't ask. "Mum, just because I've met Donna doesn't mean I'm replacing you."

Her gaze shot to mine.

"She might be the woman who gave birth to me, but you're my mother. It's no one's fault. This is just the life we've been dealt and we need to accept it. I'll always have you, and I hope I'll always have Donna too. I have two families now. That doesn't mean I love you any less."

A tear spilled down her cheek and she smiled and sobbed back a breath. "Thank you. I love you too, Israel. I do. I always have. Even in the years when I felt nothing…"

Her words trailed away and she looked back out over the garden. Sam squeezed my hand. He looked pained and took a steady breath.

"Mum?"

She looked back at me but said nothing.

"So, I want to tell you something." Still nothing, but I pressed on. "I've been seeing a psychologist for a few weeks. It hasn't been easy, but some wounds need to be opened so they can heal."

Her eyes never left mine, and the depth of sadness there squeezed my heart.

"If you think we could all benefit by seeing someone together—you, me, and Dad—then we can do that."

"Doctors haven't helped me..." She finished by mumbling something I couldn't understand.

"Things are different now," Dad said, his voice hoarse. "They have different ways to treat people nowadays. I've researched a few things, and there's a clinic in Melbourne that does specialist healing, it's more like a health spa. We'd stay for a week at a time. Israel can look after iCon while we're gone. He's more than capable." This was news to me. He obviously saw my surprise because he nodded, looking at me. "You're more than capable."

I put his words away to process later.

"Is this an intervention?" Mum's eyes darted between me and my father. "Is that what this is?"

"No," I said quickly. "Not at all. We're not making you do anything. It was just a suggestion because we care." No one said anything for a long second. "Just think it over," I added. "You don't have to do it alone."

A long drawn out silence filled the garden, though eventually my mother smiled. "Your father asked if I wanted to see Israel." Then she clarified, "The country. Not you."

I knew what she meant, and I liked that he'd asked to make a dream she'd once had come true. "You should go," I said. "I hear it's an amazing place."

"I don't know," she fussed. "It's so far, and I'm busy with my social clubs and charities."

"Make the time," I said with a smile. "Do something for you."

"Your father can't leave the office for that long," she countered.

"Yes, I can." My father said gently. "Like I said, Israel can fill my shoes while I'm gone."

I tilted my head. "Sure. With about twenty years of training, the board of directors making all decisions, and Nigel sitting beside me, I'm sure I can."

My father smiled a genuine smile. His eyes crinkled at the corners, and in the sunlight, sitting in the garden, he looked ten years younger. "You'd be fine. I saw how you handled the Hallicott case. I couldn't have done a better job."

Hearing my father say that made my heart swell. I wasn't used to hearing compliments from him, and I instinctively wanted to talk myself down, tell him it was a team effort, that I was only as good as the weakest link or some other cliché buffer I could think of. But something stopped me. Maybe it was the way Sam squeezed my hand. Maybe it was because I knew my father was right.

"Thank you."

My father gave me a nod, then stood up. "Can I get anyone a drink? Sam, want a beer? Water?"

"Oh no, I'm fine, thanks," Sam replied. This time, I squeezed his hand. My father had just included him. It was such a small gesture, but it meant a lot to me.

My father looked at me. "Drink?"

"No thanks, Dad. We have to get going." The afternoon had gotten late, and after Sam and I had said goodbye, we drove in silence for a while. Until I said, "Well, that was weird."

Sam scoffed. "Uh, yeah. Though I see exactly what you mean, before when you said getting on well with your old man was weird, sometimes a little awkward, but still really nice. That's exactly what that was."

I chuckled and shook my head, half in wonder, half in shock. "I know! So weird."

Sam nodded as he drove. "A little awkward."

He let me finish. "But really nice."

He laughed. "And I don't mean to brag or anything, but your father totally spoke to me like I was a human being. In his house."

"I know! I never thought I'd ever see the day that I brought my boyfriend around and he acted like a normal person and asked if he could get you a beer." I was grinning hugely.

"And he said you were awesome at your job, and that you could do his job better than him," Sam said excitedly. "I'm paraphrasing but that was the gist of it."

I laughed, then he laughed, and I'm pretty sure I grinned for the rest of the day.

EIGHTEEN

We sat in the café, and my father let out another nervous breath. My mother smiled at him, but the way her eyes kept watch on the doors told me she was nervous too. It was two weeks since Sam and I sat in my parents' garden and we spoke, really spoke, for the first time.

It had been an interesting two weeks. My mother had agreed to speak to someone about her depression. She hadn't made any official appointments yet, but it was a start. My father had been to my place again for dinner and a night in front of the TV watching ice hockey, and he'd started training me in a few areas of his work, a role myself and Prue enjoyed immensely.

My father had also organised this official meet and greet with Nick, which was what Sam and I were doing in the same café in Penrith we'd met him the first time with my parents, waiting for him to arrive.

But not just Nick. Apparently the entire Westbrook clan was coming.

I'd spoken to both Nick and Donna a few times over the last fortnight. I really liked them, and I wanted to explain my new but still somewhat tenuous relationship with my parents.

When I'd first met Nick, the impression I'd given him of his birth parents wasn't great. It was honest at the time, but this whole experience had changed us all, and they were trying to fix things, as was I.

He was happy with this development, and so was Donna. "Family is a funny thing, Israel," she'd said. "It doesn't always make sense. But no one said it had to."

Sam tapped my leg and nodded toward the window. I followed his line of sight and stood up. "Here they are."

Nick and Melissa walked in first, and he smiled when he saw me. I walked up and gave him a hug. "Good to see you again," I said.

Then I hugged Donna, and she pulled back and put her hand to my face before she realised Sam was right behind me, then she hugged him too. "Oh, look at you two!"

I felt myself blush, making Sam laugh. I ignored him and said hello to Lachie and Ash, but when a silence fell over them, I realised Nick was looking at my parents.

Shit.

I walked over toward where my parents were now standing. "Uh, Nick? These are my parents, Merrick and Julia Ingham. Mum and Dad, this is Nick Westbrook."

My dad looked nervous and happy and a little overwhelmed, but he extended his hand. "It's so nice to meet you."

Nick shook his hand earnestly. "Same."

My mother had tears in her eyes, and she put her hand to her mouth. I wondered how she'd react, but when Nick hugged her, she let out a surprised, "Oh."

Then Donna hugged her too. "Finally," Donna said, her tears falling freely. Then she hugged my father. She let go of him and waved a hand to her own face. "Ignore my tears," she said. "I'm a crier." All of her kids laughed, me included.

Introductions were made all around, and when we all finally sat down at the table, everyone took a deep breath and a moment to gather their thoughts. Then if anyone had to break the ice, it was Ashley. "Wow," she said, looking between Nick and my mother. "You two really look alike."

I chuckled and looked right at Nick. "It's weird, isn't it? Seeing yourself in a family you just met."

Nick nodded, but he smiled.

My father kept looking at Lachie and Ashley, then looking at me. I knew he saw the resemblance. "Well, you're definitely related," he said with a smile.

"I'm the good looking one," Lachie joked.

Then in perfect sync, my father and Nick both laughed and shifted in their seats, relaxing. It was an absurdly mirrored reaction. Everyone stared at them, and we all laughed at the same time.

Nick scrubbed his hand over his face, like I'd seen my father do a hundred times. "It's kinda freaky," he said to me.

I agreed. "It is."

We ordered our coffees, and my mother produced some photographs. Some I'd seen, some I'd never laid eyes on. "That's my father," she said, pointing to one in particular. She smiled at Nick. "You look a bit like him."

Donna had brought a whole album with her, showing photos of Nick from the day she brought him home from hospital up until his engagement party, and every milestone in between.

We all chatted around the table, Sam and Lachie talked about cricket and cars, Nick, Melissa, and I talked about their upcoming wedding plans, which I'm sure Ash was really planning, given her constant input.

Donna spoke with my mother, and I found myself watching them a bit. There was a world of difference between them: clothing labels, jewellery, hairstyles. But they weren't that different at all. They were both mothers who had struggled. They'd fought different fights, but in the end, still sat around the same table.

I got dragged into a discussion on football codes between Sam, Lachie, and Nick, and after about half an hour of jibes and laughter, I heard my father's voice.

"I had started legal proceedings against Eastport Hospital. But I asked my lawyers to drop it."

What?

That was news to me. Not that I'd mentioned it since I'd told him how I felt about it, but still, he'd not brought it up either.

"You did?" I asked.

Everyone around the table stopped talking and looked between me and my father.

He gave a nod. "Yes, I did." He glanced around the table, then stared at his hands. He looked scared as hell but raised his chin and steeled himself. "When we were told of the hospital's error, I wanted someone to blame. It was *someone's* fault: a doctor, a nurse, the hospital, the health department. A gross misconduct that affected many peoples' lives. I was angry." He looked right at me. "But then Israel said something that stuck with me. He apologised if having him for a son was a mistake. And I realised that it wasn't a mistake at all. Getting you for a son wasn't a mistake."

My chest tightened, my heart felt like it would burst. Tears burned in my eyes until they spilled down my cheeks. "Dad."

Donna waved her hand in the air. "Oh," she said, fussing as tears streamed down her face. "Look at us two," she said to me, handing me a tissue. "Both as bad as each other."

It made us all chuckle, despite our tears.

And that was when I knew my father was serious about trying to change. I'd spent the last twenty-six years screaming into the void, being unheard, unseen, unloved.

But now I knew he was hearing me just fine. He saw the real me. Finally.

After all this time, it finally took proof that we weren't a family to become one.

EPILOGUE

FOUR YEARS LATER

It was a perfect spring day in Sydney. The sky was a perfect shade of blue, the backyard looked a treat, and life was pretty great. Sam and I had worked hard on it since we bought the place. We couldn't decide whose place to move into, so we both sold up and bought a terrace house in Rushcutters Bay. We got great prices for both our properties but were still mortgaged up to our eyeballs, and I'd never been happier.

"Uncle Izzy," Phoebe called as she ran with her tiny hands raised in the air. I scooped up the little girl and fixed her pretty dress. She was eighteen months old and gorgeous, and the only person who could call me Izzy and I didn't care. She was born a year after Nick and Mel's wedding and melted the hearts of all who met her. "Cake?"

Nick laughed, looking fondly at his little girl. "We told her it was a party. And all parties have cake."

I bopped her on her cute, little button nose. "Of course there's cake. But later. You have to eat lunch first."

Everyone was here to celebrate Sam's and my engagement. Yep, that's right. Engaged. Sam asked me to marry him, and of course I said yes.

We had been in our new house for a week and had spent the day in the garden, digging it all up and replanting a thousand bloody plants and new lawn. By the afternoon, I was so sore and tired, I'd showered and fell onto the sofa with a book. I felt him watching me, and when I looked over the book, there he was sitting on the other sofa staring at me with a goofy look on his face.

"What?" I asked with a smile.

"Marry me," he replied.

I dropped the book. "What?"

"Marry me. This, here, right now, with you being all-cute and shit on the couch, I want that forever. I want to make it official. I want you to wear a ring on your finger that says you're mine. Always. I never want this to change. Marry me."

I picked up the book and threw it at him. "You were supposed to take me to Paris. That's how it happened in my head. Or skiing in Austria. You arsehole, it was supposed to be romantic."

He laughed and ran over and jumped on me. He kissed me quickly, then pulled back to look at me. His eyes were bright and full of love. "We just paid the price of two souls and all the tea in China for this house. We can't afford trips to Europe."

"Yes."

"No we can't. We're owned by the bank."

"No, silly." I leaned up and kissed him. "Yes, I'll marry you."

So that's how the marriage proposal of the century went down, and a month later we were celebrating with our friends and family.

Family.

Wow. All my families were here. My parents, of course. My father and I had a slow but stable relationship. We didn't always see eye to eye, but we were learning. My mother, after a few failures, finally found the right doctor and had never been happier. She was grateful for the day I sat down with her and asked her to seek some help. As she sat in the sun with Phoebe on her lap, smiling at me, I would never regret taking the hard road.

My second family was the Westbrook clan: Donna, Nick, Mel, Phoebe, Lachie and his girlfriend, Ash and her new boyfriend. It was weird, that the only one I wasn't actually related to was Nick, yet he and I were the closest. We shared a bond like no other and were brothers in every sense of the word.

Sam's family were here too, of course, which technically was my third family.

And then my fourth family arrived, loud as always.

"Are you ready, kids?" Millsy yelled from the patio doors. Jamie grinned and answered, "Aye, aye, captain." Then of course Connor replied, "I can't hear you."

Then the three of them sang the SpongeBob theme song, in harmony, like they'd practiced it.

Everyone laughed. I sighed, and Sam, who was standing behind them, having obviously just let them inside, laughed. "I had no idea they were gonna do that."

"You know when I get married, I might change my surname. Just so my initials aren't aye aye anymore."

"We would still sing that song to you, brother," Millsy said, shaking my hand. "'Bout time you two finally made it official. You've been the married couple in our group since high school."

So we ate food, drank beer and wine, and for the benefit of Phoebe, we had cake. Sam and I stood in front of all our guests, with drinks in hand. For his speech, he talked about love and dreams and what forever meant to him. My speech was much shorter.

"To family. Sometimes it's bound by a wedding ring, sometimes it's bound by blood. Sometimes we're born into it, and sometimes we're switched. It doesn't matter how we got here, only that we are."

Sam kissed my cheek, and everyone raised their drink in the air.

"To family."

The End

ABOUT THE AUTHOR

N.R. Walker is an Australian author who loves her genre of queer romance. First published in 2012, she now has over 70 books, many which are also audiobooks, and numerous translations done in nine different languages.

She loves writing and spends far too much time doing it but wouldn't have it any other way.

---

nrwalker.net

ALSO BY N.R. WALKER

Blind Faith

Through These Eyes (Blind Faith #2)

Blindside: Mark's Story (Blind Faith #3)

Ten in the Bin

Gay Sex Club Stories 1

Gay Sex Club Stories 2

Gay Sex Club Stories 3

Point of No Return – Turning Point #1

Breaking Point – Turning Point #2

Starting Point – Turning Point #3

Element of Retrofit – Thomas Elkin Series #1

Clarity of Lines – Thomas Elkin Series #2

Sense of Place – Thomas Elkin Series #3

Taxes and TARDIS

Three's Company

Red Dirt Heart

Red Dirt Heart 2

Red Dirt Heart 3

Red Dirt Heart 4

Red Dirt Christmas

Cronin's Key

Cronin's Key II

Cronin's Key III

Cronin's Key IV - Kennard's Story

Exchange of Hearts

The Spencer Cohen Series, Book One

The Spencer Cohen Series, Book Two

The Spencer Cohen Series, Book Three

The Spencer Cohen Series, Yanni's Story

Blood & Milk

The Weight Of It All

A Very Henry Christmas (The Weight of It All 1.5)

Perfect Catch

Switched

Imago

Imagines

Imagoes

Red Dirt Heart Imago

On Davis Row

Finders Keepers

Evolved

Galaxies and Oceans

Private Charter

Nova Praetorian

A Soldier's Wish

Upside Down

The Hate You Drink

Sir

Tallowwood

Reindeer Games

The Dichotomy of Angels

Throwing Hearts

Pieces of You - Missing Pieces #1

Pieces of Me - Missing Pieces #2

Pieces of Us - Missing Pieces #3

Lacuna

Tic-Tac-Mistletoe

Bossy

Code Red

Dearest Milton James

Dearest Malachi Keogh

Christmas Wish List

Code Blue

Davo

The Kite

Learning Curve

Merry Christmas Cupid

To the Moon and Back

Second Chance at First Love

Outrun the Rain

Into the Tempest

Touch the Lightning

EWB - Enemies With Benefits

Holiday Heart Strings

Bloom

The Men from Echo Creek

Method Acting

The Bait

Nothing Left to Lose

Deck the Fire Halls

Benji

Fitch

Sir

Tallowwood

Imago

Throwing Hearts

Sixty Five Hours

Taxes and TARDIS

The Dichotomy of Angels

The Hate You Drink

Pieces of You

Pieces of Me

Pieces of Us

Tic-Tac-Mistletoe

Lacuna

Bossy

Code Red

Learning to Feel

Dearest Milton James

Dearest Malachi Keogh

Three's Company

Christmas Wish List

Code Blue

Davo

The Kite

Learning Curve

Merry Christmas Cupid

To the Moon and Back

Second Chance at First Love

Outrun the Rain

Into the Tempest

Touch the Lightning

EWB

Holiday Heart Strings

Bloom

The Men from Echo Creek

Method Acting

The Bait

Deck the Fire Halls

Benji

Fitch

SERIES COLLECTIONS:

Red Dirt Heart Series

Turning Point Series

Thomas Elkin Series

Spencer Cohen Series

Imago Series

Blind Faith Series

Missing Pieces Series

The Storm Boys Series

Gay Sex Club Stories

FREE READS:

Sixty Five Hours

Learning to Feel

His Grandfather's Watch (And The Story of Billy and Hale)

The Twelfth of Never (Blind Faith 3.5)

Twelve Days of Christmas (Sixty Five Hours Christmas)

Best of Both Worlds

TRANSLATED TITLES:

ITALIAN

Fiducia Cieca (Blind Faith)

Attraverso Questi Occhi (Through These Eyes)

Preso alla Sprovvista (Blindside)

Il giorno del Mai (Blind Faith 3.5)

Cuore di Terra Rossa Serie (Red Dirt Heart Series)

Natale di terra rossa (Red dirt Christmas)

Intervento di Retrofit (Elements of Retrofit)

A Chiare Linee (Clarity of Lines)

Senso D'appartenenza (Sense of Place)

Spencer Cohen Serie (including Yanni's Story)

Punto di non Ritorno (Point of No Return)

Punto di Rottura (Breaking Point)

Punto di Partenza (Starting Point)

Imago (Imago)

Imagines

Il desiderio di un soldato (A Soldier's Wish)

Scambiato (Switched)

Tallowwood

The Hate You Drink

Ho trovato te (Finders Keepers)

Cuori d'argilla (Throwing Hearts)

Galassie e Oceani (Galaxies and Oceans)

Il peso di tut (The Weight of it All)

Pieces of You - Missing Pieces 1

Pieces of Me - Missing Pieces 2

Pieces of Us - Missing Pieces 3

Code Red

FRENCH

Confiance Aveugle (Blind Faith)

A travers ces yeux: Confiance Aveugle 2 (Through These Eyes)

Aveugle: Confiance Aveugle 3 (Blindside)

À Jamais (Blind Faith 3.5)

Cronin's Key Series

Au Coeur de Sutton Station (Red Dirt Heart)

Partir ou rester (Red Dirt Heart 2)

Faire Face (Red Dirt Heart 3)

Trouver sa Place (Red Dirt Heart 4)

Le Poids de Sentiments (The Weight of It All)

Un Noël à la sauce Henry (A Very Henry Christmas)

Une vie à Refaire (Switched)

Evolution (Evolved)

Galaxies & Océans

Qui Trouve, Garde (Finders Keepers)

Sens Dessus Dessous (Upside Down)

La Haine au Fond du Verre (The hate You Drink)

Tallowwood

Spencer Cohen Series

Thomas Elkin One

Lacuna

GERMAN

Flammende Erde (Red Dirt Heart)

Lodernde Erde (Red Dirt Heart 2)

Sengende Erde (Red Dirt Heart 3)

THAI

SPANISH

El Peso de Todo (The Weight of it All)

Tres Muérdagos en Raya: Serie Navidad en Hartbridge

Lista De Deseos Navideños: Serie Navidad en Hartbridge

Feliz Navidad Cupido: Serie Navidad en Hartbridge

Spencer Cohen Libro Uno

Spencer Cohen Libro Dos

Spencer Cohen Libro Tres

Davo

Hasta la Luna y de Vuelta

Venciendo A La Lluvia

En la Tempestad

El Toque del Rayo

Corazón De Tierra Roja

Corazón De Tierra Roja 2

Corazón De Tierra Roja 3

Corazón De Tierra Roja 4

ECB (Enemigos con Beneficios)

Floral

CHINESE

Blind Faith

Bossy

JAPANESE

Bossy

To the Moon and Back

PORTUGUESE

Sessenta e Cinco Horas

DUTCH

De Strafbank

Vijanden met Voordelen

Perfecte Vangst

De Gluurder 1 - 3